Not Deep Enough
by
Kelly Zimmer

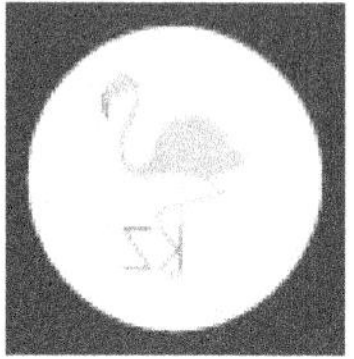

This is a work of fiction. Any resemblance to actual persons, living or dead, is purely coincidental.

Chapter One

I believe people come to you as you need them. It happened to me three times before my twenty-first birthday. The first people to save me were Sean and Melanie Mayweather. The most recent and most significant was Officer Ray Armstrong.

On the morning I met Ray, I yelled, "Cops," even before the Tallahassee police cruiser rolled to a stop in front of the office. Cops meant trouble, so a heads-up was in order. While technology played a crucial role in our work, Mayweather Executive Solutions had no intercom. My talents included cheerleading, so I was the designated intercom and was confident the team caught my warning.

I greeted our two visitors with my best "go team" smile. "Good morning, officers." One wore a suit, so he might not have been police, but I chose the safe route.

The man in the pinstriped suit produced a business card and set it on the granite reception counter at my eye level. I ignored the offered card and kept my eyes fixed on the man's broad, tanned face, and smiled as though I couldn't wait to learn how I could help him.

"Good morning." He made a show of checking out my carved wooden nameplate, "Allison, is Tony Guydan available?"

A tingle of fear curled my toes, but I didn't let the smile falter. "Let's check. It's pronounced Ghee-dan, by the way. Come on back." I stood and retrieved the card without reading it, as though it didn't matter to me who he was; we were so delighted just to have him visit.

I led our guests through the right-hand corridor, ambling past the restroom and kitchen, not rushing to give Tony and Sean time to prepare themselves. My slow stroll allowed the cops to appreciate both our ordinary office and the seat of my jeans. We turned left and passed Theresa and Emi, working away at their computers. I suspected their ears perked as we passed, but they played it cool and didn't spare us a glance as we passed their open door.

At the conference room, I waved a hand at the chairs surrounding the polished oval table and offered our guests drinks. The suit asked for coffee. The uniform requested water.

I put more sparkle in my smile. "Won't be a moment."

The sparkle evaporated as I turned left into the corridor leading to the other two offices. Tony's was dark, so I hurried on to Sean's door. The partners stood behind Sean's desk, their expressions tense and expectant.

I mouthed, "Cops for Tony," at their questioning eyes, and held out the business card.

While Sean stepped around his desk, I read the card in my extended hand. "Martin Clendennon, Detective, Homicide."

I froze.

Sean snatched the card, read it, and passed it to Tony. They shared an anxious glance before turning to me. Sean didn't whisper but kept his voice low. "Two minutes."

I fetched the drinks, reconstituted my smile, and returned to the conference room.

"Tony will be with you in a minute, fellas. He's finishing up a call." I set their drinks in front of them but didn't attempt physical contact. It was too soon.

Clendennon thanked me. "This is a quiet office."

"It is," I agreed, ratcheted up my accent to mint julep level, and babbled. "It's a nice little office park, with lots of restaurants nearby for lunch. My favorite is the Airstream Diner, on the next block. They have the best turkey club sandwich. It's not good to eat out every day, but I enjoy variety, and I'm not much of a cook, so I don't bring my lunch. I bet cops are always eating on the run, aren't they?"

The uniformed cop suppressed a chuckle. The tag on the black shirt read, "Armstrong." I guessed Officer Armstrong was in his late twenties. He had deeply tanned skin, black eyes, and shiny blue-black hair. Once Officer Armstrong curbed the chuckle, then his eyes cut back to me. He wanted to keep it professional because of the suit sitting there, but I had his attention, for sure. I filed that away.

Sean and Tony entered the conference room together, but Sean took the lead.

"Detective Clendennon and Officer," Sean read the name tag without a pause, "Armstrong. I'm Sean Mayweather." He extended a hand.

Both cops stood. They were tall, at least six feet, but at six-four and slender, Sean towered over them.

"And I'm Tony Guiden." Tony offered his hand. "How can I help you today?"

Clendennon held Tony's eyes but nodded in my direction. "It's a police matter."

Sean took the hint. "Thanks, Allison. I'll call if you're needed." He inclined his head toward Emi's office.

It was my turn to take the hint. I closed the conference room door behind me, then hustled into the next office. My friends' heads popped up with mouths open, but I said, "Cops for Tony," and tapped my ear.

Emi and Theresa pulled earbuds out of drawers and plugged them into their laptops. Emi waved a spare set at me and scooted over so I could share her chair. I plugged into her computer while she pulled up the audio for the conference room's hidden microphone.

The first voice was Clendennon's. I mouthed, "detective."

"What do you do here, Mr. Mayweather?"

"Mayweather Executive Solutions offers consulting services to businesses throughout the Southeast," Sean said.

"What sort of consulting services?"

"Executive searches, mergers and acquisitions, security and financial consulting, especially financial consulting. Tony is a former CFO."

"And you're a former sheriff's deputy," Clendennon said.

"I am."

"Unusual partnership."

"It is." Sean wouldn't give him any more than necessary.

"Mr. Guiden," Clendennon began.

"Tony."

"Tony, we're here to discuss an incident that occurred in July of this year."

Emi's shoulders twitched.

Tony responded with an amused, "In July? I'll try to help, but that was three months ago."

"I'm sure you'll remember the incident. Ray, pull up the video, please."

There were sounds of a zipper and the clunk of metal on the conference table. After a pause, there was another voice, younger, not as deep. Armstrong.

"A security camera captured this video from behind a nearby pharmacy. Note the time and date stamp at the corner; July sixteenth, at five-forty-seven. Does the date, July sixteenth, mean anything to you?" Officer Armstrong asked.

Emi squirmed in the seat next to me. It sure meant something to her.

"No," Tony replied, "not off the top of my head."

No one spoke until Clendennon broke the silence. "Isn't that you on this video, Tony?"

"No."

"It looks like you."

"It looks like two men who resemble me. Which one am I supposed to be?" Tony asked.

"You're the one chasing the other man."

Emi moaned. I kicked her to shut her up, but I'd heard enough to jog my memory too.

"It's not me."

"That one resembles you." Clendennon must have pointed at the screen.

"It's a fuzzy, five-second video of two dark-haired men my size. Both are in profile. One is chasing the other. Neither one is me." Tony's voice wasn't nervous or confrontational. I imagined him shrugging at the detective.

"Do you deny you are in this video?" Clendennon asked.

"Yes. Why does it matter?"

Clendennon ignored the question. "What were you doing that day?"

"I assume I was working, but I'll check."

After a pause during which I imagined him checking his phone, Tony said, "I worked until five, then drove home. I took my wife out for a special dinner that night. We'd argued, and I planned a reconciliation dinner. Francine will remember."

"Your coworkers and your wife will confirm your whereabouts on July sixteenth?" It was Armstrong speaking now.

Tony laughed. "I believe so, yes. Look, I'm sorry, but I can't help you."

Clendennon again. "To confirm, you aren't on this video."

"I confirm I'm not on that video," Tony said with confidence.

"We need to talk to your staff."

Sean spoke. "I'll bring them to see you myself, but I want to know why you think Tony chased a man in July and why it's important."

Clendennon said, "The man being chased is a known drug dealer. We're looking for him."

They wouldn't find him, not alive. Tony had shot him dead on July seventeenth.

When Tony spoke, he filled his voice with outrage. "We don't do business with drug dealers."

This was a lie. We were always bumping into drug dealers, murderers, and thieves.

Tony continued. "I have teenagers at home. I don't sell or use drugs."

"I'm not suggesting you do. I'm suggesting you know the man in this video." Challenge filled the detective's voice.

"I don't."

Again, everyone remained quiet until Clendennon broke the silence. "Sean, can you have your employees at the station tomorrow at nine to make statements regarding July sixteenth?"

"Absolutely," Sean said.

"Can your wife be at the station tomorrow, Tony?"

"Certainly."

There was rustling. I popped out the earbuds and rushed to the reception desk, posing as though I'd been eagerly awaiting the return of our guests the entire time.

Sean led the visitors around the corner. He shook their hands and held the door for them as they left. After the police cruiser pulled into the street, Sean bellowed, "Meeting!" so loud the door rattled.

In the conference room, the mood varied from shaken to grim. Tony leaned back and covered his eyes with one hand as though the overhead LEDs were too bright. Theresa wrapped a slender arm around Emi's shoulders. She cooed comforting words while Sean used his fingers to rearrange the blond spikes he'd gelled his hair into.

"On the upside," Sean said, "we don't know the name of the guy Tony's chasing in the video. On the downside, Tony shot him back in July."

"In my kitchen," Emi blurted. Emi's my best friend. She has an extraordinary gift for precognition and an annoying habit of blurting out whatever comes into her head, no matter how random. The blurting helps her cope with the images bombarding her brain, but it's irritating, especially when I'm trying to focus.

Theresa rubbed Emi's back. "You moved out of your apartment over a month ago. Allison and I helped you clean the heck out of the kitchen after the shooting, and the rental company cleaned it again when you left."

"Not that it matters. Clendennon doesn't think *you* killed the guy," I said. "The cops are interested in Tony, and he's for sure not telling them he shot a guy in your apartment."

Tony removed his hand from his eyes and straightened. "As far as the cops know, he's still alive. They suspect we fought, but, other than that, there's no connection between us."

"Tony's right," Sean said. "We were confidential informants working with Dave Davis, very confidential. Davis didn't know this guy's name either, or that he'd killed Pete Izary."

Emi stiffened as her panic grew. "If they connect this guy to Pete's death, they'll talk to Dave. If they talk to Dave, the cops will learn we were looking for Pete's dog. That's a connection between Tony and the dead man."

Theresa raised her hazel-green eyes to the ceiling, then leveled them at Emi. "How? There's no connection between Pete's death and this guy."

"Theresa's right. Dave knows even less than we do, and he's not likely to mention our help with his money laundering cases. Even if the police learn Pete Izary laundered the dead guy's money," Sean said, "it's quite a leap from searching for a lost dog to money laundering."

Emi wasn't satisfied. "But it's a connection to Tony, and the video is a second connection. That's one connection too many."

Sean passed his gaze around the table. "We'll continue to support Tony's alibi and deny we know the man in the video."

"What else can we do," Theresa said. "We can't tell the cops Tony and Pak chased the guy because he was waiting to kill an invisible Treasury agent."

Emi turned frantic again. "Oh my God, Pak! I forgot he was with Tony that afternoon."

"Pak isn't in the video," Tony said. "He fell before we got out of the hotel parking lot, and he didn't follow me."

Still panicked, Emi blathered on. "We need to warn Pak and Francine and get everyone on the same page. We have to discover who this guy was and what cops have connecting Tony to his death."

Sean pressed his palms toward the tabletop. "Calm down, and remember we're talking about a disappearance, not a death. Our story is we don't know this guy; therefore, we don't know he's dead."

"The detective is from homicide," I said in a *duh* voice.

"Let's not assume the cops will wait until tomorrow morning to follow up on Tony's alibi." Sean shot fingers at Tony and Emi. "Call Francine and Pak and bring them up to speed, then meet back here in twenty to work on our strategy for tomorrow morning."

I whipped up a fresh pot of coffee. I already had my strategy prepared.

My knack for mind-reading requires a three-pronged approach. I need to be in physical contact with the target. I must ask specific questions, and I have to focus on the answers. It's crucial to ask the right questions, so it helps if someone else does the questioning while I'm concentrating on the responses. Focus is a challenge, especially if a lot is going on around me during the interview.

Take the day I met Sean. A lot was going on the day someone kidnapped his baby girl.

Chapter Two

Before I became the receptionist for Mayweather Executive Solutions, I worked a register at McDonald's. I was seventeen, and that job meant the world to me.

My dad walked out when I was two. Getting dumped and left with two kids hit my mom hard. She struck back by partying and hooking up with any guy who'd pay her bills. To me, Dad was a series of lowlifes, and my home a series of cheap rental houses, apartments, and trailers. My older brother, Ben, and I got dragged from one crappy dump to another, shoved into a spare room, and warned to stay out of the way.

As a kid, I dreamed of being a high school cheerleader. My mom couldn't have cared less about my childhood aspirations, so I snuck into basketball games, football games, and soccer matches to watch the routines from the sidelines. Afterward, I'd run to a park and practice by myself, imagining how cute I'd look in the cheer uniform. The bows and sparkly makeup were so foreign to my grimy existence that the girls might have come from another planet. In this clean, happy world, everybody smiled, and people shouted for their team, not at each other. I wanted to be one of them, someone other kids looked up to instead of what I was—a trailer-trash loser in thrift shop clothes and dollar store sandals.

I wanted to be a cheerleader, but cheerleading cost money, so I ran a register at McDonald's. It helped, but not much.

On a sunny, breezy spring afternoon in my senior year, I sulked on a concrete park bench. School let out, but my shift behind the counter didn't start for an hour. I didn't want to go home to confront my mom's latest winner, Earl, so I hung out on a picnic table, watching traffic and wishing my life was different.

A voice, frantic, bordering on hysterical, drifted across the park. "Connie! Connie!"

I twisted and scanned the playground behind me. A woman spun in circles and screamed that her baby had vanished.

A white-haired man pulled out his phone, and people rushed toward the woman. I could help, but I needed someone who'd seen what happened, so I focused my attention on the people rushing *away* from the distraught mother.

A tall kid in a brown hoodie strode purposefully to the street, his hands pushed deep into his pockets. I slid off the picnic table, jogged to him, and grabbed his arm. "Did you see anything?" I asked.

"No, not a thing. Pretty sick, huh?"

His horror was genuine, and he was late for work. He'd been smoking pot under a covered pavilion and didn't see the kidnapping, so I let him go.

My attention turned to a couple pushing a stroller. My pulse quickened. The kid in the stroller might be the missing baby. I dashed after the pair.

Winded by the time I reached the couple, I rested my hands on their backs. "That woman's baby is missing. Did you see her?" The couple's eyes grew wide. They turned and hustled toward the crowd, swelling around the hysterical mother. Not them.

On the sidewalk bisecting the park, a thin woman with stringy blonde hair trotted toward the street. She peered over the right shoulder of her dirty white shirt as if she thought someone was following her. I ran to intercept her before she reached the road.

The woman in the dirty shirt didn't notice me as she rushed across the park. She paused when the mother wailed, then turned back to the road and moved faster, altering her route to take her away from the noise. Unfortunately for her, her altered path took her past me. She didn't spot me until I grabbed her.

The moment my fingers encircled her thin wrist, I knew she was in on it without asking the first question. The story was on the tip of her brain, unfolding for me like a silent film.

The baby is a girl, not even two. Blonde. Good money. Wait until the mom turns her back. Okay, she's busy with the two boys. Shit! The baby's toddling away to look at a bug. Move! Now!

Don't stop, act natural. Pick her up, cuddle her like she's your own; don't slow. Good, she's not crying. Keep moving. There he is, there's Dan outside the men's room. Hand him the baby, but don't stop. Keep moving. Don't look back and don't slow down!

She pulled against my grasp, but I caught her other wrist in my free hand and squeezed.

My eyes drilled into hers as I screamed, "Where is she?"

"Let go of me, you fucking bitch!" She kicked at me, but I held tight, focused on the words in her head, not the filth spewing from her mouth.

"Where'd he take her? Where did Dan take the baby?" I asked, calmer now.

The bitch's face went slack, then twisted itself into a frenzy. "Let me go, freak!" It was enough for me to read the rest.

Still holding her, I faced the crowd and used my cheerleader-trained lungs to bellow, "She's in a black van. He's got the baby in a black van."

I bent my knees and dropped my butt to the ground, pulling the skanky bitch with me as I screamed again, "His name's Dan. He's got the baby in a black van."

At last, the guy who'd been pushing the stroller caught my words. He shouted something, then bolted to me. His arms locked tight around the waist of the woman in the dirty shirt. We struggled with the writhing woman until a police cruiser skidded to a halt at the edge of the park. Two cops emerged. One dashed toward the crowd, the other toward me. The female officer was a tall, sturdy woman who had me and the skank handcuffed in seconds.

"I saw it all," I lied, breathless from the struggle. "She snatched the baby and gave her to a man with white hair. She called him Dan. He's wearing denim shorts, and he put the baby in a black van." I nodded to the right. "He drove off that way."

The cop talked into a shoulder mike. The wail of sirens rose in the distance, and soon the park was crawling with police.

Chapter Three

The Mayweather team didn't need much time to prepare for our interviews with the Tallahassee police. Our story was simple. Tony was in the office all day, and we didn't recognize either man in the video. While the cops interviewed us, we were to remember the guy was missing and not dead. As an afterthought, we reminded Emi not to blurt any thoughts arising from random images she might receive.

Theresa and I rode to the station with Sean. We parked as Emi and Pak climbed out of Emi's red Fiat. Inside the station, Francine and Tony Guiden sat hand-in-hand in yellow plastic chairs. Our arrival interrupted a conversation about a Halloween party their twins wanted to attend. The couple appeared relaxed, more focused on their teenage domestic drama than a police inquiry.

A cheerful officer took our names and promised Detective Clendennon would be with us soon. He didn't make us wait long. At nine, Clendennon appeared from a side door and asked for Francine Guiden without acknowledging the rest of us. Tony's wife rose and smoothed the wrinkles from the skirt of her casual suit. She and Tony parted without a kiss or even a goodbye. Her manner implied a meeting with police was merely an inconvenient errand, a box to check off on the day's to-do list.

Officer Armstrong's head of dark, wavy hair appeared from the side door. His gaze flashed to me, but he asked for Theresa Fitzpatrick, whose hazel-green eyes missed nothing. It was her job to locate any evidence the cops had against Tony, so familiarity with the station was critical.

I wiggled my fingers at Officer Armstrong as he followed Theresa through the door. I need to build rapport if I expected to put my hands on a cop. That was my job; to interview him in my unique way to learn what the police had on Tony.

Emi rested her head against Pak's shoulder, eyes closed. From experience, I knew she was emptying her mind of everything but our goal. Her job was to see the future, Tony's future.

Clendennon returned with Francine in under twenty minutes and asked for Sean, who'd been leaning against the front counter, chatting up the cop on the desk. On her way out, Francine kissed Tony's cheek and told him to call her later. If she'd seen the video, it hadn't disrupted her composure.

Armstrong returned with Theresa. She took the chair next to mine.

"Emily Watson?" Armstrong read from a clipboard.

Emi and Pak stood.

"Who's this?" Armstrong aimed a thick finger at Pak.

Unlike Emi, Pak oozed confidence, which was usually unwarranted. Beaming his warm smile, Pak shot out a hand. "Kalpak Zacharia. I'm Emi's fiancé."

My head swiveled to Emi. Fiancé? When did that happen? She raised her eyebrows as if to say, "in his dreams."

Armstrong wasn't pleased, and frankly, I didn't understand what Pak was doing there either. The cops weren't aware he'd been with Tony that day, and we didn't need to involve him. I supposed Emi needed moral support. It was her sister the dead guy had planned to kill.

At ten-fifteen, Pak and Emi followed Officer Ray Armstrong back into the lobby. I was the only one left, but he called my name, anyway. Maybe he enjoyed how it rolled off his tongue.

I popped up with a grin, eager to get started. Armstrong led me to a windowless interview room. A laptop and a small recorder rested in the center of the scarred table.

"How are you doing, Officer Armstrong?" I asked.

"I'm doing well, thanks for asking. Sorry to keep you waiting."

"Hey, it's better than working."

"You're the receptionist at Mayweather, correct?" Officer Armstrong turned on the recorder.

I smiled and aimed my response toward the device. "My name is Allison Francona, and I'm the receptionist at Mayweather Executive Solutions here in Tallahassee. I've worked at Mayweather for three years. I'll be twenty-one in April, and I'm single." Proud I'd provided so much useful information without prompting, I wiggled in my seat and grinned at Officer Armstrong.

Armstrong stifled a laugh as his professional bearing cracked. I had him.

"Do you know Anthony Guiden?"

"Yes, sir. Tony is a partner at MES, that's Mayweather Executive Solutions. Tony and Sean own the business."

"How long have you known Mr. Guiden?"

I remembered the exact hour I met Tony because I'd met Emi that day, too, but I squished my face and pondered. "I'd say almost a year now. Sean and I did a job for Knox Engineering, the big mining machine company here in town."

"Tony Guiden worked for Knox, is that correct?"

"He was the chief financial officer." I brightened as though I'd remembered something important. "MES did the executive search to find his replacement. Knox hired a super guy named Art Gates. My friends and I got to go to New York to interview him."

"Sounds exciting, but let's get back to Tony Guiden. Did your boss tell you we'd be asking about a specific incident?"

"Sean said you had a video from July sixteenth that has Tony in it."

Both of Armstrong's black brows rose. "He told you Tony is in the video?"

"No, that's crazy talk! Sean said the cops *think* Tony is in the video."

Armstrong powered up the laptop. "Watch this with me, please."

I scooted to the end of my seat, eager and attentive. Officer Armstrong played the clip. It was eight seconds long, shot from a camera mounted high, and the resolution sucked.

"Ms. Francona, do you recognize either man in the video you just watched?" Armstrong asked.

"The picture's not too clear." I squinted and frowned, then sat back in my chair. "I'd have to say no, I don't recognize either guy."

"Anthony Guiden isn't chasing the other man?"

"Why would Tony chase anyone? He's an accountant."

"He *was* an accountant. Now he's a partner in a firm that looks into all kinds of things, including money laundering." Uh oh.

"We've never done a money laundering case," I said, but couldn't help but lose the perky from my voice. I turned my concern into curiosity. "Did the guys in the video launder money? Tony wouldn't do that. He's too smart."

Armstrong huffed. "I've seen smart people do stupid things."

My opening had arrived.

"Boy, ain't that the truth," I said and rolled my eyes. "I love those forensic cop shows, the ones that show actual stories. There was one about this doctor who hired a cop to kill his wife. How stupid is that?"

Armstrong sat back in his seat. "I remember that one." We discussed the show for a few minutes before he remembered to turn off the recorder.

"Sorry, I let us get off track."

"My fault. I babble." I fanned my face with my hand.

"Are you warm? Would you like a cold drink?" he asked.

"That would be great. You don't have Dr. Pepper, do you?"

"I'll be right back." He was back at the door in two minutes with two cans of Dr. Pepper.

"Tha-ank you!" I rose and took a step toward Officer Armstrong to accept the cold drink. I popped it to give the cop time to settle himself. After taking a long swig, I seated myself in the chair next to Ray, rather than across the table. "Can I see the video again?"

I leaned close to the laptop as we watched. My upper arm rested against Armstrong's. "Which guy is the money launderer?" I asked.

He pointed to the man Tony was chasing. "Him."

"What's his name?"

"Axel Thornhill."

"Funny name."

"Not a funny man."

I let my knee bump against Ray's. "Why do you think Tony would chase him?"

"The guy had drug money to launder. Tony Guiden could do that, couldn't he?"

"I guess, but that's not Tony chasing *Axel Thornhill*." I pronounced the name like it was the dumbest thing I'd ever heard.

Armstrong turned on the recorder. No longer adversaries, we sipped Dr. Pepper, flirted, and wrapped up the interview. My chat with Ray ended with him suggesting we might see each other around.

I left the station with my head held high, confident I'd done my best to protect my friends. The last time I'd been interviewed by the police, I'd been far less sure of myself.

Chapter Four

After I rescued Connie, the cops interviewed me right there on the park bench. A detective removed my handcuffs and offered me a cold bottle of water. She asked me to tell her what happened in my own words. I sipped water and took my time because I had to make up the stuff my mind-reading hadn't given me.

I described a combination of what I'd seen and what I'd gathered from reading the skanky woman's thoughts. I couldn't mention the mind-reading, so I told the detective I'd seen the whole thing. Since I hadn't, I guessed at some of it, and the detective's frown told me I'd flubbed a few details. But they'd found Connie in the black van, driven by a man like I'd told her, so she believed me. The detective recorded everything and told me to stop by the police station the next day to sign a copy of my statement.

By the time the police finished with me, I was so late for my shift I elected to skip work and stay put on the bench to watch the sideshow. A damned news van arrived and disgorged a camera guy in jeans and a red-haired woman in a sharp blue suit. The reporter read from notes as she interviewed the detective who took my statement. The reporter's eyes kept drifting to the reunited family inside the crime scene tape.

I didn't want the reporter looking my way, so I turned my attention to the little girl's family, too. The three kids huddled with their mom in the back of an ambulance a hundred yards from my bench. Their mother was disheveled and clutched her baby to her chest. The older boy squeezed his little brother's hand and his mother's t-shirt.

When the reporter finished her interview with the detective, she gestured to the family. The police didn't let her past the tape, and the mom didn't budge. I didn't blame her.

I sure as hell didn't want to talk to a reporter, so I turned my back to the news people and pulled out my phone to call McDonald's and apologize for missing work. Once I told her the story, the manager was understanding and promised me another shift to make up the hours.

I needed those hours. There were three months of high school left, and I was one month from my eighteenth birthday. I didn't expect birthday and graduation cards stuffed with cash to help with prom, graduation photos, grad night, or the cheerleading awards dinner. My pathetic job wouldn't cover a third of it. Oh, and my mom planned to kick me out the day I turned eighteen. I had that going for me too.

Busy with my call, I didn't notice which direction the guy came from, maybe from the street behind me. He was tall and wore his dirty blonde hair combed up into spikes. He moved with confidence, marched past the cops, and past the yellow police tape fluttering in the March breeze, to embrace the woman holding the baby girl. After kissing their cheeks, he let his hands rub the heads of the two little boys clinging to his legs.

I cried, not for the family and the near-tragedy they'd experienced, but for me. I'd never had that. I'd never had a family of people who loved each other. Every night I prayed for someone to rescue me, save me from the groping, the fighting, and the filth. Help never magically appeared for me the way it had for them.

What was so damn special about them that deserved saving instead of me? I hated the whole damned family. I hated them because I wasn't one of them, but the truth was, I hated me.

Chapter Five

We didn't dare discuss Tony's problem in the office, not until Anderson checked the place for bugs, so we met at Sean's house. Since it was a school night, we waited until the Mayweather's three kids were in bed before gathering around the dining room table.

Sean sat at the head of the table as though he were conducting a board meeting. "Let's review what we learned today."

Tony began. "The dead man's name is Axel Thornhill. He was a drug dealer specializing in opioids. It's safe to assume Pete Izary laundered money for him. The police know Joanna Izary hired us to find the dog, Rascal. That's connection number one. Emi's sister recovered the dog when she found Pete Izary's body. That's connection number two, so the video is the third connection."

"That's bad," Emi said. "If they learn Thornhill wanted to kill my sister for taking a photo of him at Izary's building, they'll consider it a motive for Tony to kill Thornhill. I'm so sorry, guys."

That was another one of Emi's annoying habits. She blamed everything on herself.

"If they know Thornhill laundered money with Pete Izary, it won't take them long to bump into Dave Davis," Pak said. Pak had no special skills but was a born actor and loved our work.

"Local police may have talked to him already," Sean said. "Davis is working on money laundering cases involving three of Izary's former clients."

"Are you sure?" Emi asked.

"I should ask you that," Sean said.

Emi started as though she'd forgotten she could see the future. "I haven't thought about it yet."

"While you're thinking," Sean turned to me, "did you get anything, Allison?"

I love the spotlight, and I love teasing Sean. "Officer Armstrong is a cutie, and he likes Dr. Pepper floats." Everyone chuckled, even Tony.

"What have they got?" Sean asked.

"Not much. A narcotics team talked to pharmacists in the area, trying to link Thornhill to opioid thefts. When they showed the pharmacist Thornhill's picture, the woman said the guy resembled someone she'd seen in a security video from earlier in the year."

"Damn, that's some memory," Theresa said. "So the woman recognized Thornhill. How did she know you, Tony? Do you shop there?"

"I've never been inside the place. Are you saying the pharmacist knows me?" Tony asked.

"No, she recognized Thornhill in the video, not you."

"Then how did they get to me?"

I deflated. "That's all I've got, guys. Sorry, I wasn't with Armstrong that long and couldn't ask too many questions."

Theresa sounded deflated, too. "If there's additional evidence, Armstrong didn't bring it into the room. He was mostly concerned with Tony's movements. I told him what we agreed on; we all worked until five, then went home."

Sean cast his gaze around the table. "That's it?"

Pak dropped his bomb. "They found Thornhill's body. That's important, isn't it?"

Sean rubbed his stubbly cheeks with both hands so he wouldn't use them to strangle Pak. "Yes, Pak, it is crucial, and you might have mentioned it sooner. How do you know they found Thornhill's body?"

"This couple had a pool dug," Pak began eagerly. "The pool company ran into a body while they were digging."

I frowned. "Armstrong told you this? I got nothing like that."

"My mom told me. She and Uncle Anton were in the pool business, remember? One of her old friends called yesterday and said, 'Guess what we found in a hole the other day?' Mom mentioned it to me when we talked last night."

"How does Zabel know it was Axel Thornhill in the hole?" Tony asked. "Did the police talk to your mom?"

"No, but her friends told my mom a Detective Clendennon interviewed them the day after they dug up the body, so I'm assuming the dead guy was Thornhill."

"They're sure keeping it quiet," I said. "There's been nothing on the news."

"The detective hopes to wrap up the case before it becomes public," Sean said. He hooked his arms over the back of the chair and blew air at the ceiling.

Tony rested his chin on interlaced fingers. "The police have recovered the body of a man killed by a gunshot to the head. They've identified the deceased as Axel Thornhill. An old surveillance video has surfaced. In it, Thornhill's being chased by a man who resembles me because he is me. The cops will assume we fought, I killed Thornhill and buried the body, which has now resurfaced."

Emi pounded her forefinger into the table. "We know it's you, but how do *they* know it's you? The video is lousy. They must have more. We need to figure out what they've got, find it, and get rid of it."

"Tell me what it is, and I'll find it," Theresa assured us.

"We don't know." Emi dropped her head to the table. "We're going in circles."

Sean turned to Tony. "Allison didn't pick it up from reading Armstrong's mind. He was too focused on the video. We need your skills. You'll have to make one of them tell you."

Tony puffed out air, making the hair on his forehead ruffle. "How do I manipulate a cop? And not just any cop, a detective, a detective who thinks I'm a murderer."

It was time for me to spring my surprise on them. I smiled and sat up straighter. "I can't help with Detective Clendennon, but I stole Officer Armstrong's comb if that helps."

The team turned to me like I was Santa at Christmas. I loved being me.

My talent was nifty, and so were Theresa's and Emi's, but Sean and Tony had skills with power-ups. Tony and Sean were practitioners. They made things happen. Sean could visit places in his head, which was impressive enough, but just the tip of a creepier iceberg. If Sean forged a connection with people at the places he visited, he could manipulate them like puppets.

Once, he visited this company, Deiner Equipment, because they were spying on Knox. There was a web developer at Deiner named Mindy Li. When Sean visited, he got her to pull up stuff on her computer that told us how Deiner was getting into Anderson's network at Knox.

Tony went beyond even that. He got inside a person's head and made them do things they wouldn't ordinarily do. Tony once convinced Emi to have sex with him. I always tell her he was just helping her unlock her skill and didn't manipulate her, but the poor kid never had a chance.

As with my mind-reading, Tony's skills took focus and concentration. He had this ritual to help him get where he needed to be using something personal—hair or blood or sweat—from his target. He studied it, stared at it, I don't know what, until he got inside the person's brain. Giving Tony that comb was like giving him the keys to Club Armstrong.

*

Ray had Saturday off; he'd told me that during my interview. He planned to take his boat out, dock it down the river at Privateers, and listen to a band. I think he was trying to get me to invite myself. I didn't bite, but my friends and I planned on bumping into him at the bar. Small world.

Boats pulled right up to the dock and parked at Privateers, a restaurant and bar on the Ochlockonee River. The bar sprawled under a fake tiki-thatched roof that kept the sun from baking the customers. On Saturdays, local bands played one after the other from noon until close.

From my private conversation with Officer Armstrong, I learned he planned to be at Privateers around one. As usual, Sean's gray Odyssey van served as our HQ on wheels. Sean studied the river with high-powered binoculars. He has lots of toys like that he learned to use in the Marines.

When Armstrong's boat appeared around a bend in the river, Theresa, Emi, and I hustled out of the Odyssey's side door. I wore cutoff denim shorts and a lacy white halter top. Melanie Mayweather had done my hair in two braids that fell forward over my bare shoulders. Emi assured me I looked adorable. Theresa used a different, less flattering word.

The three of us grabbed an open table in the tiki bar. Theresa ordered a bucket of beers, and we slipped into character. We were three friends out having fun on a Saturday afternoon. Nothing sneaky happening here other than the fake ID I'd been using to buy drinks since Emi and I worked our first job together.

A decent band played southern rock on a raised pavilion decorated with maroon and gold pennants fluttering in the breeze coming off the river. I'd prepared a few opening lines to try on Armstrong when we "accidentally" ran into him.

My preparation flew right out the window when he strolled up to our table. "May I see your identification, Ms. Francona?"

I bounced up, wrapped an arm around his neck, and pressed my boobs into his arm. "Guys, look who it is!"

"Officer Armstrong, what are you doing here?" Emi sounded genuinely stunned to see the man.

"Don't call me that here." He winked at us.

Theresa pulled out the vacant fourth chair. He sat without waiting for an invitation. Promising.

"You said you don't turn twenty-one until April." Ray pulled a beer from the bucket, also without waiting for an invitation. Very promising.

"Did I say that?" I asked.

"I bought the beers, Officer Armstrong, and I'm well over twenty-one." Theresa tossed her head and parted her lips in a smile guaranteed to warm the coldest cop's heart.

Ray squinted at Theresa as though seeing her for the first time. Theresa dresses all business for work. She'd worn a black suit, gray silk blouse, and stiletto heels to her police interview. At Privateers, she wore skinny jeans and a soft white t-shirt that glowed against her brown skin. Her hair hung loose, and her eyes blazed from within the black frame. The effect pushed Armstrong's pulse to heights it hadn't visited in a while.

"Out here, I'm Ray," he said.

Emi may have been a blurter, but she got people talking. Maybe it was part of her precognition thing. She waved a hand toward the river. "Which boat is yours?" We'd watched it approach the Privateers' dock, but the question got Ray talking.

His eyes lit up as he pointed out his boat, *Miranda*. Outwardly Ray's monologue enthralled us. We didn't allow our eyes to glaze over once as he discussed anchor lockers and horsepower.

I didn't notice her do it, but Theresa ordered another bucket of beers. At the one hour mark, Armstrong drained his third beer, and Emi needed the restroom. Theresa scooted off after her. Armstrong's eyes followed her swaying backside. I got his attention with a hand on his shoulder.

He swung his head to me with a sheepish smile. "Sorry."

"You can't blame a guy for looking," I said.

"Please don't say anything to Theresa. That was unprofessional of me. Actually," he glanced at his watch, "I shouldn't be talking with you girls."

"Why not? We're not discussing the thing with Tony."

He relaxed, and his gaze shifted to my halter top, which I'd pulled low. His beer-softened eyes focused themselves on my boobs. My boobs and my chatter kept him distracted as Sean and Tony slithered up to the table.

As Tony seated himself at Ray's side, the cop rose and barked objections. Sean positioned himself behind Ray and gently eased the baffled man back into his chair, using the tips of his fingers.

I relinquished my seat to Sean, who took charge. "Good afternoon, Officer Armstrong."

"What are you guys doing here?" Ray asked.

"We're collecting our employees who've been enjoying the river view. They've had a few beers and shouldn't drive."

Ray's professional cop persona returned. "And this one," he pointed to me, "shouldn't be drinking."

"I'll have a talk with her," Sean said.

The head of black curls swung to Tony. "And you and I shouldn't be talking either."

"You're not talking." Tony gave Ray a half-smile. "You're listening."

"What?"

Tony rested two fingers of his right hand on Armstrong's cheek. The gesture was both intimate and creepy.

"You're listening to what I'm saying, Officer Armstrong. Tell me about the video and other evidence related to Axel Thornhill. After you do, we'll leave, and you'll forget we were here," Tony said.

"Except for Theresa," I said. "He should remember watching Theresa walking away."

Tony raised one brow. "Officer Armstrong, how politically incorrect of you."

Ray tried to resist. His mouth moved, but no sound came out. He pushed his arms against the chair to stand but couldn't. He did that for a while, tried to speak and stand. Soon, his eyes half-closed, and he talked. We listened.

*

Tony and Sean walked Ray to his boat and waved as he sped away, then we joined Emi and Theresa in the van.

"Are you sure he'll forget he saw us today?" I asked.

Tony shrugged. "I believe so, but it doesn't matter. If he remembers, what can he do? Admit he blabbed to a murder suspect? And when they ask why he blabbed, what does he say?"

"He says he talked because you hypnotized him in a crowded bar and crawled around inside his head. You're right. He won't say a word."

"What have they got?" Emi asked. "How do they know Tony's chasing Axel Thornhill in that video?"

"They have a personal item belonging to Tony," Sean said. "We'll retrieve it and make this mess go away. This is under control."

That was Sean. He took control.

Chapter Six

From my perch on the park bench, I watched the tall guy talk to the detective who'd interviewed me. After shaking the detective's hand, he chatted briefly with the woman holding the baby, then strode across the park aimed straight for me.

I moaned a resigned sigh. He'd want to thank me for saving his kid. I'd have to smile and say shit like "anyone would have done the same" and end up thanking *him* for allowing me the privilege of rescuing his perfect little life. Or, I mused, he might give me a reward.

The possibility of quick cash got me to pull myself together. I used the hem of my work smock to wipe the smudged mascara from under my eyes, smeared on lip gloss, squared my shoulders, and arranged my face into a shy smile. Who knows, I thought, if the guy was in the right frame of mind, I might get enough to cover graduation, a second-hand prom dress, and rent for a crappy apartment until I got a full-time job.

The promise of an apartment un-infested with my mom's loser boyfriend put the "go team" sparkle in my eyes.

"Hey," I said as he approached.

"Hey, yourself." He sat on the bench and rested his elbows on his knees. I expected him to be all over me with grateful enthusiasm, or at least give me the once-over like most guys. Instead, after a quiet moment, he asked, "How did you do it?"

"I saw the woman take the baby." How about a "thank you," I thought.

"That's what the detective said. However, that's impossible unless you have telescopic eyesight, x-ray vision, and the ability to observe activity through solid objects within a three-hundred and sixty-degree radius. Do you have telescopic eyesight, x-ray vision, and the ability to observe activity through solid objects within a three-hundred and sixty-degree radius?"

I laughed, not at his question but at myself. I'd expected gratitude, possibly a reward. Instead, he questioned me like a cop. Fine, I thought, be an asshole.

If he wanted the truth, I'd give it to him. A voice laden with sarcasm replaced the perky I'd worked up. "No, but I can read minds. I didn't see it happen, but I heard the woman scream her baby was missing. I ran around the park, touching people moving away from her in a hurry. Oh, I need to touch people to read their minds. When I reached the skanky woman, I grabbed her wrist and asked her what happened. She told me, in her head, you understand, not out loud, but I told the police I'd seen the whole thing because people don't believe I can read minds." There, I thought, fuck you. Now give me fifty bucks, then leave, I added to myself.

He stared off into the distance, nodding. "I thought that might be the case." His gaze roamed over me in an appraising, but not lecherous, manner. "Are you going to work?"

"No, I missed my shift because of this." Now give me fifty bucks.

"Will you lose your job?" he asked.

"That can't happen. I need the money."

"If money's a problem, I can offer you a job."

"I'm still in school."

"We'll work around your schedule. If you're not doing anything tonight, we could use help at the house. Melanie and the kids are a mess. Would your folks let you spend the night? I'll pay you and see you get to school on time in the morning."

The conversation wasn't going where I'd expected. I shouldn't have been surprised. Why should I expect anything but weird? I abandoned the last remaining bit of civility. "Mister, my mom doesn't give a good god damn if I ever come home, but if you're trying to get me to your house and into bed, it's not happening."

"The furthest thing from my mind." He stood abruptly. "Call your mom, and let's move. It's getting late, and the boys are hungry."

And like that, Sean Mayweather took control of my life.

Chapter Seven

Anderson hadn't yet done the pest control check on the office, so we stopped at the Guiden's house for our post-Privateers meeting on Saturday evening.

Tony's home wasn't as spacious as Sean's, but more elegant. The Guidens had decorated the living room, appropriately considering the conversation, for Halloween with jack-o'-lanterns, fall leaves, and an assortment of lurking monsters. The subtle scent of cinnamon filled the air. Someday, I told myself, I'll have a house like this and dress it up for every holiday.

Francine perched on the arm of the upholstered side chair where Tony slumped, his legs outstretched. Tony twirled a lock of hair at the nape of his neck. His other hand covered his mouth and his eyes focused on something distant, maybe in the past. I'd never seen Tony, the king of cool, so agitated, and his discomfort unsettled me. Even Theresa was edgy, and Emi was a basket case.

Sean sat between Theresa and me in the center of the comfy, corduroy-upholstered sofa, his long arms stretched across the back. Emi sat in a chair she dragged from the dining room. She refused to sit on the Guiden's couch because that's where she'd had sex with Tony. The sofa made her jittery, and so did Tony's wife.

Francine nuzzled Tony's neck. Her golden-brown hair hid his face. She straightened, draped an arm over his shoulders, and kissed his cheek. "You'll be fine. You always are."

"I've been lucky," he said.

"You've been smart and careful." She kissed the top of his head. "And you are very, very special."

Tony raised one of Francine's hands and kissed her palm. "You're the special one. I'd be dead by now if it weren't for you."

Emi drew everyone's attention back to the problem at hand. "And I'd be dead now if it weren't for Tony. Thornhill came to my apartment to torture me, to find out what we'd learned about him and Pete Izary. Tony saved my sister and me, and I won't let him take the fall for this."

Sean lowered his arms and addressed Francine. "I promise we'll stop at nothing to remove the threat to your family. Every member of the team is committed to finding a solution."

"I know, but I'd like to learn more about what's happening. I feel as though I've walked into the middle of someone else's nightmare."

"That's not a bad way to describe it," Tony said. "In July, a police task force visited pharmacists with a photo of Axel Thornhill. They were following up on a series of opioid thefts. The pharmacist at a drug store in town told them she'd seen Thornhill on a security video and gave a copy to the police."

"A month later, the task force determined Thornhill disappeared," Sean said. "Not unusual for someone in his business, but one of the task force investigators remembered the video clip. He wondered if the man chasing Thornhill made him go missing, but he couldn't identify the guy."

"Five days ago," Tony said, "Thornhill's body turned up at a pool construction site. They pulled a fingerprint off—"

"The gun, oh my god, your fingerprints were on the gun." Emi panted with fear.

I rolled my eyes at my friend. Tony glared at Emi and continued. "They pulled a fingerprint off a snap on the dead man's jeans. That's how they identified him. There were no prints on the gun. I saw to that."

"The missing person case became a homicide case," Sean said. "Detective Clendennon visited the pharmacy. The pharmacist had nothing new concerning the video. However, a clerk remembered something he'd found while taking out the trash the day after the video was shot. It didn't appear to be valuable, so he shoved it in the lost and found drawer.

"It was a gold card case," Sean continued. "There were no cards in it, and the clerk didn't scrutinize it. He figured it was cheap, like the stuff sold in the store. The engraving on the back was worn, easy to miss. The cops magnified the printing and read the 'Knox Engineering, Ten Years of Service, Anthony Guiden,' engraved on the back of the case."

"My prints are all over it," Tony said.

Theresa shrugged a slender shoulder. "So what. We'll say the case was lost or stolen years ago."

"Why didn't they confront Tony with it?" Francine asked. "Why keep it a secret?"

"At the moment, they have an altercation between Tony and Thornhill, which we deny ever happened," Sean explained. "It's too soon for them to determine when or where Thornhill died. They'll hold something back to corner Tony with if they tie the fight to the murder."

"How do they do that?" I asked.

Tony dropped his hands to his lap. "The fight is the motive, and the victim's gun was the means. They still need to prove I had the opportunity, so I'll work on my alibi."

Francine leaned across Tony and squeezed his shoulders. "What will you do?"

"We have to do two things to end this mess," Sean said. "We need to retrieve Tony's card case, and we need to give Detective Clendennon a better suspect for Thornhill's murder."

"Is that all?" Francine made a face between a smile and a grimace. "The twins will be home soon. I'll leave you to your scheming." She strode off to the kitchen. As she passed, she gave Emi's cheek a "aren't you the cutest thing" tweak.

Emi's eyes grew wide, her lips parted, and a strangled noise escaped her throat.

I rescued Emi from further humiliation by refocusing on another problem. "What if Ray remembers something from today?"

"Denial," Sean said. "We were never there."

"He could get video surveillance from Privateers," Theresa countered.

"Way ahead of you. Anderson visited in uniform and deleted two hours' worth of recordings."

"I can't believe that stripper costume works so well," I said.

Anderson wore the cop costume back in the day when he earned extra cash dancing for small groups of women. Most of the audiences were over sixty, but they tipped well, according to Anderson. I appreciated his hustle. I used to be that way when I was in high school—anything for a buck.

Chapter Eight

I'd hustled for cash since I was fourteen. Before then, my brother Ben used to give me a few bucks when he could spare it, but I hated taking what little money he made. When Ben left home, the handouts ended, and I learned to scrounge on my own.

On that March afternoon, a month before my eighteenth birthday, a night of babysitting for the Mayweathers suited me fine. It wasn't the reward I'd hoped for, but it was a night away from home, so why not? Sean rang a guy named Mike Spinelli to retrieve Melanie's Escalade. Sean loaded his family and me into a gray Odyssey van and promised the boys a stop at guess where—McDonald's.

The kids played in the ball pit as if nothing horrific had happened to their sister. Their joy and innocence jolted me out of my peevish self-pity. Despite the hard shell I'd grown, I loved kids, maybe because I'd never been one.

For a while, Sean disappeared, and Melanie provided the outpouring of gratitude I'd expected from her husband. "I'll never be able to thank you enough, never." She blew her nose into a paper napkin. Melanie had one of those perfect little upturned noses set in a perfect little round face. She'd probably passed for thirty when she was eighteen and would still look thirty when she was eighty.

"Everything happened so fast. If it weren't for you, my baby would be gone." She was working up to another round of tears.

I patted her hand. "Well, that didn't happen, so you try to forget the whole ugly thing. Relax in a hot bath. Get a good night's sleep. Everything will look better in the morning." That was from a movie I'd seen on the Hallmark Channel, and it did the trick with Melanie.

She smiled at me through eyes shiny with tears. "Sean says that you're special."

"He does?" I asked, unsure of what she meant.

"Sean said that you read that woman's mind. For someone like you to be where you were today, it's a miracle."

I didn't know how to respond. Sean hadn't mentioned our conversation during the drive. That meant he'd told Melanie about me *before* we talked. How could he have known about my mind-reading before I told him? No one believed I could read minds, not my brother, not my mom, not her loser friends. Did these Norman-Rockwell-ordinary people actually believe me?

Uneasy, I distracted myself by laughing at the boys' rambunctious play until Sean returned and blew my world apart.

"That's settled." He sat, looking ridiculously large in the small plastic chair. "You've officially resigned."

"What!" I flew out of my seat, torn between running to the manager to beg for my job back and whacking Sean with a tray. If I moved fast, I could do both. "I need this job!"

He raised a palm. "I told your manager a version of what you did for us tonight and explained I can offer you more money working for me. She understands. Relax."

I refused to relax or do anything this guy told me. "I didn't agree to that! You can't do this."

"It's done. Pull the kids out of that ball pit thing. Let's move."

I didn't move. Sean held my eyes in his laser-blue gaze until I waded into the ball pit after the boys. I promised myself I'd get big money out of the asshole.

*

I dreamed of a house like the Mayweathers' when I was a little girl shoved into the corner of a squalid apartment listening to her mom having loud sex with a stranger. A swing hung from the ceiling of a covered porch that ran the white two-story ranch's length. Light glowed from the fan-shaped window above the entry door, placed in the porch's exact center. A night here wouldn't be so bad, I thought, and Melanie was a sweetheart.

I trudged upstairs behind Melanie, who held a sleeping Connie tight to her chest. Ahead of us, Sean and the boys turned left at the top of the stairs, headed for baths. I followed Melanie to the right into Connie's nursery.

The baby didn't wake while Melanie undressed her and changed her diaper. I turned down the Noah's Ark quilt, and Melanie settled the baby. Melanie let me fold the quilt over the sleeping angel. Tiny pink lips pushed in and out while Melanie shed the last of her tears for the day. Once she'd composed herself, she took my hand and led me to the guest room.

"Yell if you need anything."

"I'm sure it will be fine," I said as Melanie opened the door. She switched on the light. Fine didn't come close to describing the room.

They'd furnished the bedroom in white wicker. My eyes drifted to a lavender patchwork quilt folded at the foot of the double bed. Besides the bed, a pair of night tables held lamps with stained-glass shades. There was also a dresser and a vanity table with a low matching bench. A white ceiling fan with carved palm frond blades turned slowly overhead. Watercolor beach scenes hung on the walls, and a porcelain doll sat in the corner of a cushioned reading nook built into a bay window.

Melanie pointed to the left. "The bathroom is there if you need to freshen up." She closed the door softly behind her, and I was alone in Wonderland.

Chapter Nine

Anderson, the chief information officer at Knox, declared the MES office free of pests, so we met around the conference table on Monday morning to finalize our strategy. We made one modification to our plan to clear Tony. We decided not to steal the card case from the police property locker, at least not exactly. We'd replace it instead.

Selecting a replacement suspect for Thornhill's murder was easy. While investigating Pete Izary's death, we'd cozied up to his three least-favorite money-laundering clients, drug dealers. We suspected one of them killed Pete, but Axel Thornhill confessed to Tony before Tony shot him.

The three surviving drug dealers were undoubtedly capable of Pete's murder; Axel just beat them to it. Juan Angel "Johnny Angel" Herrera was my favorite, so we elected him. Our challenge was to re-focus the police investigation on Johnny rather than Tony.

"Herrera's name needs to pop up everywhere the police turn," Sean said.

"A copy of the police file would help," Theresa suggested.

Sean agreed but said, "I don't want to turn to our usual source inside the station. Theresa, you're on the card case. Use whatever resources you need."

Sean turned his attention to me. "Allison, stay in contact with Officer Armstrong. Keep current with the case and make sure he follows up on the leads we plant."

"Got it."

"Emi, do you have anything yet?"

"No, I'll tell you when I do," she said.

"Are you focusing?" Tony's voice carried an impatient edge.

Emi ground her teeth. "Do you think I don't want to help?"

"We know you do, honey." I bobbed my chin at Tony and Sean. "Don't let them rush you."

Theresa shot a glare in the guys' direction. "I think you're focusing too much, especially on Tony. Focus on someone else."

Emi's shoulders relaxed.

"Theresa's right," I said. "You watched Tony kill Thornhill. You're too close to the situation already. Stop concentrating on Tony's future."

"I'd like to stop thinking about Tony," Emi said wistfully. "Who should I target?"

"Clendennon," Sean said.

After our meeting, I joined Theresa and Emi in their office.

Theresa lay on the battered old sofa, which sat in the Mayweather's living room long before I moved in. "How the hell do I steal that card case out of a police evidence locker?" she asked.

Emi spun in her desk chair. "You can't. Get someone on the inside to give it to you, then replace it with the phony."

"And how do I get someone in a police station to hand over evidence? An attorney might request a look, but there'll be a record. If anything odd happens, it will come back to whoever checked it out," Theresa pointed out.

"Does Tony have a lawyer?" I flopped into an open chair.

"Tony says he'd look guilty if he got a lawyer at this stage." Emi covered her face with one hand. "This is my fault. I should have called the cops instead of Tony when Thornhill attacked me."

I kicked at Emi's feet to stop her from spinning. "You'd be dead. Quit blaming yourself and help us think of a way to get Theresa that case."

We had a plan by lunchtime, but we didn't get to run it by Sean because we had a visitor.

When the front door chimed. I popped out of Emi's guest chair and jogged to the lobby. An African-American man of average height and average build waited. He wore a gray suit, and an irked frown. "Can't say I'm surprised to see you," I greeted agent Dave Davis.

*

Dave Davis was the Treasury agent working on the three money laundering cases linked to Pete Izary. Davis was a practitioner, and his talent was wild. He could make people not see him. Dave also played around in people's heads, but not as much as Tony. Dave's gifts were useful for an investigator, and he'd become a fan of MES during and after the Izary investigation.

One of his money-laundering targets, Juan Herrera, was our target now. Davis' appearance was our first opportunity to sow seeds of suspicion on Juan, so we invited Dave to join us for coffee in the conference room.

"You people told me Herrera didn't do it." Davis was angry, sure we'd lied to him back when we'd worked on Pete Izary together.

"The cops still don't know who killed Izary," Sean said, "and either do we. We never got that far. Maybe Thornhill killed Pete, and Herrera killed Thornhill."

"The guy Guiden chased away from my hotel room back in July was waiting to kill me," Davis said. "If he wanted me dead, it's safe to assume he killed Izary."

Tony raised a palm at Dave. "Okay, so it was Thornhill. Joanna Izary got her dog back, and you got three money cases out of Pete Izary before he died. We'd reached a dead end. We couldn't hunt down Axel Thornhill. We didn't even have a name until now."

Everything Tony said was correct. We didn't hunt down Axel Thornhill. He came to us. Thornhill broke into Emi's apartment to torture and kill her.

"So, you didn't kill him?" Davis asked.

"No, but you understand," Sean said, "why Tony can't admit to the police he chased Thornhill that day. He'd have to say he was protecting you, which gives him a motive to kill Thornhill."

Davis ran his eyes over Tony, perhaps to decide if he was a murderer. Not that it mattered. Davis was one of us. "I understand, and I appreciate you keeping my name out of it," he said.

"You can reciprocate by getting us a copy of the police file," Sean said.

Davis reared his head back. "I can't get involved in this, and you don't want me involved. If a federal agent sticks his nose into Tony's rumble with Thornhill, the cops will ratchet up the scrutiny."

"Agreed," Sean said. "But they'll let you review the file as part of your money-laundering investigation involving Pete Izary. Get us a copy of the file, do your follow up on Thornhill's money laundering, and get on home."

Davis sighed. "I'll do it, but not because you've kept your mouth shut about me. Folks like us should help people when we can. I'll do it because of what you did for that kid up in Atlanta."

The mention of Atlanta broke the tension in the room.

"How is K-T?" I asked.

"He's making millions with his music and making his mom and dad proud."

"And Auralia?" Emi asked tentatively. When she was known as Margaret Ellen Thomas, K-T's mom had been declared legally dead. We found her and brought her back to life, though it was a different life than she'd left.

Dave Davis leaned back in his chair and took a break from being a treasury agent. "Auralia is making up for lost time. She and K-T's half-sister are part of the entourage now, and you'll be pleased to know Mark Thomas sold that old house. He's finally moving on with his life."

"Is he still married to Auralia?" Theresa asked.

"For the moment. Mark's satisfied with being friends. He doesn't want to force her to choose between him and Roger Riegert. Auralia's faced enough tough choices.

"That's for damn sure," I said. "I'm glad her life is coming together."

Davis stood and chugged the last of his coffee. "It is, thanks to you folks. You'll get your police report. After that, I'm out of here."

I wanted to hug him but resisted the urge. As a kid, I'd never been a hugger. Physical contact wasn't a pleasant thing in my family. Even in my teens, when I knew I could ferret information from people with a touch and a question, I didn't hug. Personal space was an issue with me until I moved into Sean's house when Melanie started in with the damn hugging.

Chapter Ten

After Melanie left me alone in the fairy-tale room, I changed into the workout clothes I carried in my backpack, then skipped downstairs. Sean had Melanie resting on the sofa, a glass of wine within reach.

"Sean gave the boys their baths," she said. "If you'd help them brush their teeth, read them a story, and have them in bed by nine, that would be incredible."

"No problem," I said, and it wasn't. I'd made a few bucks babysitting since I was thirteen, and the Mayweather boys were fun. Chad was a super adorable four-year-old and six-year-old Connor, the know-it-all big brother. The events of the afternoon wore them out. They were asleep before I finished the second bedtime story.

As I tucked the blankets tight around them, I gave each boy a kiss on the forehead. After switching off the bedside lamp, I turned and squealed. Sean Mayweather's lean form filled the doorway, his arms folded over the front of his blue t-shirt. He motioned me out of the room with a nod.

I followed him downstairs. Melanie had gone to bed while I was caring for the boys. Sean and I sat in the darkened living room, facing each other across a coffee table that was the perfect height for coloring books.

"Thank you, Allison," Sean said. "Thank you for what you did today. Do you have homework?"

I had to laugh. Thanks for saving my daughter and did you do your homework?

"You're welcome, and I have a biology quiz on Friday and an English paper due on Monday. Don't worry, I have to keep my grades up, or I get kicked off the squad." Though that was true, my grades were good because I enjoyed school. History or math or whatever was a distraction, and extra studying kept me out of the house.

"You're self-motivated. I can use that," Sean said.

I laughed again. "Sean Mayweather, you are one weird guy." He got even funnier.

"I meant what I said about giving you a job, and we always need help around here. Would your mom give her okay for you to move in with us to help with the kids?"

My heart soared at the prospect of living in the Wonderland room, even for a weekend, and I'd make a few bucks. I snorted. "I've been signing permission slips with my mom's name since I was in eighth grade. Yeah, you've got her freaking okay."

"Good. After I pick you up from school tomorrow, we'll swing by your place to get your things. Get on with your homework. Lights out at ten." He trudged up to bed.

I sat alone in the dark and let my head spin.

*

Two things happened the next morning that clinched my decision to stay on with the Mayweathers. I had no clean clothes, so Melanie loaned me one of her shirts to wear to school. It was a fitted Anne Taylor blouse with pearl-gray buttons. Most days, I wore jeans and a t-shirt, and they weren't always clean.

While I stared in the mirror, admiring the fit of the blouse, Melanie stepped into the bathroom and picked up my comb. "A French braid would be neat and pretty, don't you think?"

I was so stunned, I couldn't speak, so I just nodded. When I cheered, I wore my hair in a long French braid. My mom couldn't be bothered, so one of my fellow cheerleaders did the braid for me. It was no big deal. We always helped each other with our hair and makeup. For me, the time spent getting ready for a game was the best part of cheerleading. That's when my sad, grimy life transitioned to sparkly and happy, if only for a few hours. Doing my hair for a game was the first step on the road to escape. When she picked up my comb, Melanie couldn't have made me feel more special if she'd plopped a tiara on my head.

After breakfast, I rounded up the boys, helped them with their shoes, and loaded lunches into their backpacks. Sean herded everyone into the van. High school started before elementary school and pre-school, so I got dropped off first. I'd never gotten a ride to school, at least not since first or second grade. That morning I slid out of the van in my designer blouse and neatly braided hair, feeling like a princess stepping out of a Cinderella carriage.

As I pulled the van door shut, Connor said, "have a nice day."

Chad parroted his big brother with "Haf a nice day," and blew me a kiss.

I was a goner.

Chapter Eleven

Dave Davis came through with the police file late the next day. He joined us as we lounged around the Mayweather's pool, enjoying the still-warm October sun. We broke up the file and passed the pieces around. I read the dry as dust narrative from the comfort of a chaise lounge.

The narcotics task force that showed Thornhill's photo to the pharmacist suspected he had coordinated the theft of opioids but uncovered no direct connection. The task force's only link was an eight-second drug store security video showing their target being chased by a man with dark hair.

The day after the chase, a store employee found a gold card case embossed with the name Anthony Guiden. Anthony Guiden resembled the man in the video chasing Axel Thornhill.

In July, Pete Izary's ex-wife hired Mayweather Executive Solutions (MES) to find their missing dog, Rascal. Joanna Izary wasn't aware Pete Izary laundered money for drug dealers. She just wanted the dog back. Treasury agent Dave Davis supplied information regarding the money-laundering case. Davis was not familiar with the name Axel Thornhill, but he confirmed there were money-laundering clients Izary failed to identify before his disappearance and subsequent death.

Jenifer Watson, the sister of Emily Watson, an MES employee, found Pete Izary's body at a Habitat for Humanity build site. Anthony Guiden was a partner at Mayweather Executive Solutions. Even dry, police-reportese made it clear the cops found this to be an intriguing coincidence.

The missing dog, Rascal, was returned to Pete Izary's widow, who said she liked the people at MES and was satisfied with their service.

Anthony Guiden denied he was the man in the video. The techs found no fingerprints other than his and the clerk's on the card case. Guiden hadn't been asked to explain how the card case came to be behind the drug store.

The police file contained tons of disgusting forensic details concerning the condition of Axel Thornhill's body. He'd been dead for approximately three months when he was dug up by a pool installer's backhoe. He'd been buried in damp soil in the middle of a hot Florida summer. There wasn't much trace evidence left. The medical examiner identified the victim from a thumbprint on a snap on the dead man's jeans. Thornhill's death resulted from one gunshot wound to the head. The murder weapon was found with the body but had been wiped clean of prints.

The number of suspects was overwhelming.

Suspects included business rivals such as Juan Herrera and Stewart Burkhalter, as well as dozens of dissatisfied customers, former lovers, and subordinates who hated the man's guts. Some of these people had names; many didn't. But Anthony Guiden's name was on a gold card case found at the scene of an alleged altercation with the dead man.

"The case against Tony is circumstantial," Davis said.

"We believe one of your money-laundering targets, Juan Herrera, is Axel's murderer," Sean lied.

Dave nodded. "He is the most likely candidate."

"We'll gather the evidence to implicate him, but execution will be tricky."

"I want nothing to do with that," Dave said.

"We understand. You focus on the money-laundering and pretend you don't know us."

"You can count on it." Dave slid his sunglasses on and slipped away into the breezy afternoon.

Once he was out of earshot, Sean said, "We've got to drop clues leading to Herrera. It will help to have forensic evidence, but Juan Herrera has seen you three, so I'm sending in Pak."

Emi fell out of her chair. She didn't so much fall as stumble while standing up from the chaise. Bits of the autopsy report landed on the pool deck as she regained her balance. "I don't want Pak near Juan Herrera; he's too dangerous."

"We'll be close," Tony said, "and listening in from the van."

I tried to reassure Emi. "Pak's not stupid. If things get weird, he'll ditch. Give him some credit."

Sean continued outlining our plan. "Sol's working on the new card case. When it's ready, he'll give it to Theresa. I understand you three have a strategy to make the switch."

"We have," Theresa said, "but we'll need you and someone on the inside, Armstrong, maybe."

"He'll be skittish around us," Tony said, "let's use Clendennon instead."

"No, not him," Emi said.

Sean arched his brows in surprise. "Why not?"

"I've seen something. I'm not sure how it will help, but we should discuss it."

All eyes turned to Emi. When she got something, whether she had it right or wrong, it was worth hearing.

"Next year is an election year. Clendennon's face is on the news because he's announced he's running for political office. Tony's picture is in the background."

Everyone drew in a breath and held it.

Sean broke the silence. "Why is Tony's picture in the background?"

"The Thornhill case must be important to his campaign. Guys like Clendennon usually run on a law and order platform, don't they?"

Sean squeezed his eyes shut, then opened them wide. "Let's focus on changing that outcome. Allison, I want you and Emi to get close to Armstrong, involve him in exonerating Tony."

"Aye, captain." I let my smile sparkle, but the sparkle was forced. It was the smile I used when our team was down thirty-zip with two minutes left in the game. My high school football team needed the first three-quarters of every game to warm up, so I had plenty of experience with come-from-behind victories.

Chapter Twelve

As a kid, I loved school but hated the end of the day when my friends waited for their rides. Eager eyes searched the lot, then lit with joy when they spotted the van or the pickup or the beat-up sedan driven by their mom or dad or grandma or big sister. Sometimes their mom or grandpa handed them a drink or a snack, and I hated them.

I'd linger until after my friends got picked up before trudging off to whatever dump we shared with whoever my mom was sleeping with. Even at age eight, I didn't want anyone to see how I lived, so a lump grew in my throat when Sean's gray van slid into the high school's parking lot. To give the lump a chance to dissolve, I slowed my walk and took my time settling into the passenger seat.

"Hey," I said.

"Hey, yourself. How was your day?" he asked.

"I got tons of compliments on Melanie's shirt."

He pulled from the line exiting the parking lot and turned right, rather than toward his house.

"Where are we going?" I asked.

"Your place to pick up clothes."

I'd forgotten. My stomach recoiled at the thought of Sean seeing the filthy dump I shared with Mom and Earl. "Don't bother. I can wash my things tonight."

Sean didn't answer. He didn't ask for directions either.

"Do you know where I live?" I asked.

"You gave your address to the sheriff's deputies. I used to be one of them."

Mention of the cops reminded me I had an escape. "Forget the clothes. I need to go to the police station to sign my statement."

"I took care of your statement," Sean said.

"Oh." My heart clenched again. I hugged my backpack and prepared for the inevitable humiliation.

Earl, my mom's current, rented a crap house on a street of crap houses with brown, overgrown lawns and unpaved driveways. Sean followed me inside and waited in the living room while I grabbed my stuff. Thank God, Mom had already left for her favorite dive, Hell's Pony. I'd be spared that awkward introduction, at least.

The house reeked of stale booze and pot, and one of my mom's bras hung from a lamp. I scuttled through the living room to my corner bedroom. Confronted with my miserable cheap trash, I grew angrier with each item I crammed into my duffle. To cheer myself, I said goodbye to all the stuff I hated. Farewell to the sheets that served as curtains, the banana boxes that held my clothes, and the peeling wooden chair I shoved under the doorknob at night.

The last thing I grabbed was the purple, heart-shaped pillow from the mattress on the floor. My brother won it for me from the grab machine at Hell's Pony when I turned fourteen. He left home three weeks later. Since then, I pretended the pillow was Ben's heart, and I talked to it when I felt low. On the dreadful nights, when I'd had to fight off Earl, I'd squeeze the pillow and sing *Silent Night* into it until I fell asleep.

When I scooted to the bathroom to collect my hair stuff and makeup, Sean was still in the living room, his head high, sniffing the air like a bloodhound. The guy was weird, but he was getting me out of this dump, so I let it go. Back in the cluttered living room, I caught him flipping twenties onto the coffee table.

"What are you doing?" I asked.

He ignored the question. "Take off the shirt."

"Excuse me!"

"Take off the shirt."

Disgusted, I flung my duffle and backpack to the floor. "Ah man, I should have known. You're like every other guy my mom brings home."

"That's not what I want, and you know it. Take off the shirt."

Hot tears filled my eyes. The humiliation of Sean seeing the house was nothing compared to what was coming. I glared up at him. At six-four, he stood a foot taller than me and stared down without lust, or pity, or revulsion. Afraid my mom or, God forbid, Earl might walk in on us, I thought, fine, let's get it over with, bastard.

I undid the pearl buttons as fast as my trembling hands allowed. When half were undone, I pulled the shirt over my head and scowled up at Sean, willing myself not to cry.

He tilted his head, taking in the bruises where my mom's fingers had dug into my upper arm and the rashy mess on my right shoulder from being dragged across the carpet by Earl. After studying the purple blotch over my right breast, where I'd been punched, he picked up my bags. "Put on the shirt. Let's move."

With tears streaking mascara down my cheeks, I pulled the blouse back over my head, leaving it unbuttoned. I grabbed my heart pillow and half-stomped, half-ran to the van.

As Sean pulled away from the curb, it burst out of me. All seventeen years of hell.

"You arrogant asshole," I heaved through a sob, "with your perfect house and your perfect wife and your perfect kids! You don't know what it's like to watch your mom get shoved around and have guys paw you like they own you because they pay the rent.

"You've got your kids doing what? Little League and that crap. I bet you're always having cute little birthday parties with pinatas and shit."

I punched a fist into the dash. Pain shot through my hand and up my arm. I hated him even more. "Guess how many birthday parties I've had. None! If she remembered, my mom bought Little Debbie Cakes and maybe a balloon if she was flush. And now you show up with your fucking white wicker furniture and your fucking family van. Well, fuck you! Fuck you and my stuck-up cheerleader buddies. Oh, they'd have me over, but come to my place? In this neighborhood? I've never had a friend over in my life, never!"

I raised a leg and kicked at the dashboard, sparing my hand. Sean turned off my street and headed east toward home.

"I should have left like my brother did when he got fed up with my mom blaming us for everything and letting guys maul me." I scrunched my eyes closed and hugged my pillow to my chest.

"That park where Connie got snatched? I slept there the night before last. That's where I do my homework, so I don't have to go home and fight off Earl or clean my mom's puke off the bathroom floor. When it's raining, I walk two miles to the library or get one of my cheer buddies to drive me in her fucking Mustang. God, I'm sick of listening to her saying, 'any time you need help, honey, you just call' as if her pity can help me."

Recalling four years of my fellow cheerleader's condescending crap brought on a fresh wave of rants.

"You know a cheer bow costs twelve bucks? A fucking bow! Every time I needed anything, I panicked. Hell, the uniform was sixty bucks. Where was I supposed to get the money? Until McDonald's, I waited until my mom was asleep and stole it from her or her asshole boyfriends. If one of them caught me at it, I'd let him grope me, then I'd blackmail his ass. Keep that in mind, Mr. Mini-van driving Mayweather. That's the shit I've been doing to survive."

For the rest of the drive, I alternated between sobbing and spewing out all the ugliness of my life. As we pulled into Sean's driveway, I screamed how I hated how my friends felt sorry for me. "And I don't want you and your little Suzy Homemaker wife gushing about taking the poor little trailer trash girl into your home so just let me out now, let me go!" I wasn't making sense anymore and dissolved into incoherent blubbering.

Sean hadn't said a word during my tirade. He parked the van in the drive, and I wiped my face with the sleeve of Melanie's beautiful ruined blouse, hiccupped, and stared at my knees.

Sean lifted my chin with one finger. "First, you are never to refer to yourself as trailer trash again. Second, as you said, my wife and I are taking you into our home. We have three small children, so clean up your mouth. Now. Third, I won't allow anyone to do that to you again, so let it go. You're better than that, better than them, and what you have is more important than all of it, so pull yourself together."

I sniffed and stared dumbly at him.

"Melanie's waiting to gush all over you, and I have to pick Connor up from school, so go, move."

I scooted out, snatched my bags from the back, and struggled through the front door. Exhausted from my rant, I let my bags drop, and stood in the entry, weak and wobbling. Empty and numb, I clutched the purple pillow to my chest and fought to remain upright.

Melanie peeked around a corner.

"Allison, come and tell me about your day. I'm making cupcakes."

I'd returned to Wonderland.

Chapter Thirteen

Johnny Angel's favorite hangout was The Dungeon, a club near the FSU campus. I'd done one of my hands-on interviews with him there when we were looking into Pete Izary's murder. There's safety in numbers, so Theresa and Emi had tagged along. That meant we were out for another face-to-face with Johnny.

Pak didn't have skills, not like mine and Emi's, but he was a born actor. He'd helped MES out masquerading as an art student, a pool salesman, and even as me with the help of a blonde wig. That night, Pak walked through a door outlined with red lines, entering The Dungeon dressed as himself but concealing an excellent wireless microphone, courtesy of Anderson.

In the convenience store parking lot next to the club, six of us crowded into Sean's van with ears on Pak. For a long time, we picked up only throbbing dance music and bits of conversation as Pak moved through the crowd, searching for Johnny. The microphone caught Pak ordering a beer, then a mish-mash of club noises for a while.

"Sorry, dude." Pak must have bumped into someone.

"No worries." My breath caught as I recognized Johnny's smooth, confident tenor.

The music and crowd noise faded to a thump of base and a hum of distant voices. When we heard a flush and water flowing, we figured Pak had followed Johnny to the men's room.

"Quiet night out there," Pak observed. His voice echoed off the walls.

"It's early, man," Johnny said. "It'll liven up in an hour or so." Sounds of water running followed by the whir of a towel dispenser.

"I'll do that. See you out there." Water ran, then the volume of the music increased.

Club sounds continued for half an hour as we watched the parking lot fill. Inside, the noise level increased, but we caught Pak's voice ordering another beer. After a brief pause, he said, "You were right. The place is rocking," Pak said.

"Hey, watch it, man," Johnny snapped, and Emi gasped. Johnny's words were sharp, tense, but there was no anger there, just a warning.

Pak made no response, but the chaotic conversation noises grew louder. He'd walked into the crowd. Five minutes later, Pak jogged through the parking lot, grinning like a fool.

"Could you hear me?" Pak asked.

"Crystal," Anderson replied. He accepted the bits of sticky tape Pak offered him. "What are these?"

"That one's hair. The other two are fingerprints. I got a good set off the sink and another from the faucet."

"Did you get any pictures?" Tony asked.

"Three, but they're not clear. The one from the men's room has him alone against a white wall."

"I can work with that," Anderson said.

Pak turned to Theresa. "When you guys met him here in July, did you notice if he was wearing a Ralph Lauren t-shirt under his jacket?"

Theresa was our fashionista. "Yeah, a black one. You think that's a thing with him?"

"He's wearing a navy one tonight," Pak said.

"A zillion guys wear Ralph Lauren t-shirts," I said.

Sean smiled at me through the rear-view mirror. "So true. Did you notice Tony was wearing one on the day he chased Thornhill?"

"And," Theresa said, "Herrera's only an inch or two shorter than Tony?"

"And," Emi added, "that he has straight, dark hair like Tony?"

The plan was falling into place.

*

Axel Thornhill's body had been processed, as had his condo, so the big question was where to plant our new evidence. The answer was obvious, but it took a call to Davis the next morning. He grumbled about hearing from us again so soon, but admitted he had considered suggesting a search of Izary's office himself.

A mass of people overrunning Pete Izary's old office might get the cops' attention, so Emi masqueraded as a real estate agent. Theresa and I were clients hoping to lease empty office space. We entered the three-story brick cube and rode the world's slowest elevator to the third floor. Emi carried a folder and waved it around as she pointed out the building's features.

Theresa's knack for finding things made her handy at breaking and entering. In under a minute, she swung open Izary's office door. We paused inside to consider the best locations for planting evidence.

Theresa stood back and crossed her arms. "Dave Davis will suggest to Clendennon that after killing Thornhill, the murderer came here looking for any evidence Pete may have left lying around that the police missed."

Emi paced the edges of the small office. "If the killer was looking for files, he'd sit at the desk and go through drawers. The top of the desk is smooth. The prints can go there and the hair on the chair back."

Emi opened her folder and got to work. After tweezing the hairs onto the chair's headrest, she paused and let her fingers rest there.

"What?" I asked.

"Someone has been here recently."

"Clendennon?" Theresa asked.

"I don't know," Emi said with a glance at the window. Below, a new low-income housing development of duplexes and quads was under construction.

"That's where Jeni found Izary's body," Theresa said with a nod to the window. "Maybe the cops have already been here for a second look."

"Or," I suggested, "they're watching the office to see if his killer comes back."

"If Clendennon's got surveillance on the office, we're screwed," Emi said. "The sooner we're out of here, the better."

We wiped Theresa's prints off the doorknob and left.

*

The next day, Davis called Sean to say, while the cops hadn't exactly been eager to do it, they'd taken him through Izary's office that morning. Clendennon himself spotted the hair, and Pete Izary's office became a crime scene for the second time that year.

Anderson did great work on the photos Pak snapped at The Dungeon.

"Look at this shot of Herrera," Sean said. We were at the reception desk, waiting for the others to straggle back in from lunch.

I studied the photo on Sean's phone.

The shot was astonishing, the same but different. "How'd he do that?" I asked. "The angle's the same as the surveillance video." Anderson's gift involved manipulating technology. His calls were untraceable, and his photo editing undetectable. Unless the cops had an Anderson on their team, they couldn't discredit the doctored photo of Herrera or determine where it originated.

"Now we have to get it in front of Clendennon at the right moment," Sean said.

"After they've found his prints and hair, they'll bump into this photo and lose interest in Tony. It's too perfect," I said, and gave Sean's shoulder a playful shove. "What do you suppose will go wrong?"

Chapter Fourteen

After seventeen years of hell, I didn't expect Wonderland to last, but it did. Melanie and I shopped for clothes, got our hair done, and bought me new makeup. Even my snootiest cheerleading buddies commented on the improvement. My cheer coach said my preppier look reminded her of a naughty angel.

Despite the bedlam at home, I'd always carried a decent average so I wouldn't get kicked out of cheerleading. In my last term of high school, I got my best grades ever, mostly because I didn't have to hide out in a park or library to study. Also, Sean enforced a ten p.m. curfew. I'd managed my time since I turned seven and found it infuriating to be told I couldn't party on school nights. Though I bitched about it, I wasn't looking for an excuse to leave my paradise of a room.

And I had money. There'd never been enough money, even for basics, like shoes and lunch. Now I had cash for everything. I ordered the full photo packages for graduation and prom, the souvenir trinkets from grad night, and bought the yearbook I couldn't afford to pre-order.

The sweetest, the absolute best thing was the cheerleading banquet. The end-of-year event recognized the graduating seniors and exceptional cheerleaders and coaches. I'd never attended one because fancy dinners cost money, and family was invited. I had neither money nor family, so why bother when I could pick up an extra shift at McDonald's?

Sean bought a table for his entire family, me, and Donnie Gordon, my senior prom date. Melanie helped me pick out an ice-blue, a-line halter-top two-piece outfit that resembled a formal cheer uniform.

I was the only girl on the squad sitting with my boss instead of family, but I didn't care. After four years of being the poor girl they pitied, everyone wanted a photo with me and the Mayweathers. My tall, handsome boss intrigued my friends. Melanie charmed and chatted with the girls and their moms, and for once, I belonged.

Six-year-old Connor asked me to be his girlfriend that night. I explained it would be rude for me to accept Donnie sitting right there and suggested he asked again when he turned ten. Donnie that that was a hoot. Throughout high school, I'd avoided complications by moving on to a different guy every three or four months, and I'd saved Donnie Gordon for last.

I first noticed Donnie during my freshman year. He was a smaller, nerdier guy then, the kid who ate lunch alone with his nose buried in a game or book. I sat next to him in the lunchroom one day, and at least once a week after that, to piss off the jocks who bullied him. Beyond saying hi, we didn't talk much, but the other guys started giving him some respect.

By junior year, Donnie had grown five inches and put on muscle, and we had genuine conversations. By the spring of our senior year, he was a bright guy headed for Texas Tech after graduation, and I asked him to prom.

I'd checked in his head and knew he'd imagined us being together since freshman year. I'd always peeked at guys' thoughts in self-defense, and the practice produced mixed results—thrilling anticipation mixed with greedy lust. Donnie's thoughts made my heart dance. He was so proud to be with me it both choked me up and seemed perfectly natural. As we walked the hallways, I clung to him extra tight when we passed the guys who had bullied him. It seemed fitting that I should end my high school days with someone who saw me as more than an arm ornament, a prize to brag about in the locker room.

Prom night was pre-teen daydream perfect. When Donnie arrived to pick me up, Melanie positioned him at the foot of the stairs while I made my entrance in my non-thrift-store dress. I suspected Melanie had coached him on the corsage because its ribbon matched the blue of the gown. Donnie's face softened into a dreamy daze as I floated down the stairs, and my heart swelled.

We made a stunning couple, according to pretty much everyone. Our friends, and even our old enemies, wanted photos with us. There must be a thousand pictures of me with Donnie Gordon from prom night. His parents were conveniently out of town, so we didn't do the after-parties. We drove straight to his house with no discussion.

Though Donnie was sweet, when I woke at two, I made him take me home. An infuriated Sean, glaring from the porch swing, greeted us at a quarter to three. We laughed, waved at Sean, and kissed goodbye. There was no spark there. We knew we'd never see each other after graduation, but it was okay. The night had been perfection.

The closest thing to a bad day I experienced came on my eighteenth birthday back in April, before the wonders of cheer banquet and prom and graduation. I'd expected to be homeless on my birthday, kicked out of Earl's dump, so I wouldn't have complained no matter what happened. And, looking back, my embarrassment was brief.

My birthday fell on a Saturday. I awoke in a quiet house, dressed, and skipped downstairs to help Melanie with pancakes and bacon, but she wasn't in the kitchen. She wasn't anywhere. I didn't precisely panic but grew anxious, assuming I'd forgotten something. After pouring coffee, I wracked my brain, trying to remember what I'd been told we were doing that day. I considered texting Melanie, but then Sean entered the kitchen through the door leading from the garage.

"You're finally awake," he said.

"It's eight on Saturday morning, asshole."

"Language."

"Language yourself. Where are the kids?"

"You don't remember?"

Now I was annoyed—annoyed and worried. "No," I admitted.

He shook his head and heaved an exasperated sigh. "Come on, let's move."

I set my coffee aside and followed him, whining that I forgot where we were going, and I didn't have my bag. One step inside the garage, I froze. Melanie and the kids sat in a white VW bug, a convertible with its top lowered.

"Surprise!"

I goggled at the two gold balloons, a one and an eight, tied to the steering wheel. Connie whacked at them from Melanie's arms as Chad and Connor bounced on the back seat.

I couldn't see what my face was doing, but the giddy smiles on the faces of Melanie and the kids faded. I was disappointing them.

"I don't know how to drive," I croaked.

The garage fell silent, and I felt I needed to explain.

"I had no one to teach me. My brother would have, but he left when I was fourteen, and my mom sure didn't have any interest. My friends offered, but I didn't see the point since I had no money for a car."

The garage remained silent for another moment before Sean took charge.

"Everybody inside. Not you, Allison. Get in the passenger seat and pay attention."

I learned to drive that weekend, and I would have done anything for Sean and his family. Anything.

Chapter Fifteen

Though Detective Clendennon had hair and fingerprints tying Juan Herrera to Thornhill, we still had one more clue to plant. That part of the plan called for two people, so just before three-thirty, Emi and I wandered into the police station. Emi's bag contained Anderson's doctored photo of Herrera. Mine held a Dr. Pepper pound cake.

I switched on my brightest smile for the officer on the desk. "Hi there, is Officer Armstrong available?" I hoped the guy at the counter would tell Ray something special awaited him in the lobby, and I didn't mean the cake. I also hoped Tony's mind tricks had worked, and Armstrong had no recollection of meeting us at Privateers.

Ray Armstrong stepped into the lobby from a side door. I didn't wait for the questions.

"Hi, Officer Armstrong. Do you remember us?" I asked.

Lines creased Armstrong's broad forehead. Tony must have done quite a job on the guy.

I prodded gently. "Allison Francona and Emi Watson; you interviewed us about Tony Guiden?"

The light bulb lit over his head. "From Mayweather. Yeah, I remember. What can I do for you?"

I extended the cake toward him. "Dr. Pepper pound cake. You said you liked it."

The perplexed expression fled to make way for greed. "That's right. Come back. We'll try a piece."

Ray led us to an open office area with lots of partitioned desks. His workspace was a mess. He pulled paper plates and plastic forks from a file drawer. "A small slice, please."

I cut out a sizable chunk of the bundt-style cake onto a plate. Emi handed him a fork, and I watched with wide, expectant eyes.

"Well?" I asked.

"Unbelievable," he said around a mouthful of cake. "Sweet, moist, heavenly. Join me."

I cut two smaller pieces of cake and distracted Ray with chatter about the welcomed cooler weather and college football. Emi ignored her cake as her eyes searched the desk for the best place to leave our evidence. When she'd decided, she dug into her slice, signaling she was ready for the second part of our plan.

I leaned closer to Ray, pulling his eyes away from Emi. "Would you like to get a Dr. Pepper float after this thing with Tony is settled?"

As I rested a hand on Ray's knee, a buzz or zing flowed through me like an electric current My breath caught, and my hand jerked from Ray's leg. No words or images attached to the sensation, which was both physical and emotional. I'd never gotten a shock when doing my mind-reading. Unfamiliar with the feeling, I couldn't put a name to it.

I raised my eyes to Ray and struggled to regain my focus.

Ray's eyes remained fixed on his knee, where my hand had been. "A Dr. Pepper float would be great," he said uncertainly, "but this case will take quite a while, I'm afraid."

"I don't mind waiting," I said. "It'll give me something to look forward to." The odd thing was, I meant it.

We held each other's gaze until awkwardness made me turn my attention to the office and the activity going on around us. Ray's also turned from his desk and from Emi. Perfect.

"You're busy," I said. "We should leave you alone."

Ray gestured around the bustling office."It's always this way. Life in the big city."

I chuckled. "Is it like TV shows? Is there a big board with pictures and strings and evidence in bags?"

"TV cops get to work on one case at a time, and they have an unlimited budget."

"Do you enjoy your work?"

Ray's head rotated back to me. "Love it more every day."

Emi stirred, stood, and offered her hand. It wasn't fair, but I wanted to kick her back into her seat.

"Thanks so much for taking the time, Officer Armstrong," she said.

I stood reluctantly and gave Ray my best smile, not the cheerleader smile, a genuine smile.

He glanced at his shoes and then at me. "Thanks for the cake. Come by any time."

*

"He won't find the photo right away," Emi explained. "I slipped it in a folder unrelated to the case so when he bumps into it, he won't link it to our visit. He'll assume it was misfiled."

We were in Sean's office, seated in guest chairs. Tony wasn't around.

"Well done," Sean said. "Did you see Clendennon?"

"Yes," I said. "His door was closed, but I saw him moving around in his office. He didn't see us with Ray."

"Then it's time for my part," Sean said. "Sol dropped off the duplicate card case while you were at the station."

"How did Sol get the clerk's prints?" Emi asked.

"He went to the pharmacy and left it on the counter after paying for his order. The kid handed it back to him without a second look. Theresa, are you ready to go?"

She patted the back pocket of her form-fitting jeans. "Say the word."

"Go on out there," Sean said. "I'll start my visit in twenty minutes. I'm not sure how long it will take me to get Clendennon to move, so hang tight."

"Will do." Theresa left us.

"You want a Coke first?" I asked.

"Later. Put the phones on silent so we're not disturbed. Emi, turn off the lights."

I flipped the open sign to closed and set the phone to go to voice mail. Back in Sean's office, Emi watched us with uncertain eyes. Sean's distance-viewing skill freaked her out.

After three deep breaths, Sean's eyes unfocused, and his eyelids drooped. His breathing slowed, and the time between blinks got so long my eyes watered in sympathy. When his breathing became inaudible, Sean's eyelids closed. After a minute, his lids fluttered open, and his eyes focused on something beyond the edge of his desk.

"Is Theresa there?" I spoke barely above a whisper.

His chin dropped half an inch.

After ensuring my phone was on mute, I texted Theresa.

"Sean's there. Clendennon?"

The reply didn't come for seven minutes.

"He's stepping outside now."

I didn't get another text from Theresa for over ten minutes. I expected her message, though, because Sean tracked something unseen with jerky movements of his eyes as he pulled Clendennon's strings.

Theresa must have worked fast because her next text came within three minutes. *"He's got it. He's headed to the parking lot."*

Less than a minute later, my phone vibrated with a new message. *"He's going back into the station."*

Theresa was done for a while, so I set my phone aside. It was up to Sean now.

His lids at half-mast, Sean sat still motionless for several minutes as he mentally walked with Clendennon to the property room. When he arrived, Sean's shoulders tensed, and his eyes darted then closed as he willed the detective to request the original case. If Sean was successful, Clendennon would replace it with the one Theresa had slipped into his jacket pocket, and he'd remember none of it.

Sean's eyes opened, and his shoulders relaxed. His last task was to get Clendennon out of the building, something Clendennon very much wanted to do, so Sean could just ride along for a few minutes. Tension returned to Sean's features as he made the detective ditch the original case in the wire trash bin at the bus stop. If all went well, Theresa would retrieve Tony's card case a minute later.

Sean's breathing returned to normal as he left Martin Clendennon. Emi rose to fetch a Coke from the fridge in the office kitchen. The visitation had taken over an hour, and Sean was tired and thirsty.

Sean blinked himself back to his office. Moments later, I received the final text from Theresa.

"Got it."

I gave Emi the news as she set the Coke on the desk.

"That's amazing," she said, "you must be exhausted."

Sean downed half of the can. "He was already on autopilot. If I hadn't caught Clendennon at the end of a ten-hour workday, I don't think it would have been possible."

"What do we do with Tony's card case when Theresa gets here?" I asked.

"If they continue to focus on Tony, the cops will get a warrant to search the office, so I don't want it here. And it certainly can't go home with Tony."

"We'll use my parents' condo," Emi said. "My dad can hide it somewhere in the complex, close by but not in his unit."

"Excellent idea. Tell Drew I appreciate his help," Sean said.

"So, what do we do now?" I asked.

"The cops have Juan's fingerprints and hair from Pete Izary's office. They have a photo of Herrera looking remarkably like one of the men in the drug store video. They have his fingerprints on Tony's card case. Davis has them thinking about money laundering. Now we need to make sure they put it together."

"It's mostly circumstantial," Emi said. Emi was a first-rate buzz killer. "The missed prints will raise eyebrows, and they have no more evidence against Johnny than they do against Tony."

"Sure, but Juan is now a person of interest. Johnny Angel's a known drug dealer. Tony's an accountant with no criminal record. Who's the sexier suspect?" Sean asked.

I twirled the end of one of my braids. "Johnny Angel by a mile."

Emi brought out the buzz-killer saw again. "But how do we know they've put everything together?"

I nudged her with my elbow. "I'll visit my new buddy Officer Armstrong, and I don't want you coming with me. It's time Ray and I take it to the next level."

Sean let his head drop to one side. "A cop? Seriously? You little idiot."

"You were a cop."

He shook his head. "Let's get out of here. It's Halloween, and we've got to get the kids dressed and to a party."

"Are you going to Theresa's?" Emi asked. Theresa lived in a luxury apartment complex that often held parties in the community room. That night was the annual Halloween party.

"I'll get there as soon as I can," I said. "I'm doing the kids' makeup. Do you have your costume?"

"Not yet. I'll stop and shop on the way home. Who are you going as?"

"Little Red Riding Hood. I've got a goodie basket and everything," I said.

"I suppose you're looking for the big, bad wolf," Emi kidded.

"You know I am," I said, but I didn't bump into him until the following day.

Chapter Sixteen

I strode into the police station bearing a dish of chocolate mini-cupcakes topped with Dr. Pepper frosting. The officer on duty, a forty-ish African-American woman, eyed my offering with interest.

"Officer Armstrong, please."

"Ray's in an interview, but he'll be out soon. I'll tell him you're here. Take a seat."

I pulled out a paper napkin, slid a cupcake onto it, and passed it to the officer on the desk to ensure Ray would get my message.

Ray popped out of the side door fifteen minutes later.

"What have we here?" he asked.

I extended the plate as I stood. Ray's nostrils quivered, and his shiny eyes glowed with avarice.

"Chocolate cupcakes with Dr. Pepper frosting," I said and bounced on my toes.

Two unexpected things happened simultaneously. I assumed Ray was reaching for a cupcake, but he kept coming and encircled my shoulders with one arm. My eyes grew wide as my heart filled with surprise. My eyes grew wider still, and my jaw dropped when Juan "Johnny Angel" Herrera, followed by Martin Clendennon, stepped around Ray.

Ray said he was happy to see me and suggested we sit outside, but my eyes fixed on the drug dealer I'd cozied up to at The Dungeon back in July. Johnny's head was bent as he spoke with another man wearing a severe black suit. I turned away too late. Johnny's sharky eyes caught mine and seemed to say, "I know you," as he passed through the lobby. To make matters worse, Detective Clendennon greeted me and asked after my friends.

My mind bounced like a tennis ball from Ray to Johnny, then back to Ray. Sean sent me to ensure the cops followed up on the false clues we'd planted. Since they had pulled in Johnny Angel for questioning, I didn't need to peek inside Ray's head to see we'd been successful, so I could stop using Ray. I should leave.

Maybe it was my panic at seeing Johnny and the desire for escape, but my heart ached with the need to be with Ray, and everything else flew from my mind. Me being who I was, I didn't recognize the feeling, not right away. When it hit me, it hit hard.

We shared a bench under a massive oak. Ray ate three cupcakes while telling me about growing up in Hawaii, serving in the Navy, and settling in Tallahassee. It wasn't enough; I wanted more. I wanted to immerse myself in Ray's history and his oh-so-normal life. Like my Friday night escapes into cheerleading, I put my complicated existence on hold and listened.

It seemed mere minutes had passed when Ray wiped his icing-covered fingers on a napkin. "You don't have to keep bringing me goodies, though the cupcakes were great," he said.

"I enjoyed watching you eat them." I passed him the plate with the leftovers.

"If you enjoy watching me eat, let me take you to dinner."

Sean would say no. We had what we needed. Our plan worked, and it was time to get out.

"I'd like that. Call me at the office. You've got the number, right?"

"I've got everyone's number." Ray winked and took the remains of the cupcakes back inside. I watched until he was out of sight. This wasn't good.

*

"You're sure he recognized you," Emi fretted.

"If he didn't right away, he'll remember eventually," I said.

When I got back to the office, Sean and Tony were out, but Theresa and Emi worked away on the cases we'd set aside while dealing with Tony's issue. I buzzed Emi and asked for her help with a computer problem. She huddled with me behind the reception counter.

Emi freaked when I told her Juan Herrera spotted me at the police station. "You've got to tell Sean," she said. "He'll keep eyes on you until we gauge Johnny's reaction."

"Do you really think he'll bother to come after me? Yeah, I ditched him at his club, but a guy like that won't go after a random chick for being a bitch. He's got fish to fry, drugs to deal."

"He saw you talking with a cop, a cop who'd questioned him about a murder."

"So? Cops talk to lots of people," I countered, but I was uneasy.

"You're right," Emi said. "I'm over-reacting as usual. But if Johnny learns Tony is a person of interest in the same case, he might jump to a wild conclusion that could get you hurt. I'm worried about you."

Emi hugged me. I didn't hug back and felt terrible. I needed to explain, but how to start?

"If you're over-reacting, imagine what Sean will do."

Emi waggled her head. "He'll stuff you in a bubble until we're sure Johnny won't go after you."

"Ray wants to take me out."

She frowned in confusion. "Like on a date? That can't happen."

"What if I want it to happen?"

Emi's eyes softened, and she hugged me again. This time I hugged her back and sniffled.

"I told you I keep my relationships to under three months. When I was in school, it wasn't just to avoid getting tied down like my mom. I wanted to have fun, but I had no money. If I wanted to go to a party, to a movie, or a club, I needed a guy friend with cash. I didn't just use people like my mom. I only went with guys I liked. We had fun together, but I was never really that into any of them."

"I get it," Emi said, "Noone ever clicked."

"Do you get it, Emi? You don't understand how I lived. I couldn't invite a guy home to meet my mom or take him to my room to make out on my bare mattress with roaches crawling all around us."

"When you're in love, those things don't matter."

"Easy for you to say. You and Pak have a supportive family—two supportive families. The way I grew up, I wouldn't recognize love if it drop-kicked me for a field goal from fifty yards out."

"Until now," Emi said just above a whisper.

"Yeah, and I don't want our stupid secret gifted-thing to kill it before it starts."

She was quiet for a moment. "It was the same for me. It took me a while to acknowledge my feelings for Pak, but nothing else mattered once I did. I'd have done anything to be with him."

"That's why you asked Tony for help," I reminded her.

"Let's hope you don't get that desperate."

That made me laugh. "You won't tell Sean about Ray?"

"He needs to know about Juan Herrera."

"He'll lock me in a box."

"Don't get pissed at the guy because he's concerned for your safety. If Ray cares for you, he'll wait until the time's right."

I wasn't convinced, but as soon as Tony and Sean walked into the office, I screamed, "Meeting!" and stomped back to the conference room.

*

His expression was bland and impassive, but Sean responded as I'd expected. "Well, our plan worked. Unfortunately, there's a chance Juan Herrera could link Allison to Tony."

"Is that really a problem?" I asked. "Johnny doesn't understand what kind of people we are, that we're different. To him, I'm just a dumb chick who got cold feet."

Sean ticked off the points on his fingers. "Emi's sister found Pete Izary's body, and Emi works for MES. Tony is a person of interest in the case, and he works for MES. You work for MES, and you ditched him in a club a few weeks before he became the target of Dave Davis' money-laundering investigation. It's not far-fetched to assume he'll have questions, Allison. If you're not here or at home, you're with me, Mike or Tony."

Blood rose to my face. "I'm too old for this babysitting crap, Sean!"

Theresa, the diplomat, urged me to relax. "Johnny will beat the Axel Thornhill murder. The cops have no more evidence against Johnny than they did Tony, and I'm sure he's got a sharp lawyer. This thing will blow over, and Johnny will forget little-old-you."

Despite Theresa's confidence, Tony disagreed. "The police may have no case against Herrera for Thornhill's murder, but he's still looking at money-laundering charges."

"Allison's not a witness to any of that," Theresa said. "None of us are."

"Herrera doesn't know that. If he even thinks Allison's connected to the case, he'll have questions," Sean said. "None of us wants to deal with Herrera or his questions. Sorry, kid, until we're clear on Herrera's intentions, I want you close."

Frustrated, I crossed my arms but said nothing. I let my eyes slide to Emi. There was a worried, distracted frown on her face that unsettled me. When we were alone again, I asked if she'd saw during our meeting.

"You see me banging on a door?" I asked. "Where is this door?"

"I don't recognize the location. I see you using a mallet or rock to pound on a metal door, then there's a loud boom."

"A boom?"

"Like something heavy falling or an explosion," she said.

"Do I get hurt?"

"No, you're hiding behind the door."

"Weird. When does this happen?" I asked.

Emi rolled her blue eyes one way and then the other, and we both laughed. Of all our talents, Emi's was the most annoying because her visions provided only pictures without context. Details like when and where could only be guessed at.

"I bet you're seeing me breaking out of Sean's house," I said.

We laughed again, but we shouldn't have. My life was about to change, and my relationship with Sean pushed to the breaking point one more time.

Chapter Seventeen

Sean wouldn't discuss his business with me until I finished school. It didn't matter how much I nagged at him; working was off-limits until the day after graduation. His caginess filled me with a combination of curiosity, resentment, and eagerness.

I'd got in from grad night after three, but Sean shook me awake at eight. After a five-minute shower, I pulled on my best school outfit, accepted a brown-bag lunch from Melanie, kissed the kids, and trailed Sean out the door. My smile threatened to tear my face in two. I'd gone from hopeless fast-food cashier to preppy office drone in three short months.

I bounced with excitement during the drive to the office on that warm June morning. For three months, I'd imagined what Sean did to provide the money he threw away on me. While studying for exams and caring for the Mayweather kids, I daydreamed about Sean's business. My curiosity spawned fantasies of billionaires dropping by in Bentleys and Lamborghinis. I'd meet people from all over and be privy to secrets that would keep me awake at night.

I wasn't too far off the mark.

The company was Mayweather Business Services back then, and it sat in a freestanding building in the middle of a block of small strip plazas and restaurants. Clumps of professional offices bordered it on both sides, with a large, shared parking lot in the back, which Sean said he never used. The five slots at the building's entrance were seldom filled, though that would change.

The reception area featured a mahogany desk behind a high granite-topped counter. I glowed when Sean referred to the lobby as my office. My desk held a laptop, not a register, and I had a coat rack, not a locker. I officially felt like an adult.

The tile floors gleamed, and the walls wore fresh paint. To the left of the reception desk, a corridor ran past two offices. The first office was Sean's. The second office had belonged to Sean's former partner, Constance Albies, Connie's namesake.

A right turn at Constance Albies' old office brought us to an impressive conference room. Ten high-backed upholstered chairs surrounded a glossy oval conference table. A matching credenza held a coffee tray bearing heavy white mugs. The television or monitor or whatever it was hanging above the credenza was at least sixty inches.

The next room was a dumping ground for miscellaneous junk, including an old sofa, broken toys, and Christmas decorations. A right turn brought us to a small but clean kitchen stocked with Mayweather-household castoff dishes, glasses, and flatware. A variety of partially filled booze bottles huddled under the sink. Sean explained that his clients sometimes needed fortification.

We passed the door to the bathroom off the reception area to end the tour.

Sean shows me how to operate the coffee maker. We took our Disney mugs to the conference room. I remember mentally kicking myself for forgetting to bring a notebook.

"I started Mayweather Business Services with Constance five years ago," Sean explained. "We met early in my career as a sheriff's deputy. Constance was a Leon County prosecutor. We recognized each other as practitioners but didn't discuss partnering up for over a year."

"Practitioners of what?" I asked.

"You read minds. You're a gifted person, and your skill is useful. Practitioners possess similar skills, but they can use those skills to influence people, things, or events. Practitioners make things happen."

I laughed and sipped coffee. "Are you telling me there's a bunch of people roaming around who can read minds?"

"Certainly not. That's what makes you so special."

I studied his face over the rim of the coffee mug. He didn't appear to be lying, but trust didn't come easy to me. I set my mug aside. "So, you're a practitioner. What do you practice?"

"Distance viewing, and, if I've had contact with a person, I can control them from a distance, too."

"You mean like a puppet?"

"It depends on the person. It's hard to get total control, but I can convince people to do small but useful things such as leave a door unlocked or open an email I want to read."

It sounded like bullshit to me. I'd never met a single soul who could do what I did, and Sean was telling me he did it for a living. I stretched a hand toward the center of the table. "Let me hold your hand while you tell me more."

His lips formed a wry smile. "Sure."

I took his hand. "Tell me how your distance-viewing works."

"I have to visit physically before I can visit from a distance. I can control a person with only casual contact, but the greater the connection, the greater the control."

I squirmed and frowned. Sean hadn't a thought in his head. I got nothing other than his words, so I tried a more personal topic.

"How's Connie been since her kidnapping?"

"She's unaffected as far as we can tell. Thanks to you, we got to her fast."

Nothing. Not a hum or buzz. A white wall. I pulled my hand away.

"I can't read your thoughts."

"Practitioners can control the traffic inside their heads."

"Do all practitioners have that?" I asked.

"Most of the ones I've met do. That's something we'll work on, recognizing skilled people and practitioners. A quality practitioner will recognize your skills. You need to be cautious around them, so they don't manipulate you."

The thought of someone playing around in my head made me queasy. "Who are these gifted and practitioner people?"

"There aren't many of us. Going into business with Constance put me in touch with more than the average person might meet in an entire lifetime. We used them when we needed extra help."

"How do they help?"

He raised a shoulder. "Depends."

I sipped coffee and sighed. Sean didn't trust me yet, and I didn't blame him. I had trust issues myself. "Why did your partner leave?"

"Constance sold me her share of the company eight months ago and return to Chicago. Since she's left, I've had to rely on other resources, people I met while working with Constance. Now I have you."

"I can't do that weird shit."

"I don't expect you to do what I do or what Constance did. You're quite valuable as you are."

My ears perked. "Do I really get paid?"

"I promised you a job, didn't I?"

"Yeah, but you've supported me for over three months. You bought me a car, paid for my insurance. Melanie buys my clothes. I haven't so much as paid for a pack of gum. I don't expect a salary on top of that."

"Do you think I've done all that because I'm such a noble guy?"

My fake cheerleader smile faded. Emotionless blue eyes returned my gaze with glacial indifference. Sean was a family man with a wife and three kids, yet he considered me without warmth or empathy. His were the eyes of a hawk fixed on a field mouse. The mouse in me wanted to flee, and my heart filled with disappointment. I'd been thinking of Sean as family, not an employer. The reality was worse. I was a tool.

I shifted my gaze to the surface of the shiny table and wiped at imaginary dust. "Silly me, I thought you liked me."

"I do, and Mel loves you, so do the kids. But make no mistake, you're a valuable asset, a rare commodity, and I intend to exploit you, so don't feel bad about getting paid. As for living with us, it makes it easier for me to protect you."

My head jerked, and my eyes shot to his. "Protect me from what?"

At last, humor warmed his iceberg eyes. "Yourself, mostly."

I laughed, but Sean proved to be almost as good a fortune teller as Emi.

Chapter Eighteen

Despite Sean's concerns about Juan Herrera, the mood in the office lifted the following week. I rode with Sean to and from the office and stayed home at night. Though I ached for my handsome Hawaiian, I had no time to pursue Ray Armstrong. With the cops focused on Juan rather than Tony, we were no longer distracted by Axel Thornhill's murder. In the days following my encounter with Juan at the police station, we wrapped up two cases and made progress on four more.

Ray didn't call or text, and I concluded that what I felt was just me, and it wasn't the same for him, which was a shame because I had it bad. My first brush with genuine love, if that's what I'd felt, left me shaken and preoccupied. In my few free moments, I checked out airfares to Hawaii. I shopped for bikinis and sarongs and created elaborate fantasies of walking hand-in-hand with Ray along moon-lit beaches.

On Friday morning, we made two healthy deposits, which improved the mood in the office even more. As long as Mike Spinelli chauffeured, I got Sean's okay for a girls' night out at Theresa's apartment that evening.

Already excited about getting the weekend started, my mood lifted like a hot-air balloon when Ray Armstrong strolled into the office at three. I directed my eyes to the silky black hair curling over his collar and smirked.

"Officer Armstrong, you need a haircut."

"I'm considering letting it grow and applying for undercover work."

"What can I do for you today, officer? We're closing up shop early."

"I'm here for Tony Guiden," he said.

My smile melted away, and a hand flew to my mouth.

Ray burst out laughing. "I'm not here to arrest him. We're closing our investigation into his possible relationship with Axel Thornhill."

I was around the desk, and my arms were around Ray before I could stop myself. Sean chose that moment to turn the corner from his office.

Ray backed out of my embrace and extended a hand toward Sean. "Do you and Tony have a moment?"

Sean shook Ray's hand and shot me a questioning look. "We can use the conference room." Sean let Ray precede him down the corridor with a backward glance at me. Hopefully, he thought I'd been interviewing Ray using my unique method.

Still convinced Tony was in deep shit, my stomach churned. I struggled to stay in my seat and not run back to Emi's office to eavesdrop on the conference room conversation. My battle for self-control wasn't long. Sean, Tony, and Ray returned to the lobby less than ten minutes later, shaking hands and patting backs.

"I'm sure it's been disruptive, and we appreciate your help." Ray's eyes lit on me. "You and your staff have been great."

"I'm glad we could help," Sean replied.

"Tony, Martin asked that you call him at your convenience. It doesn't concern the case. He says it's a business matter."

"I'll get with him in the morning," Tony said.

"One more thing," Ray continued.

Sean's eyes narrowed. He suspected Ray was pulling a Columbo on him.

"It's been a genuine pleasure getting to know all of you and," Ray glanced at me, "I'd like to get to know one of you even better. I assure you your case is closed. Anything that develops between Allison and me is unrelated."

Ray said his goodbyes and stepped outside.

Sean locked the door behind Ray and flipped the sign to "closed."

Sean's icy blue eyes and Tony's blazing brown eyes fixed on me. I was a bunny facing off against a polar bear and a wolf.

Tony leaned an elbow on the reception counter. "What might develop between you and Ray Armstrong?"

"None of your business, Tony." I tried to hiss out the words but sounded like a four-year-old refusing to eat Brussels sprouts.

Sean remained calm and in control. "You are our business, Allison. Your safety is our business."

"What's safer than going out with a cop?"

"It would be better if the cop weren't pursuing a case against Juan Herrera." Tony's tone was gentle, not terse, but he still pissed me off.

"I thought we wanted the cops to chase Johnny," I said through clenched teeth.

"But we don't want Johnny chasing you," Tony continued. "For your safety, this fledgling relationship should wait."

"Agreed," Sean said.

"Not agreed, dammit!" I screamed.

"You're too vulnerable." Sean remained calm, but his volume increased.

"You're ridiculous. Even if Johnny comes after me for some half-assed reason, Ray's a cop."

"Drug dealers are paranoid," Tony said. "Herrera may view your relationship with a cop as suspicious, even dangerous."

Emi and Theresa must have heard my shouts. Bags hanging from their shoulders, they hovered at the edge of the lobby opposite Tony and Sean.

"I won't negotiate with you on this," Sean said. "You're too valuable an asset."

That set me off. "I'm not a fucking asset!"

"None of us are," Emi said. "We're women. We want normal lives."

"You'll never have normal lives," Tony snapped. "Your skills are extraordinary, and your work brings you into contact with dangerous people."

"And," Sean added, "you're making uncommonly good money for women your age."

Emi scoffed. "And you and Tony are making more. You have homes, families, and friends. We want the same."

"Tony and I want to keep you alive long enough to have what you want, and I'd say you and Theresa are well on your way, with safe homes and supportive partners."

"Homes and partners who've been background-checked and approved by you and Tony," Emi said.

"Why is that a problem?" Sean asked.

"Allison isn't one of your kids," Emi said, and I wanted to kiss her.

Sean sighed. He raised his face to the ceiling then back to Emi. "I don't disapprove of Ray Armstrong, and for what it's worth, his background check is clean."

The color rose in my face, and my mouth opened, but Emi spoke first. "So, your objection has to do with Juan Herrera, not Ray."

"That's what Tony and I explained. Until we're sure of Juan's intentions toward Allison, we'd prefer she waits."

"I disagree," Theresa said, "I say she goes ahead and has her relationship with Ray Armstrong as publically as possible. It proclaims to Juan Herrera and the world she has nothing to hide."

I was ready to kiss Theresa, too, until she added, "But I agree that we should keep an extra pair of eyes on Allison. Even when she's with Ray, there should be at least one other person watching."

"Excuse me!" I bellowed.

Emi turned to me and set her bag on the reception counter. Her flamingo charm swayed, the cheap pink crystals catching the late-afternoon sunlight. "I'm sorry, Allison, I agree with Theresa. You're too valuable to risk, and not because you're an asset for Mayweather, but because you're our friend."

"To kick things off," Theresa suggested, "why don't we make tonight's girls' night at my place special and ask the guys to join us? I'm sure Reggie can make it. Hell, he never goes home anymore."

"Pak never turns down an invitation for a girls' night," Emi said. "And we can up our game by getting Mike Spinelli to pick us up in the limo."

Theresa punched a fist in the air and hooted. "I love it! I can't wait to see my neighbors' faces when my guests drive up in a limo."

The angry flush faded from my face, and I turned on the charm. "What do you say, Sean? Can I ask Ray to come to the house to meet Melanie and the kids, then go to Theresa's with Mike? Will that satisfy you?"

Sean crossed his arms over his chest and heaved an exaggerated sigh. "I suppose."

I could have kissed him, too.

*

Ray jumped at the chance to go with me to Theresa's and agreed to pick me up from Sean's at seven. I didn't mention the limo. I wanted to enjoy the surprise.

While I dressed, Sean leaned against my door and regaled me with the list of topics I shouldn't get into with Ray. Melanie shooed him out. When the doorbell rang, she kissed my cheek and told me to wait three minutes to make my entrance. Melanie loved entrances.

I controlled myself enough to take the stairs one step at a time rather than skipping ahead of myself like a kid on her first date. Ray's eyes glistened as he took in the fit of the sleeveless sundress Melanie loaned me.

"Hey, you," I said.

"Your hair looks nice braided in the back."

"Thanks. Melanie does it for me."

"Cute."

"You're pretty cute yourself." Ray wore a bright floral shirt over jeans, and he'd parted his longish hair in the center. He was an adorable teddy bear, just begging to be cuddled.

Sean asked Ray if he wanted a beer, which reminded me we weren't two thirteen-year-olds on our way to a birthday party.

Ray declined, which pleased Sean. "Let's sit out on the porch while we wait for Mike," he suggested.

"Who's Mike?" Ray asked.

"Our ride to Theresa's," I said, but Ray didn't hear me because the kids had discovered we had company and were all over him.

We sat on the porch, talking and messing with the kids until the black Lincoln Town Car turned onto the street. Ray's cop eyes latched onto the limo and followed it up the drive.

The kids dashed to the car. "Uncle Mike!" At the limo, their excitement shifted into overdrive when Pak and Emi emerged.

Ray spun to me. "This is our ride?"

I nodded and grinned an evil grin.

On the drive to Theresa's, Emi told Ray how Mike Spinelli had been Ricky Jacob's chauffeur back when he was CEO of Knox.

"Ricky used the commuting time to get extra work done," she explained. "When he retired, and Maggie took the CEO job, she preferred driving herself." Emi paused. "Maggie prefers doing most things herself. Anyway, that's how Tony met Mike."

"Tony and Sean have Mike drive us around when we're out on jobs together," I said. "That way, we can focus on work." I didn't mention that Mike also provided bodyguard services.

"Mayweather must be quite a business to afford a limo driver," Ray said.

"Don't let the modest office fool you," Pak said confidentially. "Mayweather is very successful. These three travel so much I get jealous of Emi sometimes."

Emi rolled her eyes. "And sometimes he tags along totally uninvited."

At Theresa's, we took our time emerging from the limo to give her neighbors a good look. Once inside, Ray was blown away by Theresa's spacious luxury apartment. Theresa supplied the guys with beers and provided what she called a buttery Chardonnay for us girls.

Though he was an outsider and a cop, my friends got comfortable with Ray. Reggie was a wanna-be restaurant reviewer, Pak loved to cook, and Ray liked to eat, so that's where the conversation went.

We monitored our discussions carefully. Though Pak wasn't a gifted person, he understood our world. Reggie did not, and Theresa didn't want that to change, so discussions about talent, practitioners, and special skills were out. Still, we relaxed.

We'd finished our second drinks and Theresa's fancy-schmancy hors d'oeuvres when Theresa asked, "Is everyone ready for a dip?"

Theresa thought of everything.

Emi fumbled in her backpack. "I've got our swimsuits, babes. We need to borrow towels, though."

"Oh man, I forgot the pool. Sorry, Ray, I forgot to mention we were going for a swim," I said, which was a total lie. Theresa had invented the ruse so Ray and I could be alone.

"No worries," Ray said. "We'll go down with you guys and watch."

"That's okay," Theresa said. "You and Ray can hang here for a while. It'll be too cold to swim soon. I want a quick dip, and the pool closes at ten."

"We can watch from the balcony," I said.

Emi popped up and handed Pak his trunks. "Let's go change."

From Theresa's balcony, Ray and I watched the two couples stroll from the building to the lushly landscaped pool below us. The water sparkled ghostly blue and green as my friends splashed around under the colored patio lights.

Ray slipped an arm around my shoulders. "I like your friends."

"They're incredible," I said. "I used to not have any friends."

"I don't believe that."

"It's true. I mean, I got along with people, but I was too embarrassed to have people visit, so I never got too close to anyone. My mom's a drunk and refused to work, so we were always broke. You need to know that."

"Why?"

"In case I'm crude or something, you'll understand I don't come from the best of families."

"I don't give a shit about your family."

"Sean's family is my family now."

He removed his arm and held my hand in both of his. "You're the only one I'm interested in right now. Come here."

I let him pull me close, but paused before we kissed. "It's okay if I'm kind of different?"

"You're the kind of different I've been looking for all my life."

We kissed as he wrapped his arm around my shoulders again. We didn't rush. The pool didn't close until ten.

*

I love my friends. There were no lewd jokes or suggestive remarks. After changing into dry clothes, Theresa made coffee. Ray declined, saying he had to be at work at seven-thirty. I texted Mike, and by a quarter of eleven, we were saying our goodnights to Theresa and Reggie.

Emi and I let Pak and Ray handle the conversation on the way home. I stepped out of the limo, holding hands with Ray. Sean and Melanie waved at Mike from the porch swing as he drove off, and I walked Ray to his car. We didn't drag out the goodbye. I just kissed him on the cheek and said goodnight.

Sean's eyes followed me up the porch steps, but it was Melanie who said, "Don't even think of going inside until you tell me everything."

Sean moved to a side chair and stared out into the night while Melanie and I rocked on the porch swing. We chatted and giggled like kids until well after midnight.

It was the best night of my life.

Chapter Nineteen

What I told Ray about not having many friends was accurate. While still in school, I avoided close relationships because of my home situation. After graduation, I had no friends other than Sean and his family. For over a year, we used gifted "consultants" recruited for the job at hand. At seventeen, I believed I was a freak who read minds. By the summer of my eighteenth year, I'd learned my talent was pretty tame.

In the beginning, Sean used my gift cautiously. He didn't want me to put my hands on the clients or targets but, since I had to touch people to do my thing, it was necessary to put me out there, and I loved it, despite his concerns.

The tricky part was finding a reason to put my hands on a stranger. Being young helped. People aren't that surprised when young people do stupid, unexpected things, and their reactions made it fun. The best part for me, though, was reporting what I'd learned to Sean. For those few moments when I told him what I'd gotten from the target, I had his full attention.

For most of my life, male attention had been unwelcome. When I figured out men and boys' attention got me what I wanted, I understood I had that attention only until the guy got what *he* wanted. That was another reason I didn't like long relationships. I avoided hanging around long enough to get dumped.

Sean's attention had nothing to do with my body. He was interested in who I was, what I did, and how clever I was while doing it. He was proud of me and valued me. I'd never had that before and appreciated his respect, but it didn't mean I didn't hate his guts most of the time.

Though we were friends and coworkers, the evening I met Emi didn't start well. Sean and I got home from the office a few minutes after five. I rushed to change and charged out again for a pedicure I'd promised myself for a month. As I breezed through the kitchen toward the garage, I yelled to Melanie that I'd be back in an hour. Sean was at my heels, talking on his phone. He grabbed my elbow with his free hand and pulled me along to the garage.

When he unlocked the van with the remote key, I edged around to my VW.

"In the van, Allison, let's move," he said.

I waved my keys at him. "Got a pedicure. Catch me up when you get back."

"I might need you."

"It can wait an hour."

"No, it can't. In the van, let's go."

I stomped to the passenger side door, yanked it open, and pulled myself into the seat. "You should at least ask if I've got something planned before you drag me off to these things."

He started the van, hit the remote for the garage door, and backed out. "This is business, and the business pays for whatever you've got planned, so suck it up and get with the program."

"What, I can't have a life?"

"Knock it off, Allison. Sol has an emergency. I'm in no mood for drama."

"Who's Sol?"

"A friend and a resource. He's helped me identify stolen articles."

"He's like us?"

"He handles objects and reads their history. He can tell you who owned them, and sometimes how they used the item."

That sounded fascinating. "Can this Sol tell you who used a weapon?"

"I suppose. Sol's selective about who he works with and the side jobs he takes. He has an art and antique shop. If people knew what he could do using his skill, it might hurt his business."

Even I understood how that was a problem. Some people might prefer no one know how they really acquired "Aunt Millie's" priceless vase or whatnot.

I sent a text canceling my appointment and kept quiet for the rest of the drive. Sean pulled into the parking lot of an upscale shopping center off the Apalachee Parkway. Once inside, he sprinted, dragging me to keep pace with his long strides.

Gold script across a double-door glass entry proclaimed "Sol's Fine Art and Antiques." Brilliantly colored porcelain figurines and dolls filled a case inside the doors.

"Oh, look at the dolls!"

Sean pulled me away from the door and toward a white wrought-iron bench occupied by a sullen, preppy-looking girl my age. He aimed me into the open corner and released his grip on my arm. "Wait here. Talk to no one."

Sean entered Sol's Fine Art and Antiques without me. I crossed my legs and arms and huffed, letting my gaze drift to my seatmate, who studied me back. Her eyes cut away, so I checked her out. Warm cinnamon-tinted brown hair framed a roundish face dusted with a faint sprinkling of freckles across her cheeks. Her skirt, blouse, and pumps were frumpy for someone her age. I was thinking she could use highlights and a new wardrobe when she turned and caught me looking. I twisted around and pretended to look into the antique shop.

After a peek into the shop, she said hey, and scooted over an inch. "I'm Emi Watson."

I scooted an inch her way. "Allison Francona."

We began a halting conversation, but the proximity to Sean made me edgy. I didn't know what he had going on inside, and she could be part of it. Emi appeared ill at ease as well and suggested a trip to the restroom.

Away from the possibility of prying eyes, we relaxed. By the time we returned, we'd shared where we lived, where we'd gone to school, and that we'd both been dumped there by our bosses, who we were mortally pissed off with at the moment. I suspected we had more in common.

Emi confirmed that suspicion when she asked, "Do you use any special skills in your work?"

I nodded. "Do you?"

"I can see that we'll be friends. Really, I see it."

Something bounced and tumbled in my memory. I'd overheard Sean telling Melanie about an executive we'd done a job for a few weeks back. The guy worked for Knox Engineering, one of our more lucrative clients. Sean said this guy brought a new gifted person on board who predicted the future, a real-life fortune-teller. Could this be her?

I explained my mind-reading, but before we had time to get into her talent, an amused voice interrupted us.

I spun my head to check out the owner of the voice. He was a fortyish guy with dark brown eyes so unfathomably deep, they sent a shiver through me. It was like the shiver I got when I watched a scary movie, and the heroine started down the basement steps alone.

"Who's your friend?" he asked Emi.

His question struck Emi speechless. I figured he'd given her the "speak to no one" nonsense, too. I extended a hand. "Allison Francona."

He ignored my hand and said, "Hello, Allison. Sean and I will be longer than expected. Someone's coming to take you to dinner. We'll catch up with you later."

My heart skipped a beat as I realized this was the guy at Knox Sean mentioned, the one with mega-skills. This must be the guy who, according to Sean, could kick ass. He was good-looking in a way but radiated such unsettling energy my fake smile flickered then failed. I gave Emi credit for standing up to him when he told us to ride off with Mike Spinelli.

Mike was a throwback to an era of cartoon Mafia muscle. Short and stocky, his face had lost more than a few fights. He wore a black suit over a white turtle neck and a black fedora over wavy white hair. Emi balked when Tony told us to go with him, but our objections evaporated once we saw his Lincoln Town Car limo.

For the next hour and a half, Emi and I got acquainted while directing Mike all over Tallahassee, anywhere we wanted to go. Mike stocked the limo's bar with wine, bottled water, and real crystal. Emi and I watched the city slip by in comfortable privacy. I can't say seeing my hometown from the back of a limo was a dream come true because I never dreamed of being chauffeured anywhere in a limousine.

Amiable Mike took us to the drive-thru at Taco Bell, then on past my old high school where I'd had to beg for rides home or hoof it four miles in the rain. Eased by the wine, our tentative awkwardness gave way to comfortable conversations about our lives and families.

Emi came from a small, close-knit family. She had a college education and a good job. Given my history, it was astonishing we hit it off. By the time we drove past Emi's old high school, we were deep into school days and guys but stayed away from discussing our work. We didn't want Spinelli telling Sean and Tony we'd blabbed stuff meant to be private.

Twilight faded into night as Mike pulled the limo into a deserted park. We rocked side to side on swings while I described my crummy childhood and how I met Sean. She told me about this guy she liked and how another girl was moving in on him. By the time Sean and Tony arrived to scoop us up, we were well on our way to best friend status.

Over the next few months, Emi and I worked on two jobs, one right after the other. By the time they were over, I'd been kidnapped, rescued, and had two more new friends—Emi's boyfriend Pak, and Theresa, the chick moving in on him.

Chapter Twenty

The morning after my first night with Ray, Pak and Emi stopped by the house. I assumed Emi wanted to catch up on Ray and me. She surprised me by asking to speak with Sean.

"Jeez, you two, it's early. Melanie and I talked until one, and the boys woke me up at seven."

"Sorry, Pak wants an appointment with Sean for his dad."

"Is Andrej in trouble?" Pak's dad had been out of prison for less than a year.

"Nothing like that," Pak scoffed. "He wants to talk to someone, that's all, Monday morning if possible."

"Why?" I asked.

"He has a friend with a problem."

I raised a brow at him. "A friend?"

Pak raised a brow right back at me. "Yes, a friend. Someone he knew in prison."

Sean would love this. "Let's find the boss."

We found Sean dozing behind sunglasses in a lounge chair by the pool. Connie played in the sandbox with her herd of plastic unicorns while the two boys attempted to drown each other in the pool. The kids loved it when their dad watched them.

"Customer, Sean!"

He removed the shades and opened his eyes unwillingly. Seeing it was Pak and Emi, he replaced the sunglasses and folded his hands over his chest. "Good morning. What's up?"

Pak pulled a chair around to face Sean. "My dad wants to discuss a friend of his."

"What did this friend do?" Sean asked.

"Nothing since getting out of prison. Dad thinks someone's planning to kill him."

Sean dropped his bare feet to the pool deck, sat up, and adjusted the lounge back. "Tell me more."

Now that he'd captured Sean's attention, Pak warmed to his topic. "Dad was friends with a man in prison, Leon Clipper. He got released four years before Dad and hasn't been in touch. Last week, Leon looked Dad up, and they got together for dinner. They laughed, remembered old times, and then out of nowhere, Leon tells my dad he doubts he'll see him again because his wife is setting him up to be murdered."

Sean shook the morning fog from his head. "Prisoners tell tall tales to kill time. Are you sure he wasn't just winding up your dad?"

"Dad didn't believe him at first. Since that night, he's turned the conversation over in his mind, and Dad's thinking Leon might have been serious."

"We can discuss it. Does Monday morning work for Andrej?"

"That's perfect; he's off work. Emi can give him a lift."

Sean turned his attention to Emi, who'd pulled up a chair next to me. "What are your thoughts?"

"I've only heard Pak summing up the phone conversation with his dad. It'll help to listen to Andrej tell the story."

"Okay, Andrej Zacharia, nine Monday morning." Sean aimed his chin at me. "Put it in the book, Allison."

Mentally I put it in the book, then mentally kicked the lounge chair out from under Sean.

*

Sean and I got to the office at a quarter of nine on Monday. I started the coffee and made it back to the reception desk as Emi's red Fiat pulled into the lot. She'd bought the car second-hand from Sabrina Pryor. Sabrina tried to have her step-grandmother killed, then attempted to poison her grandfather with erectile dysfunction pills. It was an ugly situation, but we got it sorted.

I greeted our first visitors of the week with a cheery, "Happy Monday."

"Back at you," Emi said. "I'll show Andrej around the office. He's never been here."

"You bet. Can I get you some coffee, Andrej?"

"Yes, thanks." Andrej Zacharia bore little resemblance to his son. He and Pak were the same height, but Andrej was blue-eyed and fair. Pak had his mom's deep brown eyes and inky hair. Emi said while Pak might resemble Zabel, he took after his Uncle Anton, Andrej's brother. Uncle Anton must have been one funny guy.

Emi and I made Andrej comfortable in the conference room until Tony got in at nine. We waited another ten minutes for Theresa, who tottered in on stilettos, apologizing and blaming an upset stomach.

Andrej was practically Emi's father-in-law, so there were no formalities. Sean began. "Pak said you had an interesting conversation with a friend recently."

"It was exactly that," Andrej said. "I met Leon Clipper in prison. He killed a man in a fight and was convicted of manslaughter, but he was a good enough man. We had a lot in common. While he was in prison, his wife divorced him and kept him from his child, a daughter."

Sad stuff before a proper breakfast, but it paid the bills, so I kept an open mind.

"We were friends in prison," Andrej said, "until Leon was released four years ago. He didn't stay in touch, and I didn't blame him. It took me by surprise when he showed up outside the distribution center where I work."

"How did he locate you?" Tony asked.

"My idiot son put me on Facebook," Andrej said. We all laughed. That was so Pak. "He built me a profile and everything. I never look at it, but Leon found me there and learned I worked at the distribution center. We went to dinner and discussed what we'd done since getting out of prison. Our conversation scared the server, I think."

We chuckled again, and Andrej smiled. The smile looked terrific on him.

"At the end of dinner, I said, 'good to see you, let's keep in touch,' ut then he looked away and said, 'I hope so, but I think my wife is setting me up to be killed.' I laughed, and so did he. He paid for dinner, then dropped me home."

"Have you heard from him since?" Sean asked.

"No, but I've replayed that conversation in my head a dozen times over the last week. I assumed he was joking, but the more I recall things he said and his face when he said them, the more I wonder if it's not true."

"Did you call him?" Tony asked.

"I left a voice message the other day, but he hasn't returned the call. I don't want to push. He might want the past to go away, and I don't want to embarrass him if he was joking. That's why I talked to Pak. He told me you people are good at ferreting out information, and you're discrete. I don't make a lot of money, but I don't have many expenses either. I can pay."

"Out of the question," Sean said. "If anyone pays, it will be Leon Clipper. Does Emi have his contact information?"

"She said you'd need it."

"Good. Now tell us everything you know about Leon."

It took under thirty minutes. Andrej and Leon were friends for over six years, and it sounded like they had a lot in common. As with Andrej, Leon was intelligent, hard-working, quick-tempered, and devoted to his family. That was the hell of prison for them—being separated from their kids. Andrej didn't even do what he'd been convicted of doing. I was amazed he stayed sane.

Before prison, Leon was a developer. He built warehouses and industrial facilities, mostly on land he owned. When he got out, he started a landscaping business. In Florida, landscaping is a year-round challenge, and Leon built up a roster of steady customers fast. In no time, he had nine employees and a fleet of three trucks. He also married again.

"When we talked, he raved about Kelsey," Andrej explained. "That's another reason his comment at the end of the evening was so unsettling. Leon said she has an excellent job working for the City of Tallahassee, and she handles the bookkeeping for the landscaping business. Leon is so busy he has to turn down work, but his wife never complains about the hours he puts in. He said her attitude is great considering she'd been widowed twice before him."

Emi's gaze slid to mine. Our eyes met, and I knew I'd be having a private chat with Kelsey.

Andrej gave us more detail and answered dozens of questions. At ten, Emi took him back to the furnished by-the-week place he rented. Sean said we'd meet when she returned, but I didn't want to wait. I was ready to go on this case.

When Emi's Fiat pulled back on the lot, I yelled, "Meeting!" and jogged back to the conference room. On the way, I passed Theresa lying on the lumpy old sofa.

"Hey, kid. Still feeling bad?" I asked.

She lowered her feet and shoved them into her shoes. "I haven't been right since Saturday morning. Nobody else got sick at my place, did they?"

"Not sick, just a little hungover. It was a fun time. Thanks for including Ray."

Theresa stood and stretched. "I like Ray. He's not the usual Allison boy toy."

I made my eyes big. "He's not a boy at all." We giggled and stepped next door to the conference room.

"So," Tony asked, "are we dealing with a black widow?"

"We shouldn't jump to conclusions," Sean said, "but Kelsey Clipper is uncommonly unlucky in love. Let's figure out a way for Allison to do one of her quick interviews."

"Theresa can get me into the Clipper's home while they're at work," Tony suggested. "Maybe the problem is with Leon's business. Once Theresa locates his records, I'll review them for anything unusual."

"Perfect," Sean said. "Do we agree we should learn more before approaching Leon?"

"Yes, I prefer we not talk to Leon Clipper until we're sure," Emi said. "It could be nothing, and Andrej would feel foolish about over-reacting."

"Where do we find these people?" Sean asked.

"East of town off highway ninety. It's an upscale area, with plenty of customers for Leon's landscaping service. One more thing," Emi added. "Pak wants to be a part of this. He wants to help his Dad."

Sean didn't like it but said, "We'll see what develops. Step one is to interview the wife, are we agreed?"

Sean handed out the assignments. "Emi and Theresa, start your research on Leon's wife. Tomorrow, Allison and Emi will bump into Kelsey Clipper. While Kelsey's out, Tony and Theresa will visit the house. In the meantime, let's find out what security monitoring company the Clippers use, if any. Anderson will get us around whatever system they have."

Over lunch at the reception desk, Emi filled me in on what she'd learned about Kelsey Ryan Magnusson Ellison Clipper. Kelsey was thirty-eight and had lived in Tallahassee for nine years. She'd been born Kelsey Ryan in Cleveland, where she met and married her first husband, Michael Magnusson. Husband number one was killed by a drunk driver. Kelsey remarried three years later. Scott Ellison, a truck mechanic, got a job with a fleet logistics company in Jacksonville, so the couple left Cleveland. Scott Ellison took his life not long after they moved. After Ellison's death, Kelsey moved to Tallahassee and took a job with the City.

"Could she have faked Scott Ellison's suicide?" I asked Emi.

"Doubtful," she said. "Scott kissed Kelsey goodbye when he left for work that day, as usual. He hung himself in one of the service bays while everyone else was out to lunch. The obituary suggests he suffered from post-traumatic stress syndrome. He served in the Middle East and suffered bouts of depression."

"Sad," I said, "Kelsey really has terrible luck with guys. It would be a shame if she lost another one."

"We should keep that from happening."

"Did you get anything from Andrej while he was filling us in on Leon?"

"I did. I relate well to Andrej."

"You're tuned into his entire family."

"Yeah, that could get tricky, but we'll cross that bridge another day. Anyway, while Andrej was talking today, I had this vision that Andrej was with Pak, having another conversation regarding Leon. Andrej seemed pleased with what he was hearing. It's not much, I know, but I'm taking it as a sign everything is okay."

It wasn't.

Chapter Twenty-one

Kelsey Clipper worked in the Permits Department for the City of Tallahassee. Mike Spinelli parked the limo on the opposite side of the street from her building. Emi and I watched Kelsey step through the double doors with a group of three friends, heading out to lunch.

"She's not my idea of a Black Widow," I said between bites of my burger. Mike had taken us through a drive-thru on the way to our surveillance gig.

"Because she's not a skinny blonde with too much makeup and expensive clothes?" Emi quipped.

Kelsey Clipper was blonde, but not naturally. Her over-frosted hair frizzed at the ends. She wore comfortable knit slacks and a jersey top that accentuated her lumpy bits. She appeared chunky and happy. Kelsey laughed with her friends as they crossed the street. The group turned right at the end of the block.

"Hey Mike," I called, "can you follow those women who just crossed in front of us."

"No need, I'll bet they're having lunch at the Cuban restaurant we passed on the way."

"Bet you're right." Emi and I slipped out of the limo and followed.

They sat around a table for four inside the small, heavenly-scented café. Emi and I ordered coffee and listened to the lunch group's chatter. Kelsey was a significant contributor. Her laugh was loud and distinctive and carried throughout the small restaurant.

We didn't get Kelsey on her own until the lunch break was almost over. She hustled to the restroom, and it surprised us when not one of her buddies joined her, unusual behavior for a group of women. Emi stayed at our table to observe them. I followed Kelsey.

I posed at a sink until she came out of the stall. She patted at her fried hair in the mirror, then washed her hands. I did the same, but studied Kelsey's hands as I lathered mine.

"My goodness, what a beautiful ring!" I was a sucker for bling and was genuinely impressed by Kelsey's round-cut diamond. It sat in a wrap-around rose gold setting with the center stone held by delicate gold leaves filled with tiny diamonds.

Kelsey held out her damp hand. I grasped it, eager for a closer look.

"It is, isn't it? Leon insisted I design it myself, Kelsey said.

"Leon's your husband?" I asked.

"He's my third and absolutely the best. I didn't want a big wedding—I'd already had two—but Leon said I deserved the perfect ring at least."

"You've been married three times!"

The full bosom rose and fell. "Unfortunately, my first two husbands died. I pray every day I go before Leon. I couldn't stand to lose another husband."

I wrapped both my hands around hers and made sad puppy eyes. "I am so sorry. I didn't mean to pry."

She slipped her soapy hand from mine, her eyes still focused on her ring. "You didn't pry, sweetie. I tell everyone how much I love my husband and that I hope he outlives me. Strangers think I'm crazy, but I figure the more I say it, the more likely it will become a reality."

She returned to her group, and I rejoined Emi, but we didn't speak until they settled their checks and the coworkers left the café.

"They like her," Emi said. "They're taking her out for her birthday next weekend."

"She loves Leon," I said, "and she loved her first two husbands. She's emotionally fragile. She can't handle losing another husband." I shook my head to drive out the images of Kelsey's grief. "I wonder why Leon thinks she wants to kill him?"

"It could be something he's doing that she's unaware of, and it's his guilty conscience talking."

"Even if Leon is into something rotten, Kelsey doesn't strike me as the vengeful type. She's more of a rainbow and unicorns chick."

Emi signaled for our check. "I wonder how Theresa and Tony are doing with the house? Perhaps there's more there."

There wasn't. Other than having lame passwords, Tony found nothing troubling in the information on the two laptops.

"Leon's business records are simple and straight forward," Tony said. "They pay business and personal expenses out of separate accounts. Income and expenses are well-documented. His taxes are current."

We were back in the office conference room by late afternoon. I stifled a yawn. If Tony started going on about accounting and taxes, I'd slip into a coma.

"And he's busy," Theresa said. "His teams are booked solid. He has nine permanent employees, and the business owns three trucks. His people work in teams of three, and he bounces from team to team throughout the day."

"Life insurance?" Sean asked.

"Fifty thousand," Tony reported, "not enough to drive his wife to murder."

"Not Kelsey," I agreed. "She'd pay ten times that much to keep Leon alive."

"So, why does she want to kill him?" Usually unflappable, Sean sounded exasperated.

Emi turned to me. "How long have Kelsey and Leon been married?"

"Not long," I said. "Nine or ten months."

"When Leon was talking to Andrej and referred to his wife, could he have meant his first wife?"

Tony leaned back in his chair and threw his arms wide. "We're looking at the wrong woman."

"But what's the ex-wife's motive?" I asked. "They've been divorced since Leon went to prison ages ago."

Emi reminded us that Pak's mom wasn't thrilled about Andrej's release from prison. "Maybe Leon's first wife was just as pissed when Leon came home," she said.

Sean stood and stretched. "Excellent catch, Emi. We start over in the morning."

"I'll start researching the first wife this evening," Theresa said.

"Are you sure," I said. "You look done in, honey."

"Reggie's got a workshop tonight. I'll slip into PJs, grab a glass of wine, and get on my laptop for an hour."

"Don't do that," Emi said.

Theresa frowned. "Why not? It'll give us a head start in the morning."

"Not that," Emi replied. "Don't do the wine."

Theresa's frown turned cynical. "Why? Am I putting on weight?"

"You will be. You're pregnant."

Theresa stared blankly at Emi, then her eyes slid to the side. Lines creased her brow, and her eyes narrowed in concentration. One hand covered her lips as the other reached for her cell. She swiped at her phone, opened an app I suspected was a calendar, and studied it for a full minute.

Our eyes were on Theresa when the tears began. Tony and Sean fled, Emi and I scooted into chairs on either side of Theresa.

"How could I have been so stupid?" She wailed.

"You didn't do this alone," I said. "Were you and Reggie planning a family?"

"Yeah, but we were waiting until after we got married in December."

If I were a cartoon character, the top of my head would have blown off into a zillion pieces. "You and Reggie are getting married in December, and you didn't tell us?"

Emi punched her fists into her hips. "What else haven't you mentioned?"

Theresa laughed and swiped at her eyes. "We didn't want to go public until Reggie told his mom. That's where he is tonight, not at a workshop. He's taking his mom to dinner to tell her he's getting married."

"You'd better call him," Emi said.

"I want to be sure first. Not that I doubt you, Emi, but—"

Emi raised a palm. "You should absolutely double-check. Tony always advises independent verification of my hallucinations. Allison, buzz Mike."

I pulled out my phone. "To the drugstore!"

*

We selected three tests. By five-thirty, all three confirmed Emi's vision. Theresa's best guess based upon her calendar was that she was six weeks along. She texted Reggie and told him to meet her at the apartment before he picked up his mom. ASAP. Emi and I left her with hugs and promises we'd support whatever she decided.

Sean had gone on home to avoid pregnancy talk, so Emi gave me a ride. "Describe the vision. Did you see Theresa giving birth or something yucky like that?"

"I saw her holding the baby, a boy," she said.

"You sure blew that gender reveal."

"Sorry. I had another vision involving this baby last year. In that vision, Zabel held a baby on the balcony of her new condo. It worried me at first because I thought it was mine and Pak's, but when I revisited the scene in my head, I knew it wasn't. Until today, I didn't know whose baby Zabel held in her arms."

"And what a way to find out. Did you stop to think," I asked softly, "that blurting out 'you're pregnant' in front of everybody might not be the best idea you've ever had?"

Emi's jaw dropped. "Oh. Oh." Her head and hands wavered, and I begged her to pull over before she ran us off the road. She eased the car back into the lane and tightened her grasp on the steering wheel until her knuckles turned white.

"What an idiot. When she mentioned the wine, I needed to warn her. She must hate me," she said.

"Are you kidding? She'll tell that story forever. You'll be the subject of ridicule for generations to come."

Emi continued to oh and ah until she dropped me off at Sean's. I felt terrible for her, but she needed to get the blurting under control.

I joined Melanie in the kitchen where I helped her pull dinner together. She wasn't all over me with questions, so Sean hadn't shared Theresa's news. After dinner, I got the kids bathed and in bed. Sean and I didn't discuss work that evening until we were alone.

I was curled up in the window seat with a book on my tablet when Sean tapped on my door. I invited him in and set the book aside.

He pulled my desk chair around and sat in it backward. "Is it true? Is Theresa pregnant?"

"Yep, she's telling Reggie and his mom as we speak."

"Will she have the baby?" he asked.

"Worried you'll lose another asset?"

"Don't be a smart ass."

"Theresa said she and Reggie have discussed a family." I pulled the porcelain doll onto my lap. "And, get this, they're getting married in December. A baby was part of the plan, but not so soon."

"Theresa's never mentioned marrying Reggie or having kids?"

"No, she's always said the opposite, that she wanted to wait."

"Does that bother you?" he asked.

I fiddled with the hem of the doll's dress. "Some. I thought Theresa and I were closer."

"Is there anything else?" he prodded.

I glanced up at him. Practitioners could be so annoying. "Do you mean, am I jealous? Yes, you know I love kids, and I'll have my own when the time's right."

"With Officer Armstrong?"

I whacked him on the shoulder. "That jerk? He hasn't texted me since Saturday night. The boy needs to work on his communication skills."

"He's probably working."

I waved that away. "No excuse. Now scram while I send Ray an angry text."

Ray responded to my how-you-doing text within minutes.

"Sorry. Working. Call you in the morning," followed by a sweet happy face emoji with hearts on the eyes.

*

Emi remained in self-kicking mode the next morning. She huddled with me at the reception desk, afraid to face Theresa alone. But when Theresa strode into the office, she was all smiles and hugs. As she lowered herself into one of the cushioned guest chairs facing the reception desk, Emi and I rolled our chairs around to her.

"I am so freaking tired! Reggie dragged me to dinner with his mom," she said.

"How did the joyous news go over with Geraldine?" I asked.

"Are you kidding? This is her first grandchild. By the end of the night, that's how I considered my pregnancy. I'm not merely having a baby. I'm carrying Geraldine's grandchild."

"Sounds like a heavy responsibility," Emi said.

"The pressure is real," Theresa agreed, but her voice was chirpier than it had been in days.

"So you're not mad I blurted your news in front of everyone?" Emi asked.

"That's how your thing works. You can't help it, and you saved me from having to tell the guys. How are they handling the news?"

"Sean's fine," I said. "I haven't talked to Tony. Has he said anything to you, Emi?"

"No, but we don't chit-chat outside the office. Can I tell Pak?"

"Now that Reggie and his mom know, you can tell anybody you want."

"Have you called your folks yet?" I asked.

That wiped the pregnancy glow right off her face. "No, I'll wait until after Reggie and I are married, then I'll have one awkward conversation with them instead of two."

Theresa wasn't close to her folks, but it surprised me she'd keep her pregnancy from them. "You're not inviting your mom and dad to the wedding?"

"They wouldn't come if I asked them."

"Are you sure?" Emi pressed.

"I don't want them here. My parents kicked me out when I told them about my psychometry skills. When they bother to call me, they ask if I'm still following Satan."

"It's your wedding. You can invite, or not invite, whoever you want," Emi assured her, "As long as Allison and I are your bridesmaids, that's non-negotiable."

"Damn straight," I agreed. "And I'm not wearing an ugly dress, so pick out something cute."

We discussed dresses until Sean and Tony rounded the corner.

"Sorry to interrupt this important conference, but what have we learned about Leon's first wife?"

Theresa wasted no time in playing the pregnancy card. She pulled the little table that sat between the two guest chairs around for her feet before reporting.

"Her married name is now Madeline Myers, and she goes by Maddie. When Leon got sent up for manslaughter, she divorced him pronto and married an orthopedic surgeon, Barney Myers. Maddie's face is all over the internet. She's one of those gown-wearing types who's at every gala and opening night, anywhere she can get her picture taken. And, get this, she had her daughter's last name legally changed from Clipper to Myers."

"She already considers Leon dead and gone," I said. "No reason to kill him again. What was Leon's story?"

"Leon's family owned a bunch of property and made a fortune in commercial and residential development. He inherited enough from the family, and his building projects were successful. Leon met Maddie at a fancy resort down in Marco Island where she was, ahem, dancing. He built them a house in a ritzy area out by Lake Hall. Leon still owns the house outright.

"A neighbor, George Tauchman, had a thing for Maddie. Leon warned him off, but the gossips suggested Tauchman's advances weren't entirely unwelcome, though Maddie denied any relationship. Tauchman staggered into Leon's house one night, looking for Maddie. Leon had been drinking too, and punches were thrown. One of Leon's landed wrong, and Tauchman died. Leon got ten years. He also settled the civil suit with the victim's family for two million bucks."

"And he still has the house in Lake Hall," I said, "and he's built a new business. How'd he manage that right out of prison?"

"As I said, he inherited a good-sized chunk of change," Theresa said.

Sean turned the conversation back on track. "The death of this supposed boyfriend ended the marriage?"

"I suspect the marriage was in trouble long before the fight happened," Theresa said. "Neighbors say Maddie left the house and started over before the trial even began."

"The manslaughter charge must have devastated her," Emi said. "On top of losing her husband to prison, she must have been embarrassed by the publicity."

"There's no sign she wasted a moment standing by her man," Theresa agreed. "She didn't even try to get the house."

"Perhaps the guy Leon killed wasn't merely an obnoxious neighbor," Emi said. "Maybe Tauchman and Maddie had a serious relationship."

Theresa frowned. "You'd think Leon's attorney would have brought that up in his defense. The media hinted at gossip, but an extramarital affair wasn't mentioned in the trial coverage."

I shrugged. "It's possible Leon wasn't aware of the relationship."

"But," Sean said, "what if Maddie cared for the guy Leon killed and has been silent? That rage eating away at her all this time could be a motive for murder."

"Where do we find Madeline Myers?" Tony asked.

Theresa flashed him a grin. "Wherever designer handbags are sold."

Chapter Twenty-two

We planned an in-depth interview with Maddie further down the road, so our initial introduction to the doctor's wife needed to be incognito. Emi guessed, and she was our best guesser, that if Maddie left the house in the morning, it would be for shopping or exercise class. We dressed for upscale shopping but brought yoga clothes.

Mike parked the limo on the street three houses beyond the Myers' mini-mansion. At ten-thirty, our target's heels clicked on the flagstones leading to her garage. The heels and the upswept red hair told us shopping, followed by lunch, was the likely agenda. Mike cranked the limo as Maddie maneuvered her Audi to the edge of the drive. He allowed her to pass us before pulling from the curb to follow.

Mike trailed the Audi to a tree-lined street filled with brick-faced shops bearing sweet names such as She-Sells Beach and Resort Wear. Wearing wigs in improbable colors, skinny jeans with heels, and huge sunglasses, we stalked our target, masquerading as a trio of spoiled college kids. The disguises were wasted. Madeline Myers only had eyes for herself.

Armed with recording devices in otherwise empty shopping bags, we caught a few choice tidbits as we followed the tall, slender woman and her matching friend from boutique to boutique.

Maddie blamed the five pounds she'd gained on her daughter, who was being a bitch. Thank God the girl left for Harvard in August. Maddie's husband, the doctor, was considering early retirement. He was only fifty-seven. What the hell was he thinking? His best earning years were ahead. Also, she hoped someone named Miles liked the panties she'd bought at thirty bucks a pop.

When the friends stopped for coffee, we ordered lattes and settled at an adjacent table. All our eavesdropping got us was a tedious outpouring of complaints.

"I'm telling you, Kim, if Barney doesn't get the snoring under control, I'm moving into another room."

"At least your husband's home at night; mine doesn't come home for days at a time. When he does, he stinks of marijuana and massage oil."

"Do you really care that he's not home?" Maddie asked.

"Not so much, but I'd appreciate having his schedule in advance so I could plan my own entertainment."

They laughed and verbally shredded the men paying for their shopping expedition. After coffee, they air-kissed and strolled off in opposite directions. We climbed into the limo, kicked off the heels, and said, more or less in unison, "What a bitch!"

We changed into our comfy clothes at the office and reported to Sean.

"She didn't mention Leon," Theresa said. "As for Barney Myers, she's way more interested in his money than him."

"It could have been the same with Leon," Sean observed. "His arrest limited his earning power, so she was finished with him."

"I don't see her doing anything violent," Emi said. "She might ruin her manicure."

"But she can afford hired help. This is worth pursuing," Tony said. "We're ready to talk to Leon and find out why *he* thinks Maddie wants him out of the way. Emi, can Andrej arrange an introduction?"

"Pak and I are organizing a casual get-together with Leon and his daughter on Friday night. Everybody come. The more crowded the party, the easier it will be for Allison to cozy up to Leon."

*

Emi and Pak had bought their house only two months before, so they didn't have much furniture. Sean and I hauled extra chairs from his dining room, and Melanie followed in the Escalade with the kids and a handful of tray tables. At five, Emi's mom and dad showed up with three deli platters and Emi's sister, Jeni.

Francine and Tony arrived with a spiral ham and their twins. Tony's fourteen-year-old twins take after their mom with light brown hair and gold-brown eyes. They were smart, good-looking, and sociable. If I'd been in high school with them, I would have hated them.

The boy, Dave, bolted for Pak's video game setup. His sister, Liz, flounced off with Jeni to complain about how boring the party was, though it hadn't even started. Emi's home buzzed with the noise of conversation, kids, and exploding zombies.

Sean shouted "showtime" when the guest of honor arrived. Emi, Theresa, and I gathered on the porch as Pak pulled his ancient Honda to the curb. I recognized Leon from his picture on the internet, but he was shorter and rounder than I'd imagined. His daughter was Jeni's age, eighteen or nineteen, and resembled her mom, willowy and graceful. She lacked her mom's jaded bitchiness, though. Justine wore a sweet smile and linked her arm in her dad's as they strolled up to the house.

Theresa and I stood on either side of Emi on her bare front porch. Andrej kissed Emi on the cheek. "This is my old friend Leon Clipper and his daughter, Justine."

"Nice to meet you, Leon. These are my friends Allison and Theresa. I'm sure Pak and Andrej have told you about them," Emi said.

Pak hugged Theresa. "This one's the little mother."

Theresa squeezed back, then shoved Pak away, embarrassed by his enthusiasm.

"Oh my gosh, congratulations!" Justine said and hugged Theresa though she'd only just met her. I already liked Justine and looked forward to my private interview with her later.

The party mixed well, with small groups ebbing and flowing like festive amoebas. Andrej, usually the quietest guy in the room, introduced Leon to one person after the next. Pak's dad was a man with a secret, but he'd rejoined the stream of life.

My opportunity to interview Leon came when Pak challenged Justine to a dumb shooting game. Pak's man-cave featured the game setup front and center with four gaming chairs facing dual monitors. A bookcase loaded with cookbooks filled one wall. Another bookshelf loaded with games sat against the facing wall. I didn't get it, but Emi said the room kept Pak out of her hair for hours.

A battered but comfortable loveseat sat against the wall behind the gaming chairs. Emi sometimes lounged on it while she pretended to be interested in whatever game Pak was playing. Leon settled on the loveseat to watch his daughter, and I got comfy next to Leon.

I squished in close and whispered, though it wasn't necessary with the shooting and shouting coming from Pak and Justine. "Justine's better at this game than Pak thought."

Leon's face widened into a smile. "Justine's a whiz at everything, smart as a whip, always has been." Even in profile, I could see his chest puff with pride.

I rested a hand on his arm and brought my lips closer to his ear. "You must have missed her while you were away."

To my relief, he took no offense to the question. "You have no idea. Justine's bitch of a mother never let me see her. Okay, I got it when I was locked up. Who wants to see their dad in jail? But when I got out, Maddie told me my daughter wanted nothing to do with me and pretended I was dead, never even existed."

"It doesn't look that way to me."

He gave a small nod. "Six months ago, Justine called the number on one of my landscaping trucks. She wanted to call me sooner, the day I got out, but her mom wouldn't let her. We'll never get that time back."

Leon's voice had grown small and tight, and a tear escaped. "Justine called me on her eighteenth birthday. She told me it was her present to herself," he said.

"That so sweet! How does her mom feel about you and Justine reconnecting?"

"She hates it and me. She wants me dead."

My focus shattered when a colossal explosion shook the man-cave, and Pak howled in frustration. He was out of lives. Game over.

*

We left Emi's house a mess that night, but promised to return in the morning to clean up and compare impressions. With so many hands helping, we were seated around Emi's thrift shop dining room table by nine-thirty the next morning, eating leftovers and gossiping.

When we finished eating, I poured myself fresh coffee and reported the results of my interviews. "Maddie's threatened Leon, and Leon believes she's serious."

"Because of the daughter," Tony suggested.

"Yeppers, I got that from Justine, no mind-reading required. Justine reached out to Leon on her eighteenth birthday. Two months later, Leon ran into Maddie and Justine at a community fundraising affair. Maddie was livid, humiliated that her ex-con, ex-husband showed up at such a fancy-schmancy event. She told him she didn't want him anywhere near her life, including her daughter."

One corner of Tony's mouth twitched. "I take it Justine didn't agree."

"She did not. Both Leon and Justine told Maddie they wanted to reconnect, and Justine said giving her Myers' name didn't mean Leon wasn't her dad anymore."

"I bet Maddie hated hearing that," Theresa said.

"She smacked Leon in the face and told him she wished he'd died in prison."

"Wow," Emi said, "and this person's big into charities?"

"The only charity that matters to her is Maddie Myers. He didn't say it out loud, but Leon believes Maddie married him because of his trust fund and earning power. From the day they married, she kept her eyes peeled for more lucrative opportunities."

"Was the guy Leon killed more lucrative?" Sean asked.

"Leon thinks Maddie had the dead guy lined up to be husband number two."

"How did they leave it at the fundraiser?"

"Justine called her mom a bitch and left with friends. Leon told Maddie that Clipper Landcare was expanding, and he was getting to know his daughter, no thanks to her, so get used to seeing him around town."

"And she said?" Theresa prompted.

"Get out of town, or I'll get rid of you myself."

We considered that for a moment.

"We know what's in Leon's head," Sean said, "now let's see what's on Maddie's mind. Any ideas?"

Theresa had a killer idea.

Chapter Twenty-three

Operation Maddie began with a phone call to Anderson on Monday morning. After listening to the plan, he said, "Easy-peasy" and offered to come along as the sound engineer. We agreed because, for this job, the bigger the entourage, the better.

The *Coffee with Cath* website was up by nine the following morning, and Theresa called our target at ten. The team listened to the call on the speaker in the conference room. Theresa used a breezy, confident Boston accent that filled the room.

"Maddie, Catherine Baxley, from *Coffee with Cath*."

"Who?"

Maddie sounded on the verge of hanging up, so Theresa got right to the sales pitch. "Tallahassee's premier lifestyle video blog, *Coffee with Cath*. You'll remember our coverage of Florida's new First Lady, I'm sure. We're hoping to include you and your beautiful home in the Home and Garden segment next month."

"I've never heard of you. What are you selling?" Maddie snapped.

Theresa injected a combination of impatience and persistence into her voice that said Maggie must live under a rock. Still, she understood the doctor's wife was in such demand, a blog might slip her mind. She gave Maddie another nudge. "We featured Doctor Missy Rider's home last month."

"The dermatologist?"

Theresa brightened. "That's right. I've caught you at a bad time. If you're interested in doing the piece, my number's on the site, coffeewithcathdotcom, bye." Theresa ended the call.

"You think she's hooked?" I asked.

"She will be when she visits the site," Emi said. "That was brilliant mentioning another doctor, Theresa. She'll want to make sure Barney doesn't miss an opportunity."

"Anderson did a fabulous job on *Coffee with Cath*," Theresa said. "There's a Q and A with the governor and his wife and ads from the best restaurants. I clicked on them myself. *Coffee with Cath* is as real as anything on the internet."

We worked on our parts while waiting for Maddie Myer's return call. Our strategy was shock and awe. We'd distract and overwhelm Maddie with as many people and disruptions as possible so her resistance would crumble like dry cornbread.

Theresa would pose as Cath Baxley, the internet's newest celebrity blogger chronicling the lives of Florida's rich and famous. Tony would be the director, Sean, the camera operator, Anderson, the sound engineer, and Emi, a production assistant. I'd pose as the hair and makeup artist so I could put my hands all over Maddie without her suspecting a thing.

The wait was under an hour. Theresa answered the *Coffee with Cath* cell phone and put it on speaker. "Cath Baxley."

"Hi, it's Maddie Myers. We spoke a few minutes ago." Maddie sounded eager.

"I appreciate the quick call back. I hope this means we'll be working together."

"Yes, absolutely."

"Super. We've had a cancellation. The mayor's wife has gone into labor, damn her. Is there any way we could fit you in at two today? It should only take ninety minutes."

"Today?" Maddie hesitated, but not for long. "Do I need to wear anything special?"

"With your red hair and fair skin, you'll kill them in emerald or teal. See you at two." Theresa ended the call.

"Wasn't that abrupt?" Emi asked.

"We don't want to give her time to talk to her friends who've never heard of *Coffee with Cath*," Sean said. "Anderson will be here at one. Theresa, Tony, and I will be in Mike's limo. The rest of you will be in Melanie's Escalade. Let's change and do a walkthrough."

*

The Myers home was stunning, totally worthy of a lifestyle blog, even an imaginary one like *Coffee with Cath*. I suspected Maddie was watching from one of the second-floor windows as the seven of us exited the Lincoln and the Cadillac. Laden with borrowed equipment, we made our way to the door of the elegant Spanish Colonial.

Theresa rang the bell. She'd chosen a white silk pantsuit that accented her long legs and temporarily tiny waist. Tony posed casually at her elbow in a black leather jacket over a black t-shirt worn with black jeans and heavily tinted shades. The bold light vs. dark contrast between Theresa and Tony made Maddie jump when she opened the door.

"Cath Baxley," Theresa shot out her hand. She held a Plexiglas clipboard in the other and aimed it at Tony. "My producer-director, Reggie Balfour." Theresa thought naming Tony after her fiancé was a hoot. Theresa introduced the rest of us with names we'd selected for ourselves. I picked Yvette. I always wanted to be Yvette or Colette or something French-sounding.

We flowed past Maddie, busy people in a hurry, as Theresa outlined the program. Maddie's eyes darted after us, already flummoxed.

"We'll start in the kitchen," Tony ordered and strode off with the rest of us in his wake.

The two-story foyer opened into a spacious formal dining room, separated from the gourmet kitchen by an arch covered in blue and yellow tiles. The spotless white and stainless steel kitchen featured a large center island, dry bar, and walk-in pantry. I'd lived in houses half the size of that kitchen.

"Perfect," Theresa enthused. "We did most of the First Lady's interview in the kitchen," she confided to Maddie, who wore a confused smile.

"You," Tony pointed at cameraman Sean, "Let's get the pool through those windows there for background." He waved a hand toward the palm-edged oasis with its own waterfall. "You," he pointed at Emi, "move the table and chairs out of the way."

Maddie puffed herself up and objected. "Don't move—"

Anderson dumped a bulky black box on the quartz countertop of the kitchen island.

Maddie's head spun his way, and she sputtered an objection. Anderson cut her off by putting on a headset and playing with dials.

Theresa moved our victim into place. Maddie winced as Emi scraped chairs across the tiled floor.

"Yvette," Theresa snapped at me, "she's shiny."

I hoisted my makeup kit onto the counter, opened it, and reached for a sponge. I dabbed at the smooth, practically poreless skin of Maddie's face.

"Don't let this chaos bother you," Theresa told the jumpy woman. "You'll do great. Let's start with a few warm-up questions while Reggie and the cameraman set up."

Maddie frowned at Anderson. "What's he doing?"

"Sound," I said, and rested a hand on her shoulder while scrutinizing her perfect skin.

Theresa began the questioning. "Your home is incredible. Who lives here with you?"

The tension left Maddie's shoulders. "There's me, my husband, the surgeon Dr. Barney Myers, and my daughter, Justine Myers."

Theresa's head dropped to her clipboard. "Is Barney Justine's father?" She scowled at her clipboard. "My research said her father's name is Clipper."

Maddie tensed again. "My ex-husband hasn't been in my daughter's life for years. She was delighted to take Barney's name."

"How sweet," Theresa said with a fake smile.

A crash followed by a series of rattles shook everyone. Emi crawled across the floor to retrieve a pewter plate that had fallen from a shelf. Theresa hissed impatiently at her.

Tony, Sean, and Anderson got into a loud discussion regarding sound and light levels. Maddie's pulse raced under my fingertips. I grabbed a makeup brush and swept it over her forehead, and focused on Maddie's responses to Theresa's questions.

"Who are some notables you've entertained?" Theresa asked.

Maddie rattled off a list of doctors, people from the hospital board, and names from the arts. I didn't recognize any of them. I didn't know a guy named Miles either, but Maddie had him front and center in her thoughts.

"Let's get started, people, we haven't got all afternoon," Tony shouted.

I stepped aside. For three minutes, Sean posed with the camera while Theresa interviewed Maddie about her latest gathering, the guests, and what food and wines they had served.

Tony ended the shoot with, "That'll work. Out to the pool."

We gathered our equipment, and Theresa hustled Maddie outside, not giving her a chance to breathe.

We went through the same setup charade. This time Theresa said, "The poor woman's washed out by the sun. Maddie, have a seat."

I settled Maddie at a glass-topped table in the shade, opened my makeup kit, and pulled a chair around to face her. "You take excellent care of your skin," I said. "Your complexion is beautiful. If Cath hadn't told me, I wouldn't believe you had a teenage daughter."

Her shoulders un-hunched, and the muscles of her face relaxed.

Anderson slammed the black box on another glass-topped poolside table, ratcheting up the tension in Maddie's face and neck again.

Tony barked at Emi, "Move that potted palm. It looks like it's growing out of her head."

Emi scraped the terra cotta pot across the brick pool deck. Ten feet from us, Theresa and Tony talked nonstop, not pausing when interrupted by Anderson with a stupid question meant only to unsettle Maddie further.

I laid a hand on Maddie's shoulder again and used the fingers of my free hand to tilt her chin this way and that. "It's crazy, I know, but it won't take long."

Maddie didn't respond. She seemed like the type who didn't chat with the help.

"Your pool landscaping is exquisite," I said. "My daddy owns a landscaping company. He does lots of beautiful homes around Tallahassee."

A vein throbbed in Maddie's temple. I reached for a fluffy brush.

"I help my dad with the landscaping, but it's such hard work. This is much more fun." I scrunched up my face at her and selected a sponge to pat the sweat from her forehead.

"Who does your landscaping?" I asked. "I bet I know them."

She still didn't respond, not out loud. Inside, she was screaming.

"There, you're perfect." Other than dabbing at sweat, I hadn't done a darn thing.

"Let's go, people," Tony bellowed.

We repeated the performance in the Myers' bedroom and at the entrance to the house. By the time we left the poor woman, she desperately needed a vodka tonic and that Miles guy.

Chapter Twenty-four

Exhausted by the elaborate con, we convened at Sean's house around his not-so-exquisitely landscaped pool.

"How you holding up, Theresa?" I asked.

She rubbed her toes. "My heel-wearing days are done. Those shoes were growing into my feet."

"Spiky heels aren't good for your back, and you need to take care of your back," Emi said. "You'll need a strong back to carry a baby."

"That's it, Emi," I said, "make Theresa feel like an old woman."

"Wearing comfortable shoes doesn't make you an old woman. I always make a point of wearing comfortable shoes," Emi said.

Theresa faked a sob.

Sean passed around bottles of cold beer and water. "Everyone was great, especially our star," he tipped his beer in Theresa's direction. "Where did you get the recording equipment, Anderson?"

"Knox," Anderson said. "They use it for training videos, 'Safety Glasses and You,' that sort of thing."

"How's the security at Myers' place?" Sean asked.

"The security system's decent, but there are only two cameras; one on the front entrance and one at the entrance from the pool. It's silly of them to go cheap on the cameras." Anderson chugged the beer, then slid his glasses up the bridge of his nose with a forefinger. "Oh, and the *Coffee with Cath* website will be down the day after tomorrow."

"That should give us enough time. Emi?" Sean prompted.

"I didn't get any clear visions, but I have this feeling Maddie won't be living in that house much longer. Also, it was mean of Tony to make me push that heavy plant around."

"Noted. Allison?"

"She has a dish on the side, a guy named Miles," I said.

Anderson whistled.

I continued. "Maddie hates Leon, thinks he ruined her life by knocking off Tauchman and embarrassing her in front of her ritzy friends. She started over with Myers, but that's gone sour."

"Is she getting ready to leave him?" Sean asked.

"She's getting ready to kill him, and Leon too, and she's talked Miles into doing it."

"Why?" Theresa asked. "She's a superficial bitch with all the trimmings. The doctor makes a ton of money, and the house is gorgeous."

"She loves the money, but she doesn't love Barney, never did, I said. "Justine goes off to Harvard next fall, and Maddie doesn't want to be alone with, quote that toad, unquote."

"How does she plan to do it?" Emi asked.

"I didn't get any of that. She's leaving the details to Miles."

Sean sucked back his beer. "Okay, then. Tomorrow we find Miles."

When everyone else had gone home, I slipped up to my room, considered texting Ray, but called instead.

"Hey, you, how's crime-fighting?" I grabbed my heart pillow and flopped on my back.

"Busy. I'm sorry we haven't been able to get together," he said.

"Don't be. I've been busy with work too."

"I've missed you." He nearly whispered the words.

I hugged the pillow tighter. "I miss you, too. When are you off next?"

"Friday. You want to come over to my place on Friday night?"

"No," I said. "I want to come over to your place on Thursday night. What time do you get off?"

He laughed a full, warm laugh. "Three-thirty. I'll pick you up at four."

"Until Thursday, then."

"Can't wait."

"Goodnight."

"Goodnight, beautiful."

I fell asleep on my back, with my phone in one hand and my purple heart pillow clasped to my chest with the other. Goodnight, beautiful.

*

"Green," Emi said. "Green works with my hair."

"Blue works better for me," I said. Emi and I did a stare-down until we laughed.

"I'm thinking," Theresa said in a dreamy un-Theresa voice, "of pleated Grecian gowns, in sea-foam green blending into deep teal."

Emi's eyes grew wide. "I love it!"

"Outdoors at sunset."

"I love it!" I said.

We loved it until Sean called for a meeting to ask what Theresa had learned about Maddie's dish on the side.

"Miles Standish," Theresa said.

"You're kidding," Tony said.

"I am. His name is Miles Tennant, an attorney with one of the big personal injury firms."

We groaned.

"He's a member of the bar in good standing," Theresa reported. "Married and divorced. No children. He jogs through Cascades Park after work. He's posted tons of selfies there and at a restaurant called Arnold's."

"Do we follow him from the park?" I suggested.

"We follow him from the park," Sean confirmed.

Arnold's was a place for rich people to get blitzed in a casual, plant-filled atmosphere. The evening called for expensive but laid-back attire, so I struggled into my snuggest designer jeans and borrowed a blouse from Melanie. Mike's Lincoln rolled up as I got the kids sat down for dinner.

At six-thirty, Sean stepped out of the limo dressed for an evening jog. He blended in with the other runners while Mike and I followed from a discrete distance. After his run, Miles strolled back to his condo, and a sweaty Sean joined me in the back of the limo.

"What do you think? Will tonight be a dinner at Arnold's night?" He toweled the sweat from his face.

"I don't do odds," I said, "but I'm going with yes."

I squeezed my eyes shut while Sean changed. He'd barely gotten his shoes tied when Miles appeared on the sidewalk wearing khakis and a pink polo shirt. Mike rolled behind him until our quarry stepped under Arnold's black and gold awning.

Sean tested the sound quality coming from the wireless mike taped between my boobs. I slid out the door, swinging my bag and ready for action.

Miles selected a table in the black and white lounge. He wasn't a big guy, but he was fit and moved with confidence. He wore his light-brown hair long and wasn't a bad-looking guy, but at least fifteen years younger than Maddie Myers.

I chose a stool at the bar where I was sure Miles could get the full view. I flashed my fake ID, ordered a vodka cranberry, and asked for a little paper parasol. The guy behind the bar wore a nametag that said 'Ray.' That made me smile. I sipped my drink, twirled the little umbrella, and aimed my smile at the handsome lawyer, even when he wasn't looking my way.

Miles gave his dinner order to the server, then strolled up to the bar. "Hi, Ray."

"Good evening, Mr. Tennant. Can I get you anything?"

"A beer and another one of whatever this young lady is having."

"You don't need to do that." I pouted in a way that suggested that's exactly what I wanted.

"It's my pleasure," Miles said. "I'm at a table. Care to join me?"

"Sure." I hopped off the tall bar stool and reached the table just ahead of Bartender Ray, who deposited a cold draft in front of Miles and a fresh drink in front of me. Miles extended a hand.

"Miles Tennant."

I shook his hand. "Carla Roper." I made that up right there on the spot. "Is this a good place for dinner?" I asked.

"I eat here three, four times a week."

"The food must be good."

"It is. I've never seen you here before. Are you a working girl?"

"Excuse me?" Was he suggesting I was a whore?

"Are you a professional?" He was suggesting I was a whore.

"I'm a landscape architect." I made that up right there on the spot.

He laughed. "Sorry, I hope I didn't offend you, but I couldn't figure another reason for someone so young and pretty to be here alone."

The tips of my ears burned. I hoped the lighting was dim enough to hide their glow. I laughed. "That's funny. I'm thirty," I lied.

"Impossible."

"It's true," I lied some more at the pig. "I've designed gardens and pool enclosures all over Tallahassee. You've probably seen my work."

"Anybody as beautiful as you must do beautiful work."

I dropped my hand to his wrist. "Let me landscape your place. I'll show you what I can do."

He grinned at me, then paused and smiled to himself at a private joke. "I live in a condo, but I may be in a house soon."

"I'd love to see your house. Call me when you move."

"I'd like to call you sooner."

We chatted about this house he expected to move into. Its description matched the Myers Mansion. When his dinner was delivered by a server in a white shirt and a black apron, I was ready for the distraction but wanted to learn more.

I tore a roll apart and nibbled while he bragged about his boring lawyer job. When he went to the men's room, I requested another round of drinks from Bartender Ray. I instructed him to replace the vodka in mine with sparkling water.

After the drinks, Miles ordered us a dessert to share, Tiramisu, and brandy to go with it. Halfway through the brandy, the barriers crumbled.

I let him put his hand on my thigh. He squeezed. "You are an incredible-looking girl."

"You're pretty hunky yourself for a lawyer."

He moved his hand higher on my thigh. Not only did I not resist, I slid a hand up under the back of his shirt and caressed his lower back while gazing into his eyes. "Tell me about your house."

"It's not my house, not yet. It won't be until I do a couple of guys."

I stopped massaging. "You're funny." I rotated my hand and slid my fingers below his slacks' waistband, letting the tips rest on top of his firm butt.

"The woman I'm seeing is married to a rich doctor. She wants him and her ex gone. I'm helping her out. She's not bad for her age, I'll give her that, but you're something special."

"You're not killing anybody," I shoved his shoulder with my free hand.

"Wait and see. And I'll make sure you get the contract."

"Contract for what?" I pulled back, shocked.

"Landscape architecture, of course." He slid his hand further up my leg. I moved in closer despite wanting to puke in his lap.

"When you say you'll do these guys, you mean?" I asked.

"Take them off the board. Get them out of the way so I can marry this socialite bitch."

That should do it, I thought. I removed my hand from his pants, sat back in the chair, and finished my brandy. "You're either messing with me, or you're going to jail. Either way, it's not funny."

He wrapped one hand around my waist and pulled me so close his brandy-scented breath warmed my face. His eyes fixed on mine. "I won't go to jail. I'll do this, then marry the rich bitch and move you in. There's a pool house that no one ever uses. You'll be right under her nose."

I laughed but pressed my palms against his chest. "One, you just met me, and two, I'm not impressed with this talk about killing people."

"Something went through me the moment I spotted you. There's something about you. Do you believe people are meant for each other and recognize it from the beginning?"

"Love at first sight? No. Now let me go."

His arm snaked around my waist again. He pulled me in and kissed me. It wasn't a bad kiss, but I didn't want it and pushed against him.

I was considering biting him when I was thrown back into my seat, as though Miles and I were magnets being sucked apart. I blinked up at Sean, who towered over Miles. Miles leaped to his feet, found he was still being towered over, and sat.

"Who the hell are you?" Miles' voice trembled, his arrogant confidence gone.

Sean grabbed me by the wrist and dragged me from the bar.

Miles didn't follow. Sean shoved me in the limo and barked, "Drive," at Mike.

"You didn't need to rush in to rescue me. I had it under control," I said.

"Do you have what we need?"

"You heard him. Yes, I think it's enough."

"Then, we didn't need to let him keep pawing you."

"It's a public place. The bartender would have helped me out, I'm sure."

"Eventually." Sean studied my face hard.

"What?"

"I'm not using you to come on to guys for information anymore."

"It's my job, and I enjoy making assholes like Miles trip themselves up."

"Your mom threw you at men for rent money. You grew up that way, so you think it's okay. It's not. No more."

My annoyance at the sudden interruption faded, and I wished Sean was a hugger like his wife. He wasn't, so I sucked back the pooling tears and kept my mouth shut until I was sure my voice wouldn't tremble. "I appreciate your concern, but don't feel bad. I have to get close to people to do what I do. A few will be pigs like Juan Herrera and Miles Tennant. I can always say no to a job."

He didn't respond.

"I like undercover work." I poked his arm with a fingertip. "Not that I would have gotten under the covers with Miles Tennant."

His shoulders relaxed as the thaw began.

"I won't be this adorable forever. Take advantage of it while you can."

He turned to me and smirked. "Tell me what you got from him."

I told him what I got from Miles, the stuff he didn't say out loud. Sean called the team and scheduled an early meeting for the next morning. Time, I'd learned, was of the essence.

*

Sunrise peaked through the blinds as we sat down to breakfast around the office conference table at seven.

"He plans to lure Leon to Myers' house by requesting a landscaping quote," I reported.

"Leon will recognize Maddie's address," Emi objected.

"Miles will give him a phony address and do the driving. On the way, he'll dose Leon with a drug to make him woozy but won't knock him out. Difena-something."

"That's a weak point," Sean said. "Leon's a bulky guy. Estimating the dose will be tricky and administering it in a moving vehicle impossible."

"He may be a lawyer, but Miles isn't the brightest light in the hall," I said. "He sees himself as a bad-ass, but he's just a desk-jockey with delusions."

"What about Barney?" Emi asked.

"Maddie will make sure Barney's home alone."

"They'll do it on a Saturday afternoon then," Theresa reasoned. "Barney is home by mid-afternoon, and the housekeeper leaves at one on Saturday."

"He'll have Maddie turn off the cameras and the alarm," I said. "Miles will bring Leon in through the back, and they'll walk through the house looking for the owner, but Miles will knock Leon out before they get to Barney. While Leon's out, Miles will shoot Barney with a gun he brings along, then shoot Leon with a different gun."

"Provided by Maddie." Tony grunted a laugh. "He plans to stage the scene to suggest Leon was breaking in to kill Barney and Barney shot in self-defense."

"It won't work," Sean said. "They won't find gunshot residue on the hands of the two men who supposedly fired the shots. Miles will never get the bodies staged believably, and we know at least one of Maddie's friends is aware she's having a fling with Miles."

"Like I said, he's not the brightest light in the hall."

"Maddie recognized Miles as a perfect patsy," Theresa said. "She'll deny everything if he's caught."

"The plan may still be in its early days," Emi suggested. "Maddie won't want to do this until Justine is safely away at Harvard. Miles has time to work out the kinks."

"I'm afraid not, Emi. They're doing this weekend," I said.

She gasped. "Miles is killing Leon this Saturday? You got that from him?"

"That's his plan."

"The plan ends now," Sean said. "Anderson's cleaned up the audio file. Check your email, Allison, then we're off to disappoint Barney's expectant widow."

*

Barney had left the house at six-thirty as usual. The Myers' housekeeper didn't come in until nine, so we pulled up in the Escalade and limo at eight-fifteen. Sean knocked twice before Maddie answered. She wore yoga pants and an oversized t-shirt. Sweat glistened on her forehead as she blinked at us in confusion.

"Remember us?" Sean asked.

Her eyes narrowed, but she stepped back from the doorway. Tony appeared from behind Sean, ready to manage any hesitation Maddie might have about talking with us.

"What do you want? Aren't we done?" she asked.

"We're just beginning," Tony said. He ran the back of his hand over Maddie's fine-pored cheek.

She jerked her head away and repeated. "What do you want?"

"Excellent question," Sean said. "Let's sit out by the pool."

Her lips moved, and she shook her head as though asking herself why she wasn't calling the cops. Maddie led us through the now-familiar kitchen, trailed closely by Tony. Anderson wandered off to ensure the security cameras malfunctioned. We wanted no digital recordings of our visits.

I helped Emi pull chairs around one of the glass patio tables. She kicked at the potted palm Tony had made her move.

"What do you people want now?" Maddie asked.

Tony extended both hands toward Maddie, palms up. "We want you to abandon your plans to kill your husband and ex-husband."

A spasm ran through Maddie. "Get out before I call the police." She rose on shaky knees, grasping the edge of the table for support.

Sean placed his phone at the center of the table, swiped, and pushed play.

"I won't go to jail. I'll do this, then marry the rich bitch and move you in. There's a pool house that no one ever uses. You'll be right under her nose."

Maddie's head swung to the sound of Miles' voice, and her bony ass fell back into the chair.

Sean swiped at his phone again.

"The chick I'm seeing is married to a rich doctor. She wants him and her ex gone. I'm helping her out. She's not bad for her age, I'll give her that, but you're something special."

"You're not killing anybody."

"Wait and see. And I'll make sure you get the contract."

"Contract for what?"

"Landscape architecture, of course!"

"When you say you're going to do these guys, you mean..."

"Take them off the board. Get them out of the way so I can marry this socialite bitch."

"Bastard," Maddie hissed, but quickly pulled herself together. "Is this a joke? Who are you people?"

"We're people who don't want Leon killed," Tony said with a half-smile. "If you don't believe us, call Miles. Ask him how he enjoyed his dinner at Arnold's last night. Ask him how he enjoyed the company of the lovely blonde landscape architect."

I wiggled my fingers at Maddie. "That would be me."

Maddie flushed. "What do you want?"

"Call Miles right now while we listen. Tell him it's off," Tony continued. "Guarantee us that Leon and Barney won't be harmed and write a check for ten thousand dollars made payable to MES for counseling services. If you prefer not to deal with us or the check doesn't clear, we'll send copies of the recording to your intended victims and to Miles. The memory of their responses will keep you entertained while you're in prison."

Her smooth face was blank, devoid of emotion. "You're blackmailing me?"

"I prefer to think of it as life coaching, but you could say we're blackmailing you into not killing your husband," Sean said. "That's odd, isn't it? The blackmailing is usually done *after* the crime has been committed. We're progressive in that regard."

Chapter Twenty-five

We dropped Maddie Myers' check at the bank on the way back to the office. Theresa and Emi spent the rest of the morning digging into the backlog of open cases. That's what they told Sean, but Theresa's wedding was a higher priority. I took part via text from the reception desk.

At one, Tony and Sean turned the corner. I thought they were headed to lunch together, but they were calling it a day since we'd had such an early start.

"We told Emi and Theresa on our way up," Sean said. "We'll lock up when they get here."

I gathered my stuff and said, "I'm spending the night at Ray's."

"Fine," Sean said, "Mike will drive you."

"Ray can pick me up and bring me home." I made big naughty eyes at him. "When I'm ready to come home."

"I want multiple sets of eyes on you."

"Chill, I'll be with a cop."

Sean shook his head. Theresa and Emi rounded the corner.

"How's the wedding planning going?" Tony asked as if he didn't know they'd been wasting time on it all day.

Theresa smiled a sweet smile. "Planning is coming along fine, Mr. Guiden. I'm putting you down for flower girl."

"Hey," I said, "why don't you two come to the house? Melanie can help organize the wedding planning."

They agreed and followed me home. Melanie worked with us on wedding details until it was time to pick up Connor and Chad from school. I used our last few quiet moments together to discuss Ray.

"Is it nuts, a person like me, seeing a cop?" I asked.

"Nuts because you're a gifted person or nuts because we're perpetually up to our necks in illegal shit?" Theresa asked.

"Nuts because I'm a trailer trash, mind-reading, twenty-year-old kid, living with her boss because his family is the only decent family she's ever had. Not to mention my relationship experience has been limited to high school boys blinded by my cheerleading uniform and my mom's loser boyfriends who I let grope me then hit them up for twenty bucks."

My friends shared an uncomfortable glance. The struggle for the right words was written all over their faces.

Emi broke the silence. "Allison," she paused again and rested both her hands on my shoulders. Her eyes were soft, full of empathy and sadness. "Allison, it's time to get your head out of your ass."

"Excuse me!"

"Seriously," Theresa added, "how long are you planning on playing the poor-little-trailer-trash girl? You're smart, you're surrounded by people who love you, and you've met a wonderful guy. Get over yourself."

"Last year, I was where you are," Emi said in a confessional tone. "Remember listening to me whine about my sister and Tony and fretting over Pak hanging with Theresa? Here we are a year later. My sister has graduated from high school, Theresa and I are friends, and Pak and I live together in our own home."

"You still whine about Tony," I countered.

"True, Tony's a developmental opportunity, but I'm not letting it interfere with Pak and me. We don't know where your relationship with Ray is going; nobody knows. Take it one day at a time."

"And keep us informed of every detail," Theresa added.

Tears tickled behind my eyes. "I have the best friends ever."

My friends left when Melanie returned with the boys. I jogged upstairs to my room to get ready for my visit with Ray. Sean watched me cram clothes and makeup into my backpack.

"We're going straight to his place, I promise. He's making fish tacos. I swear I'll text you if we leave the house."

"What have you told him?" he asked.

"What have I told him about what?"

"Your talent, what you do with it, and why you're living in my house. How well does this guy really know you?"

"I told him you took me in because my mom cut me loose when I turned eighteen. I still had school to finish, so you and Melanie gave me a place to live."

He nodded, temporarily appeased. "Stick close to the truth, good."

"He knows nothing about my gift or talented people. A cop won't believe that shit unless they're gifted, and he's not."

"And Mayweather?"

"He knows whatever you told him and Clendennon. Thanks to Tony almost getting arrested for murder, we haven't had much time together. Mostly we discuss root beer floats, football, and Hawaii."

Sean grunted and left me alone to finish packing. I played with Connie on the front porch until Ray's cruiser turned into the driveway. My heart danced, and I made a point of finding Sean and Melanie to say goodbye before I left.

In the car, I kept the conversation to work and kept my hands to myself. I didn't want to be picking up on any stray thoughts. My thoughts were all I could handle.

After a twenty-minute drive, Ray pulled up to a one-story, tan stucco duplex two blocks off a busy county road. His neighbor, a thin old guy with white hair poking out from under an Australian bush hat, mowed the small shared lawn. The smell of fresh-cut grass and motor oil filled the air.

Inside, the late afternoon sun threw crisp shadows through the wooden slats of the blinds. The duplex was clean and under-furnished in neutral tones. I would have killed to live in a place like Rays when I was twelve.

To my left was a small closet off the living room. The dining area was to the right, then a compact open kitchen. Further down on the right, I expected I'd find the bathroom and then a bedroom on either side. I wondered which one was Ray's and made a bet with myself that it was on the left.

Ray noticed me checking out his place. I smiled and said, "Nice, roomy."

Eyes focused on me, Ray pointed toward a tan recliner facing a sixty-inch television. "You can set your stuff there."

I let my purse and backpack slip to the floor where I stood.

"I've missed you." I wrapped my arms around Ray.

"Not as much as I missed you," he said. His arms encircled my waist, then dropped lower as we kissed. He lifted me off my feet, and I wrapped my legs around his hips and my arms around his broad shoulders. We kissed as he walked us to his bedroom. It was the one on the left.

*

An hour later, we were showered and making dinner. I sliced veggies while Ray fried the fish.

"Do you cook?" I asked.

"Mostly, I grill. Pak and Reggie have me wanting to try a few new things."

"Pak and Reggie love anything involving food. You're already one of them."

"I like your friends. They seem mature for their age, you too."

"I wouldn't say that. I enjoy playing with the kid's toys more than they do."

"You mean Sean's kids?"

"Yeah, I pretend I'm their big sister. I bet you have a big sister," I teased.

He eyed me warily. "You're right. I have an older sister, Bonnie. She's still in Hawaii, but I'm trying to talk her into moving here."

I gave the veggies another rinse and set the colander in front of Ray. "I'd love to meet her."

We chatted through dinner and into the evening. We ended up back in bed, made love, and fell asleep. After showering together in the morning, we dressed and made breakfast just like any couple Ray dropped me at the office at seven-thirty. When Sean stepped through the door at nine, I smiled my perkiest smile as if to say, "See, I'm not dead."

He said good morning and loped off to his office.

It was another busy and profitable day. We picked up another case from the Perryville Paper Mill in Georgia. We'd nabbed two inventory thieves for them back in June, but more problems had surfaced.

Theresa's morning sickness got the best of her, and she left for home before ten. Ray texted me five times that morning. Each text said the same thing—can't wait.

At lunchtime, I asked Sean to take me home so I could grab clean clothes for that evening. In the van, Sean kept the conversation on work. He respected my space, which I appreciated.

Melanie dished out tuna casserole while I played with Connor's old See and Say. It was Connie's now, and I made her laugh by repeatedly pointing it to "The cow says moo."

Connie's giggle was infectious, and I laughed along until Sean said, "You really do like the kid's toys as much as they do."

My world went black.

I didn't respond. I didn't trust my mouth and didn't want to upset Melanie, so I waited until Sean and I were in the van and on our way back to the office.

"You bastard," I said.

He scowled as he drove. He hadn't caught his slip.

"You sent Anderson to Ray's. You were listening to us!"

"Are you crazy? Anderson wouldn't bug a cop's house," Sean said.

He was right; Anderson wouldn't agree to that. But the only other explanation was much, much worse.

My mouth was dry, almost too dry to speak. "Then you visited. You bastard, you visited Ray and me in your damned head."

From the corner of my eye, I watched as his face clenched then released as he remembered. "The toys. You said you enjoyed playing with the kids' toys."

"I trusted you, Sean. Why couldn't you trust me?" My voice rose as I realized what he'd done, what he'd seen. Tears choked my eyes and throat. "Did you follow us into the bedroom? Did you watch us, Sean?"

"No! Stop working yourself up. I wanted to confirm the house was secure, that's all. I didn't invade your privacy."

The seat belt prevented me from launching myself through the windshield. "You didn't invade my privacy? You just hung around and watched me making out with Ray."

"I wasn't watching you. I was watching out for you. That's different."

I balled my hands into fists and pounded the dash. "Don't do it again!"

I avoided everyone for the rest of the day, even Emi, who had her head in the new paper mill case with Tony. When Ray came for me at five, I left without saying goodbye to anyone.

Despite being furious with Sean, Friday night was better than the prior evening. I was familiar with Ray's place, and our time together felt more natural, more normal.

I even opened up about Ben. I rarely discussed my brother, not even with Melanie or Emi. The aching emptiness he'd left was so vast it swallowed my words. But when Ray held me, my soul filled with just enough peace to allow me to remember and to speak.

"Ben thought my mom was the way she was because my dad left us. He made excuses for her until she started blaming me when her loser boyfriends started hitting on me. I turned to Ben when Willy, my mom's current, grabbed my ass. I don't know what Ben did, but Willy was gone the next day. My mom was pissed because the rent was only paid to the end of the month. We had to move again. Ben left two weeks later."

I rested my head on Ray's shoulder and closed my eyes. I pictured Ben when I'd seen him last, wearing his McDonald's uniform and sharing his cheeseburger and fries with me.

Ray kissed my forehead and distracted me from my pain by describing the little places along the river he wanted to visit with me after I turned twenty-one. I reminded him to save the date for Theresa's wedding, and he made me laugh by describing a series of awful weddings he'd been forced to attend.

While drifting off to sleep, I realized it had been days since I had read anyone's thoughts, and I didn't care if I never did it again. Maybe with Ray, I could be a normal human being.

Saturday morning was back to work for Ray. It was still dark when he dropped me off at home.

The kids had missed me. I made up for my absence by fussing over each of them, finding their clothes, making their breakfasts, and spoiling them rotten.

It was Saturday morning, but we had to work on the paper mill job, so the team planned to put in a full day. I'd been so busy with the kids I had to zoom to be ready to leave for work with Sean, who waited patiently in the van. Our drive to work was quiet. I didn't ask if he'd visited with Ray and me. If he had, I couldn't put a stop to it, so there was no point arguing.

Theresa left after an hour, taken down by morning sickness again. She stacked her work on my desk before she dashed out with a hand pressed to her mouth. Tony and Emi headed for South Georgia and the Perryville Paper Mill for the rest of the day. Ray texted me at eleven and asked me to lunch, saying he'd pick me up at twelve.

Twelve came and went, and no Ray. I reached for my phone to call him when Sean rounded the corner.

"I'm running home to grab lunch. Do you want to come?"

"No, thanks. Ray's taking me out."

"Lock the door behind me and keep it locked until he gets here."

"I will," I told his back as he stepped outside.

My cell buzzed. It was Ray, and he sounded harassed. "Hey, you. Sorry, I'm late."

"It sounds like you're driving," I said.

"I'm ten minutes away. It'll have to be a quick lunch. What's fast that's close to your office?"

"The Airstream Diner, it's only a five-minute walk. I'll snag a booth for us and order for you."

"Great. See you in ten."

I took a few minutes to hit the restroom, comb my hair, and smear on lip gloss. After putting the phones on out-of-office, I locked the front door and skipped to the sidewalk where I could see the silver walls and neon sign of the diner on the next block.

I kept to the part of the sidewalk closest to the strip plaza to catch the shade of the oak trees. I'd cleared the plaza's parking lot and was stepping into the street when a battered black sedan jumped the curb, its fender missing me by inches. Shaken, I bounced out of the way.

A rear door flew open, and strong hands grabbed my arm, jerking so hard I stumbled, dropped my bag, and yelped. Before I caught my breath, I was in the back of the Ford, my arms and legs pinned. I spun my head to the window and screamed. Faces turned in my direction, but by then, the car was back on the road.

Chapter Twenty-six

It's strange where your mind goes in times of stress. When Alex Cruz drove by Sean's house to grab one of his children, he found me instead. I was alone outside, a gift. Alex shoved me into a black Chevy. In Atlanta, Roger Riegert dragged me into his black Mercedes for an intimate interview concerning his wife. Incensed by this latest outrage, I shrieked from the back of the smelly Ford POS, "What is it with people shoving me into cars!"

The two tattooed men ignored me. One drove, while the other held me in his lap, using his thick arms and legs to pin mine. Immobilized except for my head and my mouth, I screamed, using my most colorful language. They weren't interested in my opinions about them, their parents, or their IQs, so I stopped and used my skills.

"Where are you taking me? There were witnesses, and a cop expects me for lunch. He'll be looking for me. Why are you doing this?"

In response to my questions, the thug conjured images of sliding a knife from my throat to my belly to relish the slow ooze of blood from deep slashes. My empty stomach roiled, and I got out of his head fast.

Fifteen minutes of casual driving took us to an industrial park. The Ford nosed through the parking lot, bumped across a set of railroad tracks, then stopped outside a square warehouse with corrugated metal walls, the last in a line of three identical buildings. The guys didn't care that I saw where they were taking me. That wasn't good.

Both were short with hair buzzed nearly to the scalp and it was like they were trying to be twins, except the white guy had a green dragon tattooed on a forearm. The black guy had a complicated moon and stars design tattooed on his face. The tattoos were very distinctive. Those distinctive tattoos and their dead eyes told me they didn't care if I saw them. That wasn't good either.

The one holding me kept me pinned until the driver opened the back door and wrapped large, rough hands around my upper arms. They positioned me between them and dragged me toward the man-sized door set in the warehouse wall. Confident I didn't want to go inside, I dug my heels into the parking lot's sandy surface, lowered my butt, and screamed. They didn't appear concerned, and I guessed this part of the complex was deserted.

When one thug released his hold to open the steel door, I dropped to the ground, but the other guy just dragged me inside by the collar of my shirt. The door clanged shut behind us. Its echo filled the warehouse and sent dust motes dancing in the sunlight filtering through seams in the corrugated metal walls.

The men jerked me to my feet. The building was empty except for a wooden chair and table placed in its center. On the table sat an object I couldn't make out in the poor light.

Each man held one of my arms while I squirmed and kicked at their legs. They didn't speak as I squawked for what seemed like ten minutes, but was probably less than five. They tightened their grip and stood a little taller when another man entered from a door on the opposite wall. The opened door let in enough light for me to recognize the man and the item on the table. The man was Juan Herrera. The thing on the table was a blow torch. My kidnappers tightened their grip as I instinctively pulled away from both.

"Hello, Allison," Juan greeted me cheerfully.

"Hello, yourself. What the hell are you doing?" I asked.

"I have questions."

"I don't have answers. Okay, I ran out on you at the club. I'm sorry I got cold feet. I'm chicken shit, and I'm sorry. There's nothing more to say."

He laughed. "I wondered what that was about, I still wonder."

He was close enough for me to make out the glint in his sharky black eyes. He wore a lightweight gray jacket over a gray t-shirt. His resemblance to Tony in both appearance and style was uncanny.

"I wonder why I meet this girl, who is so friendly but goes away so fast." He shrugged. "It's nothing, and I got feds asking about my real estate investments, so I forget her. But now cops come asking if I killed Axel Thornhill."

I swallowed hard but kept quiet.

He smirked and shrugged again. "Getting pulled in by the cops is an occupational hazard. But then I see this girl again. Do you know what the detective said? She works for a man who beat up my dead competitor. Quite a coincidence, no?"

"Yeah, well coincidences happen. Tallahassee's not a big place."

"But there is more. This girl worked for the wife of Pete Izary, the stupid asshole who washed my money and put the feds on me. And I wonder, so many coincidences. I must talk to this girl."

"You're kidding? You think *I'm* involved in money laundering and murder? You want the guys I work for, not me, and they'd love to talk to you."

"I considered that, but our business interests don't overlap. But this girl who keeps turning up, maybe she does her own business, and I think," he paused and raised a finger, "That thorn, Stewie Burkhalter, *que latoso*. Maybe you've got a side hustle spying for Stewie."

An acid taste filled my mouth. Juan Herrera couldn't have come to a more erroneous or dangerous conclusion.

"I don't know any Stewie." The denial came out weaker than I'd intended. The last I'd seen Stewart Burkhalter, he'd been using methamphetamines and getting religion.

Juan let his gaze rove across my body. "We will find out who and what you know. It shouldn't take long." Juan smiled with his lips but not his eyes.

Panic made me stupid. "If I'm not back at the office soon, my boss will come looking for me."

Juan nodded reasonably. "Perhaps I should speak to him." He kept his eyes on me but addressed his thugs. "Ask her about him, this Mayweather. Find out if he's involved in the Thornhill mess."

Flames of fear engulfed my brain, and I squirmed.

Juan winked at me. "Such a man we can't pluck off the streets, so we'll pay him a visit at home."

The children, I screeched to myself. "Forget him! You have a bigger problem. I was meeting a cop for lunch. He's probably already looking."

"And he'll find you. You won't be as pretty as you are now." Juan Angel Herrera turned and left by the far door.

The door slammed, and iron hands dragged me toward the chair. Once in that chair, I'd never leave the warehouse alive. Energized by panic and adrenaline, I twisted to the right, then sprung back to the left and aimed my highest "go team" kick into the balls of Dragon Tattoo. His hands fell to his groin, freeing my right arm to grab the back of the chair. I swung it at the head of Moon and Stars man. He staggered but held on to me. A second swing, this one to the back of his head, sent him face down on the floor and broke the chair.

I snatched the blowtorch off the table and ran. I didn't know how to use a blowtorch, but was sure I didn't want to leave it with the tattooed guys. At the door, I turned to watch over my shoulder as I pulled. Locked. I raised the blowtorch high and banged the lock three times before trying the door again. Nothing.

Mouth dry and heart pounding, I risked another glance over my shoulder. Dragon Tattoo rolled on the dusty floor as Moon and Stars man raised himself to his knees. I had ten seconds, tops. I banged the lock harder—once, twice. On the third blow, the door caved in from the outside, pressing me against the wall.

I slid from behind the door. The hood of a police cruiser jutted into the warehouse. Outside, tires squealing and radios squawking told me more cops had arrived. I flattened myself against the wall.

Moon and Stars man ran toward the door opposite me, the door Johnny Angel had used. Dragon Tattoo was on his knees.

"Stop!" Ray shouted.

As Moon and Stars reached the door, a deafening boom echoed through the metal building. He stopped.

"Hands where I can see them!" The threat in Ray's voice made the guy on the ground release his swollen genitals and drop his face to the floor.

More cops swarmed into the warehouse. Wrists were zip-tied, and rights read. Ray lowered his gun and turned to me. It was safe to cry, so I did.

*

Ray didn't ask questions on the way to the station. I rode with my eyes shut and worked on my official story. He led me to a too-bright interview room, where another officer took my statement. Focused on keeping on my fictional account straight, I kept forgetting her name.

Juan Herrera's name wasn't mentioned during the interview. I told the officer that the two guys were strangers. They grabbed me and drove me to the warehouse to rape me and torture me with the blowtorch. I never hinted that the attack was anything but random. Medical treatment was offered but refused. I wasn't hurt. Not a scratch on me, as Emi had predicted.

Ray stayed by my side as much as possible. I repeated my story five times to two other officers. Finally, one of them slid me a printed statement to read and sign. A victim support specialist gave me her card as Sean entered the interview room. Too exhausted to repeat my story and too embarrassed to even look at Sean, I was relieved that Ray stayed to explain.

Ray reviewed the attack and filled in the parts I'd missed. Within seconds of me getting snatched, witnesses called nine-one-one. Ray was under a minute from the parking lot of the Airstream Diner when he got the call. Witnesses handed him the bag I'd dropped, so within seconds he realized I was the victim. The witnesses told him the Ford drove off to the north. Ray didn't wait for backup; he just drove.

Time of day and the warehouse's remote location worked against Juan's men. Food trucks make good money at industrial parks, the out-of-the-way ones with no restaurants nearby. Two sheriff's deputies had stopped for lunch at a food truck featuring Caribbean cuisine. The truck was parked at the edge of the complex Juan's men had chosen for my interview. The deputies spotted my kidnappers as they pulled on the lot. The two officers who reported the car's position were advised Ray was on the way. I estimated the deputies edged their vehicle next to the Ford as Juan joined my kidnappers and me inside the warehouse.

Ray was five minutes behind when he left the witnesses but caught up fast. He drove the last two miles in under two minutes. Though his patrol car went airborne when it hit the railroad tracks, Ray didn't slow until it crashed through the warehouse door.

From the Ford jumping the curb to my rescue at the warehouse, the entire event had taken under thirty minutes.

Sean listened and asked no questions. Ray walked me to the Odyssey and buckled me in for the silent drive home, where I collapsed into Melanie's arms at the door. After a lot of crying and hugging, I soaked in a hot bath while sipping tea. Afterward, Melanie sat with me on my bed and rubbed my back until I fell asleep.

I awoke to a sunny, busy Sunday morning. Sean took Connor to softball practice while I helped Melanie around the house. I sent dozens of brief texts to Ray, Emi, and Theresa, who were losing their minds with worry. I assured them I was unharmed but needed to rest and promised them details on Monday morning.

When Sean returned with Connor, I got the kids settled down for lunch and tidied the kitchen before taking a nap. I awoke headachy and queasy, so I skipped dinner and stayed in my room, reading and waiting for Sean to slip in to learn what really happened.

But he never did. Sean never asked if Juan Herrera was involved. I assumed he figured it out on his own, and I couldn't bring myself to tell him what Juan said about coming to the house, not with Melanie and the kids around. Anyway, he'd probably figured that out as well. Still, I should have talked to him, but what could I say other than sorry, you were right, I'm an idiot? I wanted to apologize, but that meant admitting I needed a keeper, someone to watch over me day and night. Truthfully, I was just plain too ashamed to talk to Sean.

On Monday morning, I slid into the van, still searching for the right words. I wanted to say I appreciated his concern but couldn't live under his thumb my whole life. I was lucky this time, I know, but all I did was walk to lunch. It was ridiculous, really, I'm twenty years old, and need your permission to cross the street?

I never found the right words, so the drive to the office remained silent. As Sean parked, I tried to spit out an apology, but as I unsnapped my seatbelt, Emi and Theresa dashed out of the office and were at the van's door before I uttered a word.

Theresa hugged me, then flapped an arm toward the street. "What were you thinking?"

"I know. I was stupid," I said.

"Stupid?" Emi said. "Those guys could have just as easily shot you on the sidewalk without leaving their car."

"Johnny wanted information."

"What if he woke up on the wrong side of the bed?" Theresa snapped. "What if he'd said, fuck it, just kill the bitch?"

"Come on, I'm here, aren't I?"

"Because the witnesses and Ray acted fast," Emi said. "A slowdown at any point, and you'd be where?"

I didn't want to consider my future with the blowtorch.

We entered the office as Tony parked his silver Lexus. I trudged straight to the conference room, not even bothering to drop my bag at the reception desk.

Sean summed up the attack while I listened, eyes focused on the table, cheeks warm.

"It's safe to say Herrera is paranoid, and everyone at Mayweather is a target. He started with Allison, but we should consider Herrera a threat to the entire team. Tony and I have our families under observation. I've talked with Drew Watson as well."

"Dad's taking Mom and Jeni out of town for a week," Emi said. "and Pak's Dad has moved in with us."

I lifted my eyes to Emi.

"We've tossed the idea around for a while. It makes no sense for Andrej to live in a furnished apartment when we have a guest room. While Jeni's out of town with Mom and Dad, I'll drive my old Focus, and Andrej can use my Fiat to get to and from work."

"No stops between the office and home," Sean said, "and you don't go home to an empty house, agreed?"

Emi nodded.

Sean turned to Theresa.

"Security at my place is great," she said, "and Reggie will drop me here on his way to Knox. I told him I'm too sick in the mornings to drive, and that's not too far off the truth. It would help if one of you two could drop me home in the evening."

"Mike will drive you," Sean said. "This is an inconvenience for everyone, but we'll eliminate the threat soon."

"Do we have a plan?" Theresa asked.

"There is no 'we.' Tony and I will handle this. You three are to stay away."

He got no argument from me. I offered a tidbit, a tiny piece of information. "Juan thinks Stewart Burkhalter's behind his troubles."

"A turf war between drug dealers often ends unhappily for one or the other," Tony said. He turned to Sean. "We can use this."

"It will be easy to get them to turn on each other if we can do it without getting close," Emi said.

"As Sean said, you're not to be involved," Tony replied.

Emi continued. "We just need to get Burkhalter and Herrera in close enough proximity to make it feasible Burkhalter could kill Herrera. The cops will fill in the blanks themselves."

"Perhaps you didn't hear me, Emi," Tony said.

"We need to get them to come together voluntarily," Emi pointed at Sean, "so he can do his puppet-master thing."

"Emi, for the last time, you are not part of this." Tony's angry eyes blazed.

Emi turned to Sean. "Can you motivate Stewart to call Herrera? Can you get him to set up a meeting to discuss doing business together?"

"If Burkhalter's as weak as you three seem to think, yes. I need to see him first, though."

Tony lost what little patience he had left. "Emi, you'll be taking a nap soon if you don't stop."

"I'll poke around the internet, see if there's someplace Stewie regularly goes, like Herrera and his club. You two can bump into him."

"Emi, you're tired. Take a nap," Tony said.

Emi's lashes fluttered. Theresa yanked the pink ombre Tahari scarf from around her neck. She bunched the fabric on the conference table, so Emi didn't bang her head when she flopped forward in a sudden doze.

The two guys moved to Sean's office to work out their strategy for approaching Stewart Burkhalter. Emi woke five minutes later.

She raised her head slowly and blinked at Theresa's scarf. "The bastard did it, didn't he?"

Theresa reclaimed her accessory. "It's not like he didn't warn you."

"I was on a roll. Don't you think it will work, getting Herrera and Burkhalter together?" she asked.

Theresa bit her lower lip. "Okay, they meet. Then what do we do? Burkhalter and Herrera will expect the other one to pull something. They'll have their own security teams. Sean or Tony won't be able to get close."

"They won't need to get close," I said.

"I see what you mean, and Sean and Tony won't know where they're going," Emi said. "If Stewart asks for the meet, won't Juan want to select the site?"

Theresa nodded. "I'd expect so. Unless Sean visits the site first, he won't be able to do a distance-viewing thing and pull Stewart's strings. He'll have to follow one of them without getting too close."

"He won't have to get close," I said again.

My friends turned to me. I sighed and explained. "I told you Sean was a Marine, right?"

"Sure," Emi said. "After that, he became a cop."

"Do you know what he did in the Marines?"

They considered. Emi's hand massaged her forehead until understanding lit her drowsy eyes. "He was a sniper, wasn't he?"

"He needs to get within a few hundred yards. Tony will get in Stewart's head and follow him to the meet, then Sean will set up so far away, not even two packs of paranoid drug dealers will spot him."

The tick of the big wall clock was the only sound in the conference room. Emi's eyes remained soft and sleepy, as though she were watching a movie in her head.

Theresa and I leaned close to catch her whisper. "Sean won't have to take one of them out. They'll hear the shot and start pulling on each other." There was another long silence while Emi mused. Her eyes grew wide, and she stiffened. "What if they get caught in the crossfire?"

None of us had an answer. Why should we? We were three twenty-somethings with wild skills but unfamiliar with the ugly world of Marine snipers and drug dealers. I finally got what Sean had been struggling to get me to understand. I knew Jack and shit about dealing with guys like Juan Herrera.

Chapter Twenty-seven

After our meeting, I returned to the reception desk and worked until Ray called me at noon.

"I won't ask what you're doing for lunch," I said.

He laughed, not a cheerful laugh. "Listen, kid, you need to know those two guys have been out since eleven this morning. I don't want you to be alone."

"Believe me, I don't want to be alone. What did they say?" I asked, worried they mentioned Johnny or the real reason for my abduction.

"Not a damn thing," Ray said. "Their lawyers did the talking, and they didn't say much but made their point. I'm surprised those two losers could afford hotshot attorneys."

"I can't believe they got them set loose. Don't they have records?"

"Minor stuff, years ago. It's surprising, guys who pull that kind of thing start bad and escalate. Maybe it was a gang thing to prove themselves."

"They failed the exam."

"What bothers me is that grabbing you in the middle of the day on a busy street makes no sense. They'd be seen. Either they're stupid, or they were targeting you specifically and took the opportunity."

Or they were stupid, *and* they were targeting me, I thought. "With those guys out there, I won't be going out much, I'm afraid," I said.

"I insist. Tell Sean to look out for you, okay?"

"He's way ahead of you."

My eyes drifted up to the window as I ended the call. Mike Spinelli's limo idled outside the office door.

All four of my coworkers entered the lobby: Sean and Tony from the right, Theresa and Emi from the left. Tony handled the talking for a change.

"We'll be out for a few hours. Keep the door locked. Mike will watch the office and take you for lunch. Questions?"

"You're stalking Stewart Burkhalter, aren't you," Emi said. "Sean will make a connection, and you'll both get in his head."

"Any other questions?" Tony aimed a frozen half-smile in Emi's direction.

She smiled right back at him. "Reading you loud and clear, Captain Voodoo."

Once Sean's van was out of sight, I opened the door and motioned Mike inside to review his part in Theresa's wedding plans.

When not discussing the wedding or doing actual work, I prepared my apology to Sean. I'd start by itemizing and thanking him for everything he'd ever done for me. Next, I'd move on to how much I loved his family. Finally, I'd get serious and say I realized how clueless I was, and then I'd apologize for acting stupidly. I wouldn't whine about him not trusting me or invading my privacy or any of that childish shit.

The guys returned to the office after four, their eyes cold and jaws set. I guessed they'd been preparing for whatever futures they planned for Juan and Stewie. We were dying to learn what they had in mind, but we wouldn't get answers. Even Emi didn't bother to ask.

Sean instructed Mike to follow Theresa and clear her apartment before leaving her alone. Tony followed Emi home, where he'd stay with her until either Pak or his dad arrived.

I climbed in the van with Sean, eager to get my apology out of the way. I took a deep breath and began, "Sean, I want you to know—"

Sean turned to me from the driver's seat and fixed me with his laser-blue gaze. "I understand you want your own life, and you know what? You're right. If you want to put your life in danger so you can have a club sandwich with a good-looking cop, that's your business. But I won't let you risk my family's safety."

"I didn't tell him anything about you or the family! Give me some credit, Sean."

"After three minutes with the blowtorch, you would have told them everything about me, Tony, even Emi."

"But. I. Didn't!" I bit off each word.

"How long before he tries again? Maybe next time it'll be Emi, or Theresa and her baby. Or maybe he'll come to the house and wait for you, let his men rape my wife to pass the time."

My hands went to the sides of my head, and I squeezed my eyes shut. "Why are you doing this? Stop," I wailed.

"You're too unpredictable. Once this thing is cleared up, I want you out of the house. Find your own place, move in with Armstrong. It doesn't matter to me. I'll cover your costs, but I'm not letting you put my family in the crosshairs of a Juan Herrera again."

I shrank from him, unable to speak. Sean started the van, and we drove home in silence. I had no words.

Sean pulled the van into the drive next to my car. Eyes on the street, he waited at the front door until I was inside, then stepped in behind me and pulled the door shut before heading into the kitchen. I heard Melanie with Connie in there and wondered what Sean was saying about me. Too ashamed to face Melanie, I scooted past the kitchen and peeked into the dining room. Two blond little-boy heads bent over homework. Tears gathered as I realized I wouldn't be their big sister anymore.

As I took the stairs one at a time, I gripped the banister, not trusting my wobbly knees or tear-blurred eyes. Inside my Allison in Wonderland room, I relived those first moments of joy when I realized this space, this clean and beautiful space, was mine.

There were no piles of dirty clothes waiting until I'd scrounged up enough change for a trip to the laundromat. I didn't need a chair propped under the doorknob to keep out unwanted visitors. Roaches didn't scuttle across my toothbrush at night.

This was my home, my haven, where I tumbled on the floor with Connie and read Dr. Seuss until I could recite the stories from memory. At the closet, I selected my outfit for the day from the dozen lined up and waiting. In the bathroom, Melanie braided my hair while we chatted. At the window seat, I curled up with my doll while texting Emi and Theresa into the early hours of another day.

I lowered myself to the edge of the bed and smoothed the lavender quilt with a trembling hand. I hoped Melanie would let me take it with me. Take it with me where? Ray's duplex? We'd known each other for what? Three weeks? If I asked to move in, he'd be freaked. What guy wouldn't be? Emi had Pak's dad in her spare bedroom now, thanks to me. Theresa and Reggie were making room for a new baby. I'd have to go somewhere on my own, alone.

Miserable and overwhelmed, I buried my face in the quilt and sobbed. Everything I'd ever wanted was in that house: a home, a family, self-respect. I'd endangered it for a club sandwich with a good-looking cop, and I couldn't say Sean hadn't warned me. We'd had that conversation before.

Sick and woozy, I rolled onto my back and threw an arm across my eyes while I led my thoughts back to the night I decided to kill a man.

Chapter Twenty-eight

It began the night before I met Sean Mayweather, the night I got the bruises I was ashamed for him to see. Earl had me pinned on the sofa when my mom stumbled into the living room from Hell's Pony.

"What the fuck!" she screamed.

Earl lay on top of me, his laugh a vile grunt. His bulk pressed me into the stinking upholstery.

Unable to breathe, I hissed. "Get him off me, Mom!"

She pummeled Earl on the back. He rolled off me and took a swing at my mom. I struggled off the saggy sofa onto my feet, grabbed the lamp from the end table, and broke it across his back. I spun as he backhanded me, falling face-first onto the couch, then sliding to the floor.

Mom reached for me, and for the briefest moment, I thought we were teaming up, fighting Earl together, but then her nails dug into the flesh of my upper arm as she yanked me to my feet.

"You fucking slut!" Her nails dug in until she drew blood. She shook me. "This is your fault!"

"My fault?" I couldn't believe what I was hearing.

"That's what you get for shaking your cheap ass all over the house, you little whore!"

Earl's hoarse laughter filled my head, and my heart screamed. I couldn't take it anymore, not another day, not another second. With a piercing howl, I raised a leg and kicked at Mom until she released my arm.

"I hate you! I hate you and Earl and all your filthy pig friends!"

I ran to the door, but Earl caught my arm and twisted. I aimed my foot at his groin, but the kick went high, and I fell on my ass. He dragged me away from the door, then kicked me in the back a few times before turning to my mom. I crawled to the coffee table and used it to pull myself to my feet, then ran from the house with my hands over my ears to drown out the screaming and cursing and sobbing.

I slept in the park that night, huddled under a pavilion bench. When I returned before dawn, Mom and Earl were passed out in the bedroom. Disgusted, I showered, dressed in long sleeves to hide the bruises, and walked to school as if nothing had happened. That afternoon, two lowlifes tried to kidnap Connie Mayweather, and my life changed forever.

A year later, the summer before I met Emi, I got bored and stupid and almost threw my new and improved life away.

Mayweather hadn't had a case for three weeks. Restless, I sat at my computer behind the reception desk, played solitaire, and let my mind wander back to those days before I met Sean. I wondered if Mom had thrown Earl out when I didn't come home that night. Did she finally stand up for me? I liked to think she did. Did she miss me or just complain about the reduction in her public aid like she did when my brother left home?

My thoughts bounced around those questions throughout that tiresome day. My life had changed for the better. Had hers? Why did I care? I thought I'd buried my feelings for her, but stray memories and what few tender feelings I'd had bubbled from deep beneath the surface of my consciousness.

That night, I lay awake, obsessed with questions I thought were long buried. Unable to sleep, I dressed and quietly slipped to the garage. Sneakiness was another skill I brought to Mayweather.

Half asleep, I steered my VW to the last place we'd lived. It was unlikely Mom was still there if she ditched Earl. It was his house, after all. He paid the rent.

I parked the car on the sidewalk at the end of a gravel driveway across the street from Earl's old place. The house appeared unchanged but felt abandoned. No lights glowed, and no cars sat in the drive.

There were only two working street lights on the entire block. Lights shone on a few dilapidated porches, and a television flickered in a distant window. The street was dark and grim. After half an hour of watching, the mosquitos, the dark, and the quiet got to me, and the heat made me sleepy. I yawned, rubbed my eyes, and turned the key to start the car.

Headlights appeared at the corner, and I killed the VW's engine. Sure enough, a car turned into the drive across the street. Two happy, laughing drunks stumbled out of Earl's old Chevy and staggered to the front door arm-in-arm. Their voices carried, and my heart sank. Mom was still with Earl. My leaving had no effect on her.

Mentally, I kicked my own ass. What did I expect? Leopards don't change their spots, as Melanie said.

Melanie. She'd be frantic if she found me missing. This was nuts. I shouldn't be here, I thought. The neighborhood was dark and dangerous. As if to confirm my fears, shouting erupted from inside Earl's rented house.

The porch light flicked on, and the argument spilled out to the dusty lawn. I couldn't make out what my mom was shrieking, but Earl had hurt her. Fumbling with the door handle, I wanted to run and help but hesitated when Mom stomped back into the house, slamming the screen door behind her. I eased the car door closed enough to extinguish the dome light. Leaving the door unlatched, I scrunched low in the driver's seat.

Earl laughed and staggered backward away from the house, shouting, "It's my house, you stupid bitch!"

When he laughed at my mom, something inside me turned hard and hot. My breathing became fast and shallow as my gaze tracked Earl's slow, staggering progress down the sidewalk.

He probably planned to walk back to Hell's Pony, but at the corner, under a street light that had long lost its glow, he bent from the waist and vomited. I snapped the dome light off with my right hand, then reached into the glove box and grasped the heavy tactical flashlight I carried for both light and protection. My movements were mechanical. Sean's MES training kicked in, and Earl was nothing but a target now. Using the noise of his retching to cover the squeal car door's squeal and waited for my moment.

As Earl finished his retching, he lost his balance and pitched forward on his knees. I slipped a foot onto the crumbled pavement, then paused, but Earl hadn't heard the gravel crunch. He was busy gagging on his puke and pushing to his feet.

I slid from the car, the flashlight in my right hand poised shoulder high. Halfway across the street, a familiar voice filled my head.

"Allison, get back in the car. Go home."

I spun three-hundred and sixty degrees, but the street was empty except for Earl and me. I turned my attention back to Earl, who was wavering on his feet and laughing weakly. My window of opportunity was closing, but before I took another step, the voice returned.

"Stop, Allison. Get back in the car."

Sean. That bastard Sean was watching me.

"Go away," I screamed. Earl's head wobbled in my direction.

I'd missed my chance. I growled and groaned with frustration, slid back into the car, started the engine, and slammed my foot on the accelerator. The VW lurched toward the opposite sidewalk but missed Earl by six feet.

I pounded the steering wheel as I drove, cursing Sean, my mother, and Earl and swearing to kill all of them.

Sean waited for me on the front porch. I swung the VW into the yard and flung myself toward the house.

"You bastard! You have no right to follow me."

He stepped off the porch. "I have a right to keep you from fucking up your life and mine."

"Bullshit! You know what he did to me. He's my business, not yours!"

"Really?" Sean planted his hands on his hips and blocked my advance to the house. "What was your plan after you bashed the guy in the head?"

"To get the hell out of there, what else?"

"And come here? What if someone saw your car?"

"It's two in the morning. No one saw shit."

"What if you didn't knock him out, and he turned on you, then what?"

My lips worked while I thought. "He was drunk. I'd pound away until..." I trailed off, confused.

"While you were pounding away, he'd yell, wake the neighbors. Would they see your car? Call the police? What then?"

The adrenaline cooled in my veins, and fast answers grew harder to come by. "I'd run. I'd come home."

"Covered in Earl's blood? How long would it take the cops to trace the car? Hell, they might have just come here to wait. They'd test the flashlight, test the blood on your clothes. How long before my kids watched you get led away in handcuffs?"

The trembling started in my hands, then moved up my arms to my shoulders. All I wanted was to sleep and forget. "You don't know what it was like, living like that." I slipped to my knees in the damp grass.

Sean dropped his arms and took another step toward me. His face floated a mile above my eyes. "I was there, remember? You said you wanted out of that life. What you were planning tonight would have dragged you right back into it. If that's what you want, fine. But don't drag my family down with you."

I swayed on my knees, considering what he'd said. I'd had a close call. Three or four more steps would have put me across the road. Two or three blows might have taken Earl out if he didn't turn on me and kill me with my own flashlight. Someone would hear the commotion and call the cops. That someone might have been my mom who'd happily send me to jail for threatening her meal ticket.

A pale hand appeared before my face. I grabbed it with both hands and hoisted myself to my feet. Dazed, I stared past Sean to the front porch swing and considered how the morning might look if I'd accomplished what I'd set out to do.

I envisioned myself on the lawn, hands pinned behind me, and head bowed as a cop loaded me into a police cruiser. Melanie sat on the swing, Connie in her lap, a boy on either side. The children called to me, frightened. Melanie's eyes were sad.

My bright idea might have brought danger and grief to her door. I swore I'd never do that to her and the children again.

Chapter Twenty-nine

Juan Herrera wanted me dead, and he knew where I lived. I'd done what I'd sworn never to do again.

When my sobs subsided, I lay on my back atop the lavender quilt and wiped my hand across my face to wipe away the shame, then stumbled to the bathroom. A splash of water on my face cleared my head a little. I tried a smile in the mirror. Not good. My eyes were red and puffy, and my skin red and blotchy. I didn't want to leave my room, but I didn't want to be alone either, and I didn't want Sean hating me.

That's what hurt the most. After all that we'd been through together, Sean had finally given up on me. If he hadn't already, he'd soon tell Melanie what I'd done and apologize to her for installing such a dumb-ass in her home. My body ached as I imagined her alarm and fear for her children.

Sean's rage and Melanie's fear; I couldn't live with either. Even if I had to move out, I needed to put things right between us. I couldn't lose the best family I'd ever had. I'd get my own place if I had to, but I'd only be able to bear it if we remained friends.

I envisioned how that might look. I'd get an apartment, a cute studio, just a place to hang out between work and visiting Ray, my friends, or the Mayweathers. The children could still call me their big sister, and Melanie would make me tea when I stopped in for a visit. I could handle that future.

My eyes returned to my disheveled reflection in the mirror. My makeup was smeared beyond redemption, and frizzy wisps of hair escaped from the braids resting on sagging shoulders. After washing my face, I pulled out the bands, untwisted my hair, and reached for my brush. I wished I had Melanie's help and longed for one more chance with Sean.

I pulled the brush through my hair and pretended I was getting ready to cheer at a big game, the last game of the season. I tried on another smile: my fourth down and goal to go smile. As I did, the game's final play came to me like one of Emi's visions, and the smile in the mirror was no longer fake.

There was still time. Energized and clear-headed, I realized that Sean wouldn't talk to Melanie while the kids were awake, so I finished pulling myself together, then skipped downstairs. I strode past Sean, who chopped vegetables at the kitchen sink, and planted myself in front of Melanie at the stove. "Sean's being mean to me, I said and threw in a foot stomp.

She turned from the pot of potatoes she'd been mashing. "Why?"

"I did something stupid, and I tried to say I'm sorry, but Sean won't listen, and he says I have to move out."

Melanie gave Sean a questioning glance. He responded with a glare in my direction.

"I think," Melanie said, "we need to discuss this first."

I kissed her cheek. "That's all I ask." I tried to make my eyes twinkle as I returned Sean's glare.

He slammed a dishtowel on the kitchen table.

"You sneaky, conniving little brat. You called an end-around, well-played."

I set the table.

*

We enjoyed a dinner of roast chicken with mushroom gravy, peas, mashed potatoes, and a huge salad. Tummy aching, I handled the cleaning up and tucked the kids into bed to give Melanie and Sean time to discuss my fate.

Melanie tapped on my door and eased herself next to me on the vanity bench. I used the apology I'd worked up for Sean and held nothing back, admitting I was angry at Sean because he'd watched me with Ray. Tears rose when I explained I wasn't thinking clearly and did something stupid that might have blown back at her and the kids.

"Sean warned me not to leave the office alone, but I didn't listen. I wanted to see Ray. I can't imagine what you must think of me."

"Don't be ridiculous. We love you," Melanie said.

"Maybe you do, but Sean's done with me."

"Nonsense, you only met this Juan Herrera in the first place because you did a job for Sean. How is that your fault?"

"Juan wanted to know why I was at the police station, and his imagination ran wild. I should have laid low, stayed out of sight like Sean said."

"Sean's worried for your safety. That doesn't sound like someone who hates you."

I scrunched up the wad of tissues in my fist. "It's you and the kids he's worried about, not me."

"He's worried about all of us; that's how Sean is. You know what the problem is?"

"What?"

"You and Sean are too much alike."

I rolled my head around on my neck, "I don't see that, Mel."

Melanie placed her hands on my shoulders and turned me to face her. "How much of Sean's history do you know?"

"He's a great dad, he's smart and has incredible skills."

"I meant, what do you know about his past?"

"He was a Marine and then a sheriff's deputy."

"Before that?" she asked.

I shrugged.

Melanie smiled slyly. "The day that you saved Connie, I pointed you out to Sean. He called you a little—"

"Idiot, I know, the little idiot. He always calls me that."

"An angel. When I pointed you out, he said, 'So that's Connie's guardian angel,' and I said that's exactly what you were. He watched you almost like he does during his long-distance visits in his head."

Melanie's gaze dropped to the floor; I assumed to remember that horrible day more clearly. "After a bit, he said, 'Melanie, that little angel needs a home,' and went to talk to you."

I froze in my seat, stunned.

"I insisted he bring you home, and I've never regretted it for a moment."

"Not even now that I've got a pissed-off drug dealer after me?"

"Allison, honey, if it wasn't a drug dealer, it would be a vengeful ex-wife, angry parents, or a frustrated client. You guys don't arrange flowers for a living."

I chuckled. "Thanks for trying to make me feel better, Melanie, but it's my fault I got nabbed. I should have sat tight. Melanie," my voice grew small as tears choked my throat, "I'd never do anything to hurt the kids, please believe me."

Melanie left me and returned with a fresh box of tissues, then hugged and rocked me while I gave into sobbing. It took a while, but I got it together.

The most painful part was behind me. I'd made my apology. I wanted to focus on something else, if only for a few minutes. "Why did you say Sean and I are alike?"

"Your stories are more similar than you realize. You were what? Thirteen or fourteen when you noticed your skill? Sean, too. His dad was abusive, mostly to his mom. One day, Sean's dad smacked Sean's mom, and Sean decided he'd had enough. Apparently, Sean was an early bloomer, physically. His dad lost a few teeth, but it wasn't the teeth that scared him."

"What happened?"

"Sean's dad swore he heard Sean in his head, ordering him to pick up his teeth and wipe his blood off the kitchen floor."

A laugh erupted, and my heart cheered for young Sean. "He must have been scared shi... witless."

"His parents were drinkers, and, like your mom, Sean's mom was more concerned about keeping her man around than her son. She sent Sean to live with his grandmother, saying the boy frightened her. After his parents divorced, Sean's mom reached out to him, but Sean never forgave her. When he turned eighteen, he joined the Marines, and that's when things got interesting."

"That's when the distance-viewing started?" I asked.

"He was on watch, and his thoughts drifted to home, like most recruits, I imagine. The way he tells it, one moment he was on base, the next he was in his grandma's kitchen. It scared him. He thought he'd fallen asleep and was dreaming, but he called his grandma's name and saw her jump. Can you imagine?"

I could. Sean had done the same to me.

"Weeks later, he called his grandmother to catch up, and she mentioned this odd experience she'd had that scared her half to death."

"She'd heard him call to her?"

"Sean was blown away and shared his dream, which we now know wasn't a dream. They laughed it off, but Sean realized it was more than a coincidence. He experimented with his skills, then he used them on the job, and his career with the Marines got interesting."

My mind boggled when I considered how useful a sniper would find the ability to visit with and control a distant target.

"After the Marines, Sean returned to his grandmother's house and entered college. That's where we met."

I squeezed her hand. "When did Sean tell you this?"

"It was after his grandmother died, not long before he went into business with Constance Albies. He's told you about her, right?"

"Yeah, she was a practitioner and a county prosecutor."

"After working on a few cases together, they realized their success rate might draw unhealthy attention, so they went into business together."

"If they were partners, why did they give the company Sean's name instead of this Constance person's?"

"That's a funny one. Sean and Connie flipped a coin. Sean lost."

"Is that when he explained the special skills to you?"

"When he left the sheriff's department, he said I needed to understand why he was taking such a risk with our future."

"Did you believe him?"

"Not until I met more gifted people and saw they were otherwise normal and usually very nice. I'm glad he confided in me, and I'm glad he insisted on bringing you home. Now," she stood and reached out a hand, "quit feeling sorry for yourself and come downstairs. Let's settle this with Sean."

I repeated my apology in the darkened living room so I didn't have to meet his eyes.

"I'm so sorry that I've made this thing you and Tony are doing tonight necessary," I said.

"You were Herrera's target because he saw you at the station. That wasn't your fault," Sean said. "I shouldn't have blown up at you, but the coincidence puts us all in danger, and I over-reacted. On the upside, Herrera's assumption that Burkhalter was involved made bringing them together easier. When Stewie asked for the meet, Juan jumped at the opportunity. Tony says Herrera plans to murder Burkhalter tonight."

"Did Tony put that idea in Juan's head?" I asked.

"It doesn't matter." He turned his attention to Melanie, "Mike will be outside again tonight to monitor things here."

"What about Tony's family and Emi and Theresa?" Melanie asked.

"Everyone's taking extra precautions. Don't worry, Mel. Tony and I are settling this tonight. When you wake up in the morning, it'll be over."

I prayed that would be true. If anything happened to Sean because of me, I'd die, not for real, but a part of me would die. I refused to accept that outcome by channeling my inner Emi and pronouncing the future. Sean and Tony would be unharmed. They'd return home to their families and be their usual, arrogant selves in the morning.

I returned to my room to give Sean and Melanie alone time before he left to do whatever he and Tony had planned. My heart hurt knowing the trouble I'd made, the danger I'd put us in, but I couldn't fix that now.

I clutched my heart pillow tight and hummed *Silent Night* to myself until I fell asleep.

Chapter Thirty

"Allison, honey, wake up."

I was shaking. No, a hand shook me.

"What's wrong?" I raised myself to my elbows.

"It's Emi. She's hurt."

Melanie's faced snapped into focus. "Hurt, how?" I asked.

"A car accident. Sean didn't say how it happened."

I tossed off the quilt. While I dressed, Melanie told me I couldn't call or text anyone until I talked to Sean at the hospital. This was bad. Sean wouldn't require such secrecy for a simple car crash.

As I threw on clothes and grabbed my bag, my thoughts flew in a thousand directions. The garage was cold, and I fumbled with the car key, shivering from cold and concern for my friend. I'd been worried about Sean and Tony, not Emi. The guys would never involve her in their plan, so what happened?

It wasn't until I backed out of the garage I noticed the rain pouring down in sheets. I wondered if Emi and Pak were out late and got in an accident. It must be bad if Sean was asking me to come, but why the secrecy? I shivered in the November chill, and ordered myself to keep calm, but still missed a turn, lost my way in the parking lot, then got soaked while jogging to the wrong entrance.

Inside, the hospital was cold and bright and crazy busy for three-thirty in the morning. People, including a surprising number of cops, ran everywhere. Were hospitals always like this in the wee hours while the rest of us slept?

I couldn't find Emi. Frantic, I approached a security guard who took charge of me. She photographed me, gave me a badge, then directed me to the family waiting room outside the trauma center. I rushed to Sean, who hugged me for the first time.

Off by himself, Tony sat in a plastic chair with his face half-turned to a wall. He twirled a piece of hair at the nape of his neck and didn't acknowledge me.

"Where's Pak?" I asked.

"With Emi's folks. They're with her now."

We sat with our heads close. Sean whispered, "She has a concussion and was out of it for a while, but she's awake now. She's got bruised ribs, poor kid, but otherwise, she's okay. They'll watch her tonight and let her go home tomorrow."

The taut muscles of my shoulders relaxed, and I drew a breath. "What happened?" I asked.

Sean rested his elbows on his knees and ran his hands through his hair. "I missed."

"You missed Johnny?"

He nodded. "I missed, but the shot started something. Herrera's dead. Burkhalter's upstairs in surgery."

I grasped Sean's wrist. "Emi saw it. She saw them shooting at each other! She worried you and Tony might get caught in the crossfire."

Sean pushed himself up straight in the chair. "So, that's why she was there."

"She followed you?" I said too loudly.

"The meeting was off a dirt road near the big interchange where Crawfordville Road becomes Wakulla Springs Road. It's open but bordered by trees shielding the area from the road—an excellent site. I found a solid limb three hundred yards away. Tony stayed on the ground. There must have been twenty people surrounding Herrera and Burkhalter. I couldn't get a clean shot. It sailed high, over everyone's heads."

A shot fired at twenty armed, paranoid men. I imagined the chaos that followed. "That's when the shooting started?"

"Immediately. Tony and I packed it in—fast. Emi had parked well away from the meet, off to the north between Herrera and us. I'm guessing she wanted to be close enough to call nine-one-one when the shooting started. She must have figured the police sirens would send the bad guys scrambling before things got too out of control, and Tony and I could escape."

"How do you know all this? Did you get to talk to her?"

He shook his head and grunted a dry laugh. "I know because she called nine-one-one. She told the dispatcher she'd broken down on Crawfordville Road and was calling her fiancé for help when she heard shots. She was still on the line with the operator when her car was sideswiped."

I sunk into myself. "Who hit her?"

"The two guys Herrera sent to nab you. With kidnapping charges pending, I guess they didn't wait for the sirens. They must have run as soon as the shit hit the fan. After they hit Emi, they panicked and floored it. Their car flipped a half a mile down the road." He bobbed his chin at the ceiling. "They're upstairs too, but not expected to make it. Tony and I were on the way back to town and saw their car in the field, surrounded by emergency vehicles. I stopped and talked to a deputy I recognized. She said it was a terrible night for Fords. There was another one, a Focus, on its hood further down the road."

I gasped.

"Yeah, we figured the same thing. Emi's old Ford was in a ditch with her inside. Tony wanted to stop, but paramedics were already there. Also, my rifle was in the back of the van, so I headed straight here instead."

I glanced over my shoulder at Tony. "He's taking it hard."

Caroline Watson, supported between Drew and Pak, wobbled our way. I dashed to her. She wiped away tears and forced a smile when she saw me.

"Is she okay?" I asked.

Caroline nodded. "She's already asking when she can go home."

"Did she say why she went there?" I was anxious about Emi's condition and curious about the story she'd told the police.

Caroline brushed her bangs from her forehead. "She said she couldn't sleep because she's so excited about Theresa's wedding and the baby. She and Pak have been discussing marriage, and she wanted to think."

Tears bloomed in Caroline's eyes. "She said she wanted fresh air and didn't want to wake Pak, so she drove around listening to the rain and thinking. That old Ford sputtered, so she pulled over to call Pak. When she heard shots, she called for help instead. That's so like her." Caroline lost her battle with the tears.

I caught Pak's eyes. They were tired and guarded. While I comforted Caroline, Emi's dad, his face set in a scowl, strode over to Sean.

Pak turned to me. "I'm taking Emi's mom for coffee. Come with us."

"Go on ahead. I'll get my bag."

I reached Sean in time to catch the end of Drew Watson's rant. "Emi's done with Mayweather. I don't want her involved in any more of your games."

"It wasn't Sean's fault," I protested. "He told her to stay away."

Drew fixed his frosty eyes on mine. "Mayweather business put her there. This whole thing, this Mayweather thing, is too dangerous. I don't want Emi involved anymore."

My lips parted, but before I objected, Sean raised a hand. "I understand."

Drew glanced at Tony. "Tell him, will you?"

Drew joined his wife and Pak. I grabbed my bag and did the same.

We took our coffee to a round table and quietly pulled our thoughts together.

Pak lightened up after a few minutes. "I'm taking a day off to get Emi settled. When I go back to the office, I want Jeni to come to nurse her while I'm at work. Do you think she'll do that?"

Caroline chuckled a little. "Are you kidding? She'll love playing nurse and bossing Emi."

"And," Drew added, "give her grief for wrecking her car."

Pak turned to me. "You'll help, won't you, Allison? Tell me you're up for Emi-sitting."

"Just try to keep me away," I said.

Drew Watson's gaze pierced me through the heart.

Chapter Thirty-one

I did no Emi-sitting because Pak never asked for help; he never called or texted me at all. For two weeks, I tried to reach Pak and Emi without success. Drew must have pulled out his biggest ax to sever Emi's relationship with Mayweather. I considered stopping by but didn't want to antagonize Emi's dad or risk my newly repaired relationship with Sean. With each day that passed without a word from my best friend, I was more convinced that Emi had left our world for good.

When you lose your best friend, it hurts because your shared history is broken, and a piece of your life ends. When Ben left home, he snapped the last thread holding my childhood together. With Emi gone, I'd lost one of the few pieces of me that felt like a normal human being. Any delusions I was an ordinary twenty-year-old with a job and a family slipped further away each day. No longer trailer-trash freak show, I'd become middle-class freak show involved in tons of illegal stuff. And my boyfriend was a cop.

With Juan Herrera out of the way, Mayweather Executive Solutions stepped down from red alert. Ray and I could get together whenever we wanted. We wanted a lot.

Things were not as encouraging at the office. I moved from the reception desk to Emi's side of the oval partners' desk she had shared with Theresa so I could help her with research. Dispirited, Theresa and I didn't talk much, and when we did, my friend's thoughts troubled me.

"Is it me or is this not fun anymore," Theresa said one day.

"With Emi gone, it's gotten too quiet. Not that Emi made a bunch of noise," I said.

"But she gave us plenty to talk about most days."

"I miss her, Theresa. I don't want to piss off Sean, but I've got to see her, at least find out how she's feeling."

"Give it more time. Once Drew Watson cools off, Sean will raise the Emi-ban."

"What if that never happens?" I asked.

"Be patient. You've got a bigger problem, anyway. You and Ray are getting serious. Reggie's got his job at Knox and believes whatever stories I tell him when he asks about my day. Ray's a cop, he'll ask questions, and he'll know if your answers are bullshit."

"We've got a lot of ground to cover before we get to that point. His sister's coming to visit from Hawaii, did I tell you that?"

"That'll be interesting."

"What if she hates me?"

"Why would she hate you?" Theresa asked.

"You tell me."

Theresa laughed and returned to her work.

We cleared the backlog of minor cases. With the pipeline empty, Theresa considered working part time or even taking two years off work to raise the baby. I'd lost Emi, and I'd be losing Theresa, too. Theresa was right. This wasn't fun anymore.

As if the prospect of losing another friend weren't bad enough, Tony and Sean insisted they handle client contact from the initial inquiry to collecting our fee. They only allowed Theresa and me to do the research and prepare reports. I missed my work, the interviews only I could do. I missed my reception desk, and I missed Emi.

The days dragged. There were no calls or texts from either Pak or Emi, and Sean ordered us not to make contact. He didn't want to give Andrew Watson more ammunition to lob at Mayweather. Tony never mentioned Emi, which was worse than odd. It was sad.

The only positive thing was the diamond job for two reasons. First, the Garrett sisters lived in Charlotte, so Sean and Tony had to let Theresa and me out of the office to fly up there. Second, we made a ton of money.

Linda and Lisa were referred to us by Bobby Tallon, a big-time lawyer and lobbyist. We'd done a job for him before the mess with Pete Izary and his dog. Bobby didn't understand the skills we used to get the job done. All he knew was Mayweather found what he'd been looking for after two other companies failed.

Bobby visited us on a chilly Monday, three weeks after Emi's accident. That's how I referred to that entire series of events—Emi's accident. Forgetting Juan and focusing on Emi dulled the pain.

Bobby Tallon looked like what he was, a wealthy, asshole lobbyist in his custom-tailored suit and five thousand dollar watch, but he was an okay guy, better than okay. He paid us a quarter of a million dollars to find a clock to make his friend smile during his last few days of life. Under the slick exterior, Bobby was a sweetheart.

We took the meeting to the conference room, where I'd set out Christmas cookies and bottled water.

"Thanks for meeting with me, folks." Bobby selected a frosted snowman sugar cookie.

"Our pleasure," Sean said, "especially if you have a job for us."

"I do, but I'm not sure how profitable it will be. It's a hopeless case, but I thought the clock was hopeless."

Sean extended his hands in Tallon's direction to indicate he should continue.

"An attorney friend of mine practicing in Charlotte has two clients, sisters who own a business they inherited from their father fifteen years ago. Their attorney handled the family business for years before the father's death and thought she knew the company inside and out. The sisters came to her with a question that blindsided her, however. She called me for an opinion."

"I'm intrigued," Tony said. "This is a business issue, not a personal issue?"

"Yes and no. The essence of it is that the clients have lost something they're not sure they ever had."

It sounded like a typical Mayweather job to me. Sean made the "go on" gesture with his hands again.

"The sisters are in their early sixties and have worked in the family business, Garrett Safety Coatings, their entire adult lives. Their father, a chemist who came to this country after the Second World War, developed coatings for various flooring types to reduce slip and falls. The business began in his garage when his daughters were children. By the time they went off to college, he'd developed dozens of coatings and created a franchise for their application. The business is still family-held and worth, I'd estimate, twenty million. Since their father's death, the girls have managed the company and are preparing their daughters to take over one day."

"I wouldn't mind taking over a business like that from my folks," Theresa said. She'd dreamed of running her own company since she was a child, and I knew it would happen for her. Theresa's skills were the most developed of the three of us minions. Emi always said if any of us became a practitioner, it would be Theresa.

"If the business isn't in trouble," Sean asked. "what's the problem?"

"When their father was growing the business from home, the children overheard their parents discuss diamonds," Bobby said.

My ears perked. I was a sucker for the shiny rocks.

"Both girls vaguely recall conversations between their mom and dad concerning a customer or family friend who paid with diamonds."

"Did they ever see these diamonds?" Tony asked.

"Never, and they forgot them for a long time. When the sisters were in college, their father moved the office from the production facility in the suburbs to an office building in downtown Charlotte. This was around the time he came up with the franchise idea. He wanted a place away from the factory to meet potential franchisees. When the downtown office opened, the girls visited from college, and their parents gave them a tour. Both sisters overheard their mother ask their father if he'd taken care of the diamonds. Their dad said they were in the safe. That's the last the girls heard the diamonds mentioned."

"Weren't the diamonds listed as assets on the company books?" Tony, the accountant, asked.

Tallon's crystal blue eyes smiled, as though Tony's astute question justified his decision to turn to Mayweather. "The diamonds weren't listed as assets and didn't exist as far as the company was concerned. After the sisters graduated from college, their dad put them to work in the business selling franchises. Their father continued to run the manufacturing segment. The sisters married, and each has one daughter."

"When their father died," Bobby continued, "their mother stepped out of day-to-day operations and lived in Florida until two years ago. She must be nearly ninety now. She's in poor health and in a memory-care facility back in Charlotte. The sisters have been running the company, training their daughters, and caring for an aging mother. They've been too busy to think about mythical diamonds."

"What made them look for them?" I asked.

"They had their father's desk refurbished."

We blinked at Bobby.

"His old desk in the family home sat ignored after his death. A few months ago, the girls were inventorying the house for their mother's estate. Their father's old desk held happy memories for them, so they refurbished it and moved it to the new office in town. Oh, I should have mentioned. They moved the company headquarters into a new office building last year when the old building was sold.

"Anyway, while refurbishing the desk, the gentleman doing the work found this." Tallon removed a folded paper from his inside jacket pocket.

Sean read out loud, "*Received from J.F.: diamonds in a green velvet pouch.*" He flipped the page over, but it was blank. "That's it, no date, no value. It's a copy of a carbon copy."

Tallon nodded. "The workman found the actual carbon copy stuck behind a drawer. Who knows how long it sat there, but Lisa and Linda take this as proof the diamonds exist."

"Or existed," Tony said. "They could have been sold long ago."

"True, but the receipt has aroused the sisters' interest," Bobby said. They believe if the diamonds ever existed, they were in the company safe."

"If you're here, then they're not in the safe," Sean said, "and I assume there's no record of their sale since, as far as the company is concerned, they never existed. I'm sorry, Bobby, but this sounds hopeless."

"That's why I've come to you."

I ran through the possibilities in my head. If their parents sold the diamonds, we were done. One sister could have the diamonds hidden, but it sounded as though they were tight. If they lost the gems in the house or office, Theresa could help with a thorough search. The diamonds would have surfaced during the office move, but searching the house seemed the most promising.

"Do the sisters know you're talking to us?" Sean asked.

"No, if you're willing to give the job a try, I'll pave the way with my lawyer friend. Can I give her an idea of your rate?"

Sean drummed his fingers on the table while he considered. "A thousand a day plus expenses and ten percent of the diamond's value if they're found."

"That's risky for you," Bobby said. "Even if they exist, the diamonds might be worth a few thousand at most."

"I suspect the Garretts will provide excellent referrals should we succeed," Sean said.

"I like the way you think, Sean," Tallon said. He rose and buttoned his jacket. "I'll call when I get the go-ahead from the Garrett sisters' attorney."

As I stood to escort our guest out, Bobby paused at the conference room door. "Where is your other associate, Emi?"

After an awkward pause, Tony said, "Emi was in an automobile accident. She's taking time off to recuperate."

Tallon caught the edgy pause that told me he didn't buy Tony's explanation but said, "I'm sorry to hear that. Please express my wishes for a speedy recovery."

Tony nodded.

"Oh, there's one more thing you should know, Tallon said. "The building, the old office building, is scheduled to be imploded in five days. Good luck."

Chapter Thirty-two

After he dropped that bombshell, I let Bobby Tallon find his own damn way out of the office. I flopped in a chair, already dejected. "Five days, if the diamonds are in the old office building, we've only got five days," I said.

Theresa raised her feet onto another conference room chair. "Just once could we not get a job that's completely impossible?"

"Leon's thing wasn't so bad," I said. "I had fun."

"Pak brought us that job," Theresa countered.

"Relax," Sean said. "Until we get the go-ahead from the sisters' attorney, we don't have a case. You two learn what you can about the Garretts and their company. And Theresa, have flights ready. If we get the case, we'll need to move fast."

"No, shit." Theresa swung her feet back to the floor. "I wouldn't mind having Emi's insight on the future of this job."

"Emi's insights aren't always accurate," Tony said.

My jaw dropped. "Emi's visions don't always make sense right away, but she gets images out of context; they're hard to interpret. God, Tony, I don't believe you're writing her off so easily."

"I'm not saying her insights weren't useful, but we can handle this job without her," he said.

A flame rose in my chest, and my voice grew louder than I intended. "That's bullshit. You love Emi, so get your freaky ass over to her house and tell her we need her."

Sean stared pointedly at me. "No one is taking their ass to see Emi. This case isn't complicated. Either the diamonds are in the old office building, or they're not. If they're not, we move on to the Garrett home and their office. We don't need Emi's vague clues. Let's do our homework and be prepared. And no more talk about Emi."

"She's my best friend, Sean," I said and sagged.

"I'm sorry it's worked out this way," he said. "I hope Emi comes back, for your sake and for mine, but now is not the time, okay?"

It wasn't okay, but I didn't see I had much choice.

Theresa and I spent the rest of the morning gathering background on our potential clients and their company, Garrett Coatings.

Heinrich, aka Henry Garrett, a chemist working in Charlotte, developed his first patented non-slip coating in his garage when the sisters were children. In his on-line bio, Henry Garrett described himself as methodical and cautious. His company grew methodically and cautiously, but profitably. He held nineteen patents when he died.

His daughters earned MBAs from the University of North Carolina and went to work for the family firm right after graduation. The company and its products were profitable and reputable and dull as dust.

The go-ahead call from Bobby Tallon came at noon. We were in the air by three. At eight that evening, we met Linda Rasmussen and Lisa Sizemore at the Garrett family home on Selwyn Avenue in Charlotte. The family estate reassured us the thousand a day plus expenses would not be a hardship for the sisters. A rambling brick and timber Tudor surrounded by fairy-tale gardens greeted us as we eased the rented Escalade up the curving drive. I was no expert on homes, but this one had to be at least five thousand square feet and furnished as if they'd bought out Sol's showroom.

We visited with Lisa and Linda in a room I couldn't label. It contained a desk and bookcases but wasn't an office. A small piano occupied one corner, and a fireplace faced with white marble sat in another. The piano's surface and the mantel were covered with family photos, which Theresa studied intently. The sisters invited us to sit on a sofa and matching chairs upholstered in a fabric with the same pattern as the draperies.

The Garrett sisters fit the house like two jewels in an antique setting, with bright eyes, unwrinkled faces, and unpretentious smiles. Linda, the younger sister at sixty-one, wore her age better, appearing at least a decade younger.

Lisa, at sixty-three, bore more signs of age and was the taller sister. Despite the age and height differences, the two women were undisputedly sisters and spent too much time together. They wore their white hair in similar short styles and wore suits by the same designer. They also echoed each other and finished each other's sentences, making them ungodly annoying to interview.

Linda served us coffee as Lisa spun the same tale Bobby Tallon had told us back in Tallahassee. "Despite the receipt, I can't guarantee the diamonds exist," she said.

"But we are curious," Lisa said.

"Very curious," Linda agreed.

"I assume you searched the office yourself," Tony said.

"We did," Lisa confirmed.

"Carefully," Linda agreed.

"And this house," Sean said.

"Top to bottom," Lisa said.

"On many occasions," Linda said.

"I feel strongly that if the diamonds were still in my father's possession at his death, they would have been at the office," Lisa explained. "And if they're not in the house or the office, it doesn't matter where they are. We'll never establish ownership if they're not found on our property or among our father's effects."

"Bobby Tallon agreed with our attorney it would be difficult without additional documentation," Linda said.

"That carbon copy of the receipt is the only documentation we've ever seen," Lisa added.

The sister act wore on Sean. He inclined his head toward me. I rose to examine a pricey knick-knack, then re-seated myself next to Lisa, who pulled away as I invaded her personal space. She shifted but settled when Sean addressed her.

"You told your attorney your parents kept the diamonds in a safe."

"Yes," Lisa replied, turning her attention from me. I allowed our legs to touch and focused on her response. "My sister and I overheard a conversation during which our father assured our mother the gems were in the safe."

"That's right," Linda said. "They didn't know we were listening." She stepped to the fireplace and selected a silver-framed photo. "These are our parents."

Sean took the picture, studied it, then passed it to Theresa. After a moment, she handed it to me. A couple in their late sixties stared back at me. They both had white hair and faces creased with lines at the eyes and lips. The man, Henry Garrett, was the outdoor type, tanned and fit with angular features. His wife was softer and wore her well-earned extra pounds comfortably. She wore red lipstick and teased her hair into a fluffy style I associated with grandmothers.

"It startled us to hear those two discussing diamonds," Lisa said. "I believe I was six when they were first mentioned. When Linda and I overheard the conversation in the office years later, it jogged my memory. I meant to ask about the diamonds but never got around to it."

Never got around to asking about diamonds? These women must have been hellishly busy.

"We were insanely busy, overwhelmed," Linda said as if in response to my thought. "We were fresh out of college and newlyweds. Our father insisted we learn the business from the ground up, from manufacturing to sales. Then Lisa and I became pregnant around the same time."

Lisa beamed. "Our girls were born six weeks apart. My baby came in August and Linda's in October."

"We named them Summer and Autumn," Linda beamed.

I wanted to smack them.

"So," Sean said, "what happened to the safe?"

"We emptied it," Lisa said, "and moved everything to the safe in the new office."

"You found no diamonds in the safe when your father died?" Tony asked.

"No," Linda said, "but that was the new safe, not the old safe."

"Excuse me?" Sean asked. "Are you saying the safe in the old office had been replaced before the move?"

"Exactly," Lisa confirmed. "Dad bought a new safe two years before he died."

"What happened to the old safe?" Tony asked.

For once, the sisters were silent.

"Did your father keep an off-site storage facility?" Theresa asked.

"No, there was secure storage in the building's basement," Lisa said.

"Did you look there?" Sean asked.

"For weeks," Lisa said. "There were over five hundred boxes of paper records; racks and racks of them."

"They went back fifty years," Linda said. "There was no safe on the racks and no mention of any diamonds in the files."

"All the same, that basement is our best bet," Tony said. "Describe the old safe, please."

"Well," Lisa began, "it wasn't big, and I believe it was a Chubb. Do you remember Linda?"

"Definitely a Chubb safe; dark brown, this big." She held her hands twelve inches apart.

"That's helpful," Sean said, "Is there a combination?"

"I never had the combination." Linda turned to her sister. "Did you?"

"No," Lisa replied. "I never went into the safe until Dad died, and by then, we had the new safe, and there were no diamonds."

"Was the old safe moved to the basement?" Sean asked.

"I don't remember seeing it in the basement," Lisa said.

"Perhaps we should visit the basement and check for ourselves," Tony suggested with a forced smile.

"You can't," Lisa said. "They're blowing up that building on Saturday. No one can go in there."

Sean hated having to drag information out of his clients. He closed his eyes, raised his face to the ceiling, and then lowered it. Opening his eyes, he said, "Lisa, draw a diagram of the basement storage area as you remember it. Linda, please show Theresa the desk and the receipt."

They may have been annoying, but the Garrett women were efficient when prodded. I sat with Lisa as she drew the basement out freehand. She produced a neat and detailed drawing. Across the room, Linda walked Theresa to her father's massive, bow-fronted mahogany desk. She watched without comment as Theresa ran her hands over every surface, inside and out.

Sean and Tony stood to conclude our interview, and our work began.

It was only a ten-minute drive to the Sheraton. After checking in, Theresa and I unpacked in the room we shared. Despite the late hour, Sean called a quick meeting before bedtime in the guys' room.

"This doesn't look good, does it?" I said.

"Did you get anything helpful from Lisa?" Sean asked.

"She's been honest with us," I said, "and she's not interested in the value of the diamonds. Lisa loved her parents, and she loves her sister. She's proud of the family and their company. The theory that one sister knows something that the other doesn't won't fly."

Tony agreed. "They may be two years apart in age, but they might as well be twins." Tony would know. He had twins, and he was a twin until a stranger murdered his sister.

"The desk gave me nothing," Theresa reported, "or rather, it gave me too much. It's been used and loved by every member of the family."

"And the receipt?" Tony asked.

Theresa pointed at him. "That piece of paper is wild with images. There's a crazy mix of emotions there, but the most prominent feeling I got was excitement, the fun kind."

"Fun?" Sean screwed up his face at her.

"Yep, as if the diamonds are nothing but a big joke," she said.

Sean puffed out a lungful of air. "It's been a long day. Let's get some sleep. Tomorrow we visit the old building and figure out how we crash the implosion site."

Theresa rubbed her palms together. "Breaking and entering, my favorite."

Tony's head spun toward her. "Not for you, Theresa."

"You're doing a search without me? I don't think so."

"This is a dangerous location, and you're pregnant."

Theresa waved a hand at Tony. "They haven't hooked the fireworks up yet. Yes, it will be dark, and yes, it's a construction site, but I'll dress accordingly and wedge myself between you and Sean."

"No," Tony said.

"Let's at least look at it before kicking me to the curb," Theresa said.

Sean said, "Fine," meaning "shut up."

*

When the three of us traveled together, we shared a room and ordered a roll away bed. We pretended to fight over who had to sleep in it, but we didn't really care as long as we could play pajama-party. Emi texted Pak, Theresa texted Reggie, and we'd laugh at their replies. The talking and laughing settled our nerves before the next day's job.

In Charlotte, Theresa and I took turns in the shower, then crawled into our twin beds. Theresa fell asleep within minutes, sleeping for two. I shot Ray a "goodnight" text, then lay awake and missed him. Emi had given me an FSU hoodie for my birthday the prior April. Since my heart pillow was back at home on my bed, I hugged the hoodie until I fell asleep.

Chapter Thirty-three

In downtown Charlotte, giant cranes dotted the landscape like bony giraffes rising from a glass-and-steel-studded plain. When Sean steered the rented Escalade to the eight-story cube squatting in the center of a block of sleek structures, I understood why it was being demolished. The gray brick building that once housed Garrett Coatings' headquarters did not blend well with the new Charlotte skyline.

A variety of trucks, vans, and machinery lined the streets surrounding the demolition site. Fences, yellow tape, and terse red-lettered signs made it clear what was going on in and around the old building wasn't a game. The public was most definitely not welcome.

While we rode to the site, Theresa explained that though the explosives hadn't been set, de-construction sites were hazardous. "Load-bearing walls are removed, and supporting columns are whacked with sledgehammers, so they give way more easily."

"More reason for you to stay away," Sean said.

Theresa surprised me by agreeing. "Now that I've done my research, I won't risk my baby by going in there, but I want to help. I'll do everything I can from a distance."

"Can we use cameras?" Tony asked. "If Sean and I wore cameras, might that help you guide us through the basement?"

"It'll have to do," Theresa said.

"Let's move on to security." Sean drove around the block. This time as we rolled past the site, our eyes searched out cameras, guards, and security vehicles. "What do we see?"

"NCS, North Carolina Security." I squinted into the knots of workers. "There's at least one guard."

Theresa read the phone number and web address from the NCS van's side and entered the information into her phone.

Sean steered the rental around the block one more time. "Tony, give NCS a call when we get back to the hotel. Try to set up an appointment for tomorrow morning, persuade NCS to give us a tour, so we can map the camera locations."

"How do we spend the rest of today?" he asked.

"We run up expenses for the Garrett sisters," Sean said.

*

After a lengthy call with Anderson, we took the list of equipment he'd recommended to a place called B and G Pro Video, where we bought wireless microphones and body cameras. We moved on to an army surplus store for night camo attire for Sean and Tony. They'd left theirs at home. That I worked for two guys whose wardrobes included night camo didn't trouble me the way it did Emi.

The real leap of faith happened during the visit to the tool shop. If the diamonds existed, they'd be in a Chubb safe weighing over five hundred pounds. Theresa couldn't be there to work her magic with the combination, and the guys couldn't risk blowing a safe inside a building being readied to collapse. Sean and Tony were fit, but sneaking a five hundred pounds safe quietly through a dark building would be challenging. The solution was a device I didn't know existed until Sean loaded it into the rental van.

I read the info on the box. "Electric stair climbing hand truck."

"Water companies use them to deliver those five-gallon jugs up and down staircases," Sean said, "and it works on any surface."

"Even a half-dug-up basement floor? Won't it be noisy?" I asked.

"It's meant for office settings. The hand truck has big pneumatic wheels, and the motor is virtually silent," Sean said.

"How do you sneak this thing past security guards and cameras?" Theresa asked doubtfully.

"You can help us with that." Sean tossed a roll of black tape over his shoulder to the back seat. "While we're visiting the security company tomorrow morning, you wrap it in electrical tape to cut down on the shine."

"Marvelous." Theresa pointed to her belly. "What are the chances of food? We're starving here."

"I take it the morning sickness has passed," I said.

"Yep, my appetite's back, and it's brought reinforcements. I want grilled fish and a baked potato, and green beans, and cheesecake, and I want it now."

"Can it wait until we unload this stuff?" Tony asked.

"No!" Theresa and I shouted.

"Very well then," Sean said. "To dinner."

*

As we were on expense money, we dined at Dressler's. Theresa moaned with pleasure throughout the meal and reminded us regularly she was eating for two. "We need one of these in Tallahassee."

"There's plenty of excellent restaurants in Tallahassee," Sean said, "but your eating-out days are at an end."

"That's right," Tony said, "you and Reggie will have to give up the restaurant circuit and cook at home unless you can afford a babysitter every night."

"I can babysit," I said.

Sean shook his spiky head at me, "No, you can't. You're already babysitting my kids, and you've got Officer Armstrong to consider."

"Ohmygod, I haven't texted him all day." I reached for my phone.

"Put it away," Theresa said. "That's rude. It can wait."

"You're getting into the mom thing a little early, aren't you?" I asked.

Theresa shook a finger at me. "Don't give me any sass and eat your vegetables."

That got the entire table laughing. We had fun, but it would have been better with Emi.

*

Back at the hotel, I called Ray while Theresa took a hot shower.

"Hey, you," he answered. "How's work?"

"So far, so good. It's cold up here, though."

"That's why tourists flock to Florida in December. When will you be back?" he asked.

"End of the week, I'm guessing. Miss you."

"Not as much as I miss you. Before you came along, I was perfectly happy living alone. Now I have to get a cat for company."

I laughed and flopped on my back. "Let's adopt one from the shelter."

"Are you serious?"

"When you're working, I'll come over and feed it and clean its box and play with it."

"If it gets you over to my place more, let's do it."

I hesitated. I couldn't discuss the job, and there was only one thing I needed to tell Ray, but I wasn't ready. "We have an early meeting tomorrow. I'll call you afterward."

"Sounds good. Night."

"Night." I smiled at my phone.

"Night, Sugar," Theresa drawled as she strolled out of the bathroom.

"Speaking of Sugar, how's Reggie getting on?"

"Great. He's invited all his Knox buddies to the wedding. Emi can visit with a few of her old friends." Theresa's voice trailed off, and she sank into the desk chair. "Will Emi even be at the wedding?"

"She's a bridesmaid; she has to be there," I said.

"Are you sure?"

"No, Sean won't let me talk to her, but what about Reggie? Hasn't he talked to Pak?" I asked.

"When Reggie asks how Emi's doing, Pak says she's resting. Reggie doesn't know about the Andrew Watson ban on Mayweather."

"Pak sure won't mention it at work." I flipped face-down on the bed and told the mattress, "This so sucks. We need Emi here."

"If Sean and Tony have to wander around in the basement of a building that could collapse on them, I'd like a hint they'll find something. And we spent, what, five grand today?"

"Easy."

"The most likely scenario is the Garrett sisters are out five grand plus two grand per diem and tonight's dinner bill, and we say, sorry, no diamonds."

"That's easier than telling Sean's kids their dad's in jail or the hospital," I said.

Theresa exhaled dramatically. "Let's call her, describe the job, and ask if she sees anything. Her dad and Sean won't know."

"You can try, but she hasn't answered my calls and texts. Maybe her dad confiscated her phone."

Theresa called Emi's number. No answer. She tried Pak. No answer.

Theresa sighed again. "Come on, let's invent you an identity for your meeting tomorrow morning."

*

Overnight I became the Assistant Manager of Risk Management at Sean's imaginary demolition engineering company. As Charlotte was colder than the hinges of hell, I wore my hoodie over jeans and baptized myself a recent FSU graduate. Tony donned a suit and introduced himself as the Chief Financial Officer. Sean wore jeans and a bulky sweater and was dubbed the Vice President of Operations.

The North Carolina Security account rep was a burly, good-humored man named Eric Avery. He had ruddy cheeks, rough hands, and he knew his stuff about construction site security.

"Each site poses unique challenges," Avery said as he wrapped up his sales pitch. "The team assigned to your project will hold daily tailgate meetings and perform random inspections. Eyes will be on cameras twenty-four seven."

I adjusted the black-framed glasses I'd selected to make me appear older. "You offer both live and virtual security?" I asked.

"In whatever mix you believe is the most effective to protect your company from theft and ensure safe work practices are followed."

"Demolition sites are complex," Sean said. "Do you have experience with a deconstruction job?"

"We've handled security for several demolitions regionally, including two here in Charlotte."

"Can you provide references?" Tony asked.

"I can do better," Avery said. "We're working a demolition here in town. We'll visit."

Bingo.

"You can't walk through the site, but you'll see how our perimeter security works, and you can talk to our people. Let's take a ride. The site's only ten minutes away."

Avery made a call, then led us to a red Ford pickup in a parking lot at the end of the block. The brief walk was invigorating in the cold, damp morning air and gave me time to prepare a strategy. As Avery unlocked the truck with an electronic key, Tony and Sean quickly loaded themselves into the back seat. That left the front bench free for me to share with Eric Avery.

"Do you visit your sites often?" I reached for the seatbelt. Avery didn't notice I never completed the action.

"I visit all of my accounts each week," Avery replied. "On a demo job, I stop in more often. Our people's safety is important to us, and demolition sites are complex like Sean said. I inspect them frequently."

"Your inspections are unannounced, I assume," Tony said.

"Fifty-fifty. Some are scheduled, some visits random."

Diligent man. If he didn't let a detail slide now and then, we were in trouble.

My opportunity came as Avery steered his truck into a sharp left turn. I slid along the bench several inches more than necessary and pressed my knee against his leg to brace myself. "Isn't it dangerous working inside a building being demolished?" I asked.

"That's why we focus on the perimeter," Avery said. "The construction company handles safety its people, though we do our best to help. Our primary goals are monitoring safety measures and keeping thieves and vandals out. We don't want our people roaming a dark, dangerous site chasing an idiot risking his life for a hundred bucks worth of copper. If someone makes it past the perimeter, we alert police and fire."

"Prudent," Sean said from the back seat.

"Cameras cover the building from multiple angles," Avery added, "and we monitor from our office. The guards on-site are notified immediately if something is caught on the cameras."

It was a tiny lie, more an evasion than a fib, but a shiver of excitement whizzed through me. It would keep until the end of our visit.

A light rain fell as I slid from Avery's truck. I noted the camera locations as we walked the perimeter. After the tour, Avery introduced us to Gary, the team lead, and one of the three guards on duty. Sean talked to both for over twenty minutes while Tony kept Eric Avery occupied with questions regarding insurance, OSHA compliance, and claims history. This was a language I didn't speak, and touching our host would be weird, so I half-listened while studying the cars parked along the street.

The parking spots at the curb near the job site were filled with contractor vehicles, but they'd be empty after dark. I guessed that those parking spaces were blocked off at night with orange cones, so they'd be available the next day and that those spots were covered by security cameras.

Sean wrapped up his conversation with the guards and thanked Avery for his time. On the way back to the NCS office, Avery offered to take us to lunch, but Tony told him we had another appointment. I liked Eric Avery and felt terrible about deceiving him.

Back at the Sheraton, we entered our rooms bearing bags of takeout chicken sandwiches as offerings.

Theresa proudly displayed her handiwork. "Not a speck of shiny showing." She waved a hand at the heavy cart. "Do you have a way to get it past security?"

"Not if all those exterior cameras are working," Tony said.

"They aren't," I sang.

"What did you get?" Sean emptied the take out bags onto the desk in the guys' room.

"Camera seven on the building's southwest corner is out of alignment," I said. "It's looking at the sky, and they can't get it fixed until Friday. Since the big boom is on Saturday, they're not bothering."

"We have our entry point," Sean said. He frowned as Theresa tore into her sandwich, possibly concerned he hadn't bought enough food. "We still need to deal with the guards. Allison, you'll be the distraction. You were seen today, so you'll need a disguise."

I loved disguises. "Explain this distraction."

"After we eat, assuming Theresa leaves us anything, you and Tony buy a beat-up car; something guaranteed to break down on command."

"I'm playing the damsel in distress. Got it."

"Tony and I slip in at the southwest corner while the guards are busy with you. Once you have the guards' attention, tell them you'll have someone pick up the car in the morning and call yourself a cab. Have the driver drop you on the next block, then walk back to the van and join Theresa. She'll be guiding us through the basement."

"Once we find this imaginary safe, how do you get it out?" Theresa asked.

"I have distraction number two covered," Sean said. "You two stay put in the van and wait."

"When are we doing this?" I asked.

Sean forked coleslaw and eyed Theresa warily. "What's the weather forecast?"

Theresa used a free hand to check her phone. "Rain off and on through the night," she said around a mouthful of chicken.

"Perfect, it's unlikely Eric Avery will pull a surprise inspection in the rain. We go in tonight."

*

After watching Theresa eat, Tony and I drove to a car dealership on Charlotte's outskirts. Chuck's Chariot's website told us the inventory held just what we needed. On the ride into the sticks, Tony explained the program. The man was a wonder, but he was also a secretive bastard. When I asked if he'd heard from Emi, he said, "we're not discussing Emi," and then didn't talk at all during the rest of the ride.

Two thousand of our clients' money bought a twelve-year-old Toyota Corolla painted primer gray. Tony handled the paperwork, including a fake identification linked to some poor fool's real driving record and a fake insurance card to match. He paid cash and promised me our meddling might improve the poor fool's credit.

Eleven was the designated witching hour. Sean and Tony drove off with Theresa and their equipment in the Escalade. I followed in the Toyota, crawling along, uncomfortable with the car's brakes, steering, and everything else.

At eleven-thirty-five Theresa's message tone chimed on my phone, and I turned toward the scene of that evening's crime.

Chapter Thirty-four

The Corolla coasted to the curb like a dying duck, coming to rest in a parking space out of camera-range but well within sight of the doomed building. I let the door remain ajar for a moment to give the guard time to fix on the dome light, then stepped into the rain, praying my temporary black hair color spray didn't streak down my face. I popped the hood, then removed the part that Sean assured me would prevent the car from starting. To confirm his theory, I returned to the driver's seat and cranked the engine. Nothing.

As I prepared to exit the car again, an adorable Asian guy in a blue-gray NCS guard uniform approached me.

"Are you having car problems, Miss?" he asked.

I loved his voice and the way he called me Miss. His name tag said 'Michaels.' I buried all traces of the morning's southern accent and said, "I think I killed it."

He frowned. "I'm afraid I'm not much good with cars."

"That's okay. I'll get a ride," I said.

"Let me get my partner over here to help."

"Please, it's no problem," I said, but Officer Michaels was already on his phone. Within two minutes, another guard joined us. It was the team lead, Gary. I stepped from the car and hoped the rain, black hair, penciled brows, and red-framed glasses did the trick. I also hoped Sean and Tony were on the move. "What's the problem?" Gary asked.

Icy rain trickled down the back of my new raincoat's collar. "It's been making noise. You don't need to stand out in the rain. I'll Uber home and have someone come out in the morning and try to get it started. Is that okay?"

Gary's eyes searched my face. I held my breath, afraid he'd recognized me. "Can we take a closer look, please?" he asked.

"Sure." I forced the quaver from my voice, so I'd sound grateful rather than nervous.

Officer Michaels had his phone to his ear. My gut clenched as he said the words "patrol car" and recited the address. Cops were on the way.

I used my phone to order an Uber and pretended I didn't notice the two guards sweeping their flashlight beams in and under the Corolla. They were concerned about explosives, and I regretted the uneasiness it caused them. Regret turned to dread when a Charlotte-Mecklenburg police cruiser eased up beside me.

The NCS guards spoke with the driver. An officer with plastic covering her cap stepped from the passenger side and approached me with her flashlight pointed in my face.

I squinted into the light. "Good evening, officer. I didn't mean to make trouble. My car just died."

"Do you have help coming?" she asked.

"I ordered an Uber. Someone will pick up the car in the morning."

"May I see your license and registration, please?"

I handed over my Tony-approved documents and read the officer's name tag. Barnes.

Officer Barnes ordered me out and away from the Corolla. As the other officer opened the patrol car's back door, I noticed the words K-9 Unit on its side. While Officer Barnes examined my paperwork, a sturdy tan and black dog bounded from the car.

"Oh my gosh, what a beautiful dog! Is it a German Shepherd?" I asked.

"Belgian Malinois." Officer Barnes couldn't disguise the pride in her voice.

"What's he looking for?"

"She. She's a bomb-sniffing dog."

Nervous laughter burst out of me. "I'm so sorry, I know this is serious."

"I understand, Miss. This isn't what you expected to be doing this evening."

I shook my head. "Not even close." Well, not the dog part.

The dog and his handler finished their search. Officer Barnes returned my paperwork, and the cops drove off into the rain. Though I kept insisting I was okay on my own, the two NCS guards refused to leave. They stood side-by-side at the Corolla's passenger door. Their heads swiveled up and down the street, searching for trouble.

As I waited, my fists bunched in my lap, and my chest heaved with each uneven breath. Any moment, I assumed, Gary's cell phone would ring with a call from the security company's headquarters. Alerted to intruders, Officer Michaels would recall the K-9 Unit. In minutes, Sean and Tony would be cornered by the Belgian Malinois in a dark basement.

Rain pattered against the Corolla's roof. Each minute that passed without a buzzing cell phone confirmed there had been no last-minute decision to adjust camera seven.

My Uber driver arrived, and I said goodnight. The driver dropped me at a hotel three blocks away. Once my ride was out of sight, I jogged back to the rented Escalade. Sean had parked it at the corner, facing the dead Corolla almost a block away. Inside, Theresa chewed a nail and focused on her laptop.

"You okay? I saw the cops," she said.

"They thought I had a bomb." I stripped off the dripping raincoat. "Are they inside?"

"Yep, making their way to the basement's northwest corner."

"You think the safe's there?"

"I've got a good feeling, and it's getting stronger," she said.

Excited, I bounced onto the bench next to her. "So, it exists? There really is a safe?"

"Doesn't mean there are diamonds in it."

Sean's voice came through the laptop. "How are we doing, Theresa?"

"Keep moving to the northwest corner. Allison's back, by the way."

"Good deal. Okay, we're looking at the north wall of the basement."

Theresa squinted. "Can I get more light?" Her screen showed a featureless gray wall.

The vague shape coalesced into a pattern of brickwork. Theresa lifted a hand to touch her screen. For a moment, she stared at her finger as though willing it to point her to the treasure. Finally, the finger traced the outline of a brick, then another until Theresa had drawn an imaginary rectangle around each one in her view.

"Move two steps to your right," she said.

Another set of bricks appeared, and Theresa resumed the process. When she traced the brick furthest to the top right of her view, she tapped. "There. It's there."

Sean's gloved hand entered the view. "This one?"

"No, one to the right, then up two."

Sean's hand disappeared, then reappeared with a hammer and chisel. Theresa had wrapped the tools in electrical tape, which dulled the noise as he chipped away at the loose mortar. A drill appeared at the bottom of the screen. Sean stepped away, and we watched Tony drill small holes in the remaining mortar surrounding the brick. The motor was quiet, a faint hum over the computer. The Garrett sisters got their money's worth on the tools.

Tony disappeared from the view, and Sean got back to work with the chisel until the brick pulled free. It had taken over five minutes to remove one brick, but Theresa had done it again.

"It's in there." Sean moved his headlamp closer until we made out a hint of brown steel. I squealed and bounced in my seat.

Theresa and I grew more excited with each brick Sean and Tony removed. Eleven more exposed the entire safe. Then the guys' heads blocked our view as they mumbled to each other.

"What's wrong?" Theresa asked.

"The safe is set in mortar inside the wall," Tony said, exasperated. "The drill isn't enough. We'll need heavier tools."

My excitement fled. "I'm channeling my inner Emi here, guys. Let's not do anymore pounding."

"No way I'm watching that building come down on you," Theresa said, "my stomach hurts more every minute you're down there. It's already been over an hour."

Sean echoed Tony's exasperation. "We won't get a second chance at this. We've got to do something." He paused and conferred with Tony in inaudible tones.

After a moment, Tony asked, "Theresa, can you work the combination from a distance?"

"Without touching the dials? No, I get the signals, the signs, through my fingers."

"You didn't touch the bricks," I said. "Try working through Sean."

"I don't do that," Theresa snapped. "I don't get connections with people."

"Have you ever tried?" I asked. "I've always said if any of us takes it to the next level, it'll be you."

"We're not getting this safe out of this wall tonight," Sean said, "We've got to open it in place."

Tony's voice interrupted. "Sean, can you use your distance skill to reach out to Theresa and bring her here to work through you?"

Sean blew air across his lips. They fluttered in a motorboat trill. "So instead of me seeing through the target's eyes, she'll see through mine? Never tried that. Let's do it."

Theresa pounded her feet on the floor mat. "I can't, I mean, I've never. It won't work."

I rested a hand on the base of Theresa's slender neck. "Let Sean try. Do what Tony always says, focus with intention. What have we got to lose?"

Her head dropped to her chest, and she groaned. "Sean, once you have me, I mean, once you're inside my head, focus on the dial. Study it like it's the sexiest thing you've ever seen, and you want to memorize its every detail."

Sean didn't reply, but the safe's dial filled the laptop's screen.

Theresa closed her eyes and breathed deeply, the way Sean did when he prepared for a distance visitation. She whispered, "Sean" repeatedly, trying to connect with him by driving everything else from her consciousness.

When she opened her eyes, Theresa focused on the image of the dial filling her laptop screen. After two minutes of intense concentration, she tentatively reached out a hand. Her long fingers twitched as if she were turning the dial.

"Turn to the left four times and stop on twenty-two," she said.

Sean's hand appeared. He spun the dial.

"Damn, I missed it. There it is. Now what?" he asked.

Theresa's thumb twitched. "To the right, three times. Stop at seventeen." Theresa exhaled and straightened in her seat as her confidence grew. "To the left, twice. Stop at fifty-one."

Sean turned the dial more slowly now.

"To the right, once. Stop at seventy," Theresa said.

Sean tugged on the safe's handle. "Not working." We sagged again. "Are you sure of the combination?"

"Twenty-two; seventeen; fifty-one; seventy," Theresa recited.

Sean tried again. Nothing.

"Try switching the seventeen and the seventy," Tony suggested.

Theresa and I bent to the laptop screen, our noses almost touching the image as Sean twirled the dial to seventeen. Our attention was rewarded with a tiny click.

Sean twisted the handle and opened the safe's door.

Theresa and I yelped and high-fived.

"There's something in here." Sean's voice conveyed the excitement that danced in my stomach. His hand reached in and swept out the contents of the safe. Two pairs of gloved hands returned bricks to the wall.

Once the bricks were replaced, the screen went black, and Tony's voice gave instructions. "We're on our way to you. Sean is working on the distraction. Allison, get behind the wheel. There will be an ambulance. When it arrives, make sure you're at the far curb waiting for us. Avoid the area swept by cameras. Got it?"

"Got it," I said, and switched seats with Theresa.

For twenty minutes, only the city's night sounds and the rain tapping on the Escalade's roof broke the silence. Outside, Officer Michaels came into view as he walked the perimeter of the building. He'd almost reached the corner, about to turn the corner, when he stopped and brought his phone to his ear. After a brief pause, he sprinted out of sight, towards whatever distraction Sean had engineered.

I cranked the Escalade, pulled into the street, did a three-point turn, then idled in a spot out of camera-range.

"I hear the sirens," Theresa said as I caught their wail myself.

Emergency lights flashed in the rearview mirror, then disappeared. As the ambulance turned the corner to the opposite side of the construction site, I unlocked the van's doors and waited with heart pounding. Two men, clad in black from head to foot, strolled up the far sidewalk with their faces turned away from the security cameras.

Tony slipped behind the passenger seat. Sean pulled himself into the seat behind me and spoke into my ear. "Drive."

"Where?" I asked.

"The hotel."

Theresa couldn't wait until we got back to our rooms. "Were they in there? Were there diamonds in the safe?"

"Not now," Sean said. "When we get to the hotel, Tony and I will wait in the car; we're too conspicuous. You two go upstairs and pack. Act casual, but don't dawdle. Pack for all of us."

"We're leaving?" I asked. "Where are we going?"

"Home," Sean said.

"But," Theresa began, "we don't have return tickets."

"We don't need tickets," Sean said. "We're driving home tonight."

My heart fluttered. "It's one-thirty in the morning. Did something bad happen in there?"

"Focus on your driving," Sean said.

"I'm focused. Who's the ambulance for?"

"Gary."

"Did you hurt him?" Theresa asked Tony.

"Sean visited with him and told him to take a nap. The cameras caught him falling, and the staff back at his office called the ambulance."

"That's why Officer Michaels tore off to the other side of the building," I said.

"Hey," Theresa blurted. "Where's the expensive electric cart thingie?"

"We left it at the site," Sean said.

"That's three grand," Theresa said, "and my fingerprints are all over it."

"So what," Tony said. "It isn't stolen. We left it with a pile of other equipment. Everyone will assume it was forgotten by another contractor."

"That's cool," I said. "It's the opposite of stealing. It's leaving a gift."

"I suppose," Theresa said, but she was not happy. "I was seeing me hauling my groceries upstairs with that."

Theresa and I packed our bags and then used the guys' key to get into their room and pack for them. Burdened with luggage, Theresa and I climbed into the rental.

In our absence, the guys had cleaned the black paint from their faces. Sean explained the program. "We're driving straight through tonight."

"It's two in the morning!" Theresa objected.

"We'll take one-hour shifts," Tony said. "You need the most sleep. You'll be last in the rotation. Allison will start, I'll drive next, then Sean, then you. As each hour expires, whoever's driving will continue to the next exit and stop. We'll gas up at each change, use restrooms, and get coffee. Are we clear?"

"Theresa," Sean said, "get in the back. Strap in the best you can and keep warm. Allison, drive."

I drove. At three, there were twelve miles to go until the next exit, so I continued, then selected a well-lit truck stop for our first break. The bright overhead lights caused Tony to stir in the seat next to me. Sean filled the tank while Tony accompanied me to the attached convenience store, where I used the restroom and washed my face. The black paint in my hair could wait. Coffee in hand, Tony took the driver's seat. I sat next to him in the front, and Sean continued his nap in the middle row. Theresa hadn't budged.

Once we were back on the road, I used my new raincoat as a blanket and rested my head against the window, watching the rain through the glass until my eyelids drifted shut. When I heard the familiar sound of Sean's snoring, I asked Tony, "Have you talked with Emi?"

"No."

"Can you make her take my calls?"

"Yes, but I won't."

"I guess that's good, but you could do it, couldn't you?"

He didn't answer. I closed my eyes. "Were there diamonds in the safe?"

"We'll discuss that tomorrow. Everyone's too tired to get wound up right now. Get some rest."

The rain intensified.

"It was brave of you and Sean to sneak around that dark basement and hammer at walls. I was afraid for you," I said.

"I was afraid for myself, but we were careful."

"The police came and brought a dog." I described my encounter with the K-9 unit.

He chuckled. "You handled yourself well."

"Thank you." I traced a heart in my breath on the window and wrote, "A.F. loves R.A." inside it, then watched it evaporate away. "You won't let Emi leave us, will you?"

"That's up to Emi, not me."

A few more miles rolled past, and I sighed.

"Tony, please make Emi call me. I miss her."

Tony stroked my cheek with two fingers of his right hand. "Go to sleep, Allison."

I went to sleep.

Chapter Thirty-five

When I woke, Theresa was at the wheel. I'd slept right through Sean's shift.

"Oh, man. Where are we?" I stretched.

"Halfway home and headed for breakfast." Theresa tossed her head toward the rear seat. "Those guys don't know it yet, but this girl's got to eat."

"And this girl's got to pee. Don't wait for your hour to expire. Take the next opportunity."

"I'm with you."

Ten minutes later, Theresa turned off at an exit that promised a pancake house.

"Rise and shine, fellas," I said. "Theresa and her tag-along need food, and I need a bathroom."

Inside, we tidied ourselves in the restrooms. The guys changed their shirts and appeared fresher than I'm sure they felt. By unspoken agreement, no one talked until Theresa dug into her breakfast.

"We found," Sean paused as he remembered we were in a crowded restaurant, "something. We need Sol's expertise to tell us exactly what it means."

Theresa hesitated as she forked eggs into her mouth. "So, there were—"

"What we were looking for," Tony said. "It seems prudent to get an estimate of value before turning them over to our clients. And there's another item we need to discuss with him."

"What's that?" I asked.

"The documentation," Tony said, "is intriguing."

We finished our breakfast and stepped out into an overcast December dawn. It was still too cold, but at least the rain had stopped.

The next four hours of driving were grueling. Theresa was last at the wheel, and we insisted she stop at her apartment and call it a day. She wanted to come along to Sol's Antiques and Fine Art to learn how well we'd done, but we put up a united front and told her to get proper food into her and go to bed.

Sean had called ahead, so Sol was ready for us with coffee and a tin of cookies waiting on his desk in the stockroom. We arranged ourselves in a variety of antique chairs. Sol centered himself behind his desk in a leather upholstered chair that creaked under his weight.

Tony produced an olive-green velvet bag from his back pocket, a pouch smaller than the palm of my hand. Sol emptied the contents onto a black cloth on his desk.

I gasped as dozens of brilliant crystals reflected the light of Sol's desk lamp. Each one glittered and winked as he used a chubby finger to spread them into a single layer on the velvet cloth.

Sol didn't use a jeweler's loupe. He picked up each tiny stone in his sausage fingers, studied it, and then set it aside. When he'd finished, there were eight piles of diamonds. Each collection contained a different number of gems. The smallest group had three and the largest a dozen.

The chair complained as Sol sat back. "You want to know if these are genuine. They are. The stones range from approximately a quarter of a caret to this one here," he used a pinky to nudge a large stone in the pile of one dozen, "which is over three carets. There are fifty-six stones. It will take me time to work up a proper estimate, but you are looking at a minimum of three hundred thousand dollars' worth here, I'd say."

I whistled. Ten percent of that made a lovely payday.

Though he was looking at a hefty fee himself, Sol didn't smile. "But there's a story here, isn't there?" Sol was not just an antique dealer. Like Theresa, he located missing objects, but Sol could tell you much, much more.

Tony removed a letter from the same pocket that had held the green velvet pouch. Sol scanned it, nodding as he read.

Sean said, "Does the letter support your opinion?"

Sol let his fingers sift through the stones. "They're stolen, all of them. They've been removed from their settings. That's how I divided the stones. Each pile represents a unique setting."

"Are they old?" I asked.

He nodded at the pile of twelve stones. "The cut tells me they're from the late eighteenth century. The others are early twentieth century but quality stuff, excellent work."

"Is the letter old, too?" I asked.

Sol's full lips formed a rueful smile. "No, but it's private."

"Private? We stole somebody's stolen diamonds, but we can't read their mail? That doesn't sound right."

Sean raised a palm. "Sol's right. Our clients will decide if they want to share the letter. When can you have a formal estimate for us, Sol?

"Noon tomorrow."

"We'll pick up the stones tomorrow then. Allison, when we get home, make three round-trip reservations for Charlotte on the three-eleven flight tomorrow afternoon."

We dropped Tony at his house, then headed home. I could barely keep my eyes open but said hey to Melanie before dragging upstairs to my room. I showered the black dye out of my hair and made the flight reservations. Despite not getting much sleep the night before, I wasn't ready for a nap, so I called Ray.

"You got a cat picked out yet?" I asked.

"I'll text you a picture," Ray said. "Her name's Cinderella, and she's two."

"Aww, that so sweet. What color is she?" I asked.

"Black and white. Do you want to visit her tomorrow?"

"Can't. We're not done yet. Will Saturday work?"

"Perfect, I get off at four. See you then."

"I can't wait." After a pause, I added, "Miss you."

"Miss you, too. Good night."

"It's two in the afternoon," I said.

"I know, but you sound sleepy."

"You got that right. Night."

I dozed for an hour, then rode with Melanie to collect the boys from school. They clung to me as though I'd been away a month. Back home, I got them changed and doing homework while Melanie made dinner. After dinner, I announced I was tired, and Chad and Connor had to put *me* to bed for a change.

After I slipped under the covers, the boys acted out Jack and the Beanstalk which had me laughing so hard my stomach hurt. Chad sang me his favorite bedtime song, "*Hush Little Baby*," before tucking me under the covers.

They left my bathroom light on for a night light and slipped out, closing the door softly behind them. Damn, I loved those kids.

*

Sean and I slept late, then loaded back into the rented Escalade after breakfast. After picking up Tony, we arrived at Sol's precisely at noon to retrieve the green pouch and an envelope containing his appraisal. We stopped at the office, where I prepared the Garrett sisters' invoice and made copies of the expense receipts. We had plenty of time to return the rental and make our three-eleven flight to Charlotte.

Two and a half hours later, we pulled up to the half-timbered Tudor on Selwyn Drive, ready to blow the minds of its charming inhabitants.

*

The sisters clutched each other and bounced the way Emi and I did when we were excited.

"You found them. I don't believe this," Lisa said. "And so quickly. You're incredible, remarkable."

"Outstanding," Linda emphasized.

The diamonds sparkled atop a blue bath towel covering the surface of Henry Garrett's bow-fronted mahogany desk. Our invoice, receipts attached, lay next to the pile.

"How did you—" Lisa began.

"The less you know, the better," Sean interrupted. "Let's say we found them among your parents' belongings."

"There is something else," Tony said.

The sisters froze in mid-bounce.

"There was also a letter in the pouch addressed to the two of you." Tony pulled the letter from an inside jacket pocket and extended it toward Lisa, the older of the sisters.

Lisa read silently until she neared the end of the one-page document when she gasped and collapsed into her father's old desk chair. When she finished reading, she extended an arm, breathlessly offering the sheet to her sister. "Linda, read this. It's unbelievable."

Linda took the letter, read it, then clutched at her chest, bunching the fabric of her shirt.

"Incredible, unbelievable." Linda's eyes flashed at her older sister. "Where are the girls? They've got to read this."

Recovered, Linda stood and bellowed, "Summer, Autumn, get down here!"

Feet pounded on stairs and, within a minute, two out-of-breath women joined us at the desk.

I'd expected girls Emi's age, twenty-one or twenty-two. These women were in their late thirties and looked enough alike to be twins with their mothers' keen eyes and athletic bodies.

Linda raised a hand toward us. "Girls, these people found something we thought we lost."

"That's not precisely true," Lisa said. "We honestly didn't believe they existed."

Summer and Autumn shared a worried glance that seemed to say, "Dementia, so soon?"

Lisa's daughter, Summer, asked, "Is there a problem with the business?"

"No, no, no," Linda chattered. "What we've learned is amazing. That's all I can say. It's amazing."

Sean interrupted before the sisters resumed their cryptic back-and-forth. "Your mom and aunt asked us to follow up on a conversation they overheard as children regarding diamonds belonging to their parents."

"Diamonds," Autumn said. "Grandma and Grandpa owned diamonds?"

"That doesn't sound like them," Summer agreed.

Lisa shook the letter at them. "That's the reason we assumed they didn't exist. You couldn't hope to meet two more sensible, down-to-earth people than Mother and Father. Diamonds and our parents and now this, it's beyond belief."

"What's beyond belief?" Summer asked.

Summer's mother and aunt looked at each other and laughed.

"Would you like me to read it?" Tony offered.

"Please," Lisa said. "I couldn't get through it, not without collapsing."

"I can't," Linda agreed.

Tony accepted the letter from Linda and pulled a pair of gold-framed reading glasses from his jacket pocket. "The date at the top, what is its significance?" he asked.

Linda glanced at the top of the page and chuckled. "That was my twenty-first birthday. I hadn't noticed before."

Tony pursed his lips and nodded. "Makes sense. My dear daughters," he began.

I scooted to the edge of my seat, as eager as Summer and Autumn to learn what the fuss was about.

"I was born in Luzern in nineteen-thirty-three. I was young during the war, the Second World War, and remember little of those days. It must sound stupid, but I was a child who craved adventure and always rather regretted that I'd missed playing a part during the war.

"In nineteen-fifty-one, my parents determined I should go to university to study chemistry. Before that happened, I made a new friend, a worldly man, so unlike my stuffy parents. He changed the path of my life. His name was Jacques Fernout. He claimed to be from Paris, but in post-war Europe, who could say.

"Jacques had studied chemistry and engineering in his youth, so we had common interests and we became friends. One day, he offered me the opportunity to make good money. I didn't hesitate. The hunger of the war years was fresh in my mind. I accepted the opportunity and, with Jacques as my mentor, became an accomplished jewel thief.

"By the early nineteen-fifties, people were traveling again. Jacques and I studied the itineraries of wealthy women. We made their acquaintance, charmed them, learned their habits, and relieved them of their excess baubles. We moved around, never staying in one place too long.

"After five exciting and profitable years, I immigrated to America to pursue my long-postponed studies in chemistry. I converted most of my earnings to cash. It was easier then. I never forgot the war, however, and set something aside just in case. The contents of the green bag were to be used in an extreme emergency only.

"You know the rest. There was college, followed by marriage and children. The business thrived, and I've never needed the green pouch. I pray that you never need it either. God bless and keep you. Your loving mother, Anna."

Summer and Autumn stared at Tony, dumbfounded.

Unconvinced, Autumn said, "Grandma was a jewel thief?"

Both hands went to my mouth to smother a laugh.

Summer made a doubtful face. "We're talking about Grandma, the lady who knitted the world's ugliest sweaters and bribed us with homemade cookies so we'd practice piano?"

Lisa nodded to the letter. "That's her handwriting."

"And there are the diamonds," Linda added, pointing to the desk.

"Those are the diamonds she stole," Autumn said.

"The ones she set aside for a rainy day," Sean clarified.

"I thought Grandma and Grandpa were the dullest of the dull," Autumn said.

"Duller," Summer said, and I realized she and her cousin did the same annoying conversational juggling act as their moms.

Once they got themselves and their daughters settled, Lisa and Linda thanked us again. The diamonds were shoved aside into a careless pile; while Lisa wrote us a check. We made the eight-fifty flight back to Tallahassee. In bed by midnight, I fell asleep at once and dreamed of a cat named Cinderella. She wore a diamond necklace and matching tiara.

Chapter Thirty-six

"If you bring a cat home, things will go badly for you," Sean promised.

"The cat's not for me, it's for Ray," I said.

"I wanna kitty," Chad said.

"No, the cat's for Ray," I repeated.

"I wanna come."

"You can come, but you're not getting a cat. You heard your daddy."

"If Chad's going, I'm going," Connor said.

"Fine, you can both come if it's okay with your dad."

"It's fine with me," Sean said, "as long as you don't come home with a cat."

When Ray arrived, we took my VW to the Leon County Shelter, where we met Cinderella, who stared at us impassively from the corner of her cage. A volunteer carried her to a visiting cubicle where she proved to be a patient and kid-tolerant feline.

Ray held Cinderella on his lap, stroking the white fur under her chin with a thick finger. She crouched and purred while the boys pet her.

"I like the name Cinderella," Chad said.

"Me too. Are you letting her keep that name?" Connor asked.

"Sure, unless you think I should name her Allison." Ray winked at me.

Chad said, "Allison's not a cat. She's a girl."

"But she's as pretty as Cinderella," Ray said.

"No," Connor said, "Allison's prettier."

"Connor, honey, that's so sweet. Let's visit the other animals so Ray and Cinderella can get better acquainted."

The boys dashed from one enclosure to the next, talking to the animals, including a pair of goats and a pot-bellied pig. After finishing our tour, we found Ray at the front desk, filling out forms.

"Adoption paperwork?" I asked.

"Yep. They're putting my new girlfriend in a carrier. Do you mind stopping at the pet store? I have a list."

On the drive home, Cinderella's carrier sat between the boys in the back seat. I crammed bags of cat supplies beneath their feet. Cramped and bored, they whined that they wanted a cat until I was ready to hit my imaginary ejector-seat button. I dropped them and my car at the house, then rode with Ray to Cinderella's new home.

We set up the cat box, food and water bowls, and a scratching post, then tossed a handful of cat toys into the living room for Cinderella to ignore. I sat on the floor, leaned against Ray, and we watched the cat explore. All we'd talked about that day was the cat. Now that we were home, I found myself at a loss for words. That was odd. Chat came easily to me. I practically did it for a living.

Ray rescued us from the silence.

"Are you hungry?" he asked.

"Not yet, maybe in an hour. What are you thinking?"

"Not about dinner."

I laughed and pulled myself to my knees to put my face even with his. I wrapped an arm around Ray's shoulders and kissed him.

When we separated, he was smiling. "Do you have to travel a lot?"

I shrugged. "Usually only a few days at a time."

"You don't talk about your job much. Do you enjoy your work?"

"I do, but it was more fun with Emi. I miss her."

"How's she doing?" he asked.

"Better," I said, as if I knew. "She may not come back to work."

"Why not? Her injuries weren't that serious. I got the feeling she loved her job, and you're all friends."

"Her family's pressuring her to take it easy." I didn't sound convincing.

"As long as she's getting better. Tell her I asked after her, okay? How was the trip? Did you find your clients' missing property?"

"Mayweather has another satisfied customer." I twisted around to sit on Ray's thighs, then wrapped my legs around his waist. "And you? Are you a satisfied customer?"

"Not yet." He pulled me close.

Cinderella ignored us.

*

After a dinner of mushroom omelets, we went to bed. Cinderella purred between us. I lay half dozing, thinking about Anna Garrett and Emi. Both had safe lives planned out for them by their families until someone appeared to alter their paths. Anna had been looking for adventure, met a jewel thief, and amassed a fortune. Emi wanted an ordinary life, won an internship at Knox, and discovered an incredible gift.

I wanted to escape my miserable life and saved Connie's. Her rescue led to a new family, a job, and friends. And now I had Ray. And we had a cat. Funny old world.

*

On Monday morning, Theresa acknowledged she had a problem. With her wedding on Saturday, she was down a bridesmaid.

"I've got to call Emi, Allison."

"Sean wants us to stay away. Find another bridesmaid, maybe one of your snooty neighbor," I said.

"I don't want another bridesmaid, I want Emi, and the dress won't fit just anybody." She shoved away from her desk. "I can manage with two bridesmaids, but what about Pak? He's the freaking best man! Reggie can't stand up there alone."

"Oh my God, I forgot." I had forgotten, which shows the state I was in over Ray. "Call Pak at work. Even if he doesn't answer his desk phone, he'll check his messages. Tell Sean first. I don't want him blind-sided with an angry call from Andrew Watson."

"I'll talk to Sean, but this can't wait. Our final dress fittings are this afternoon. I need you both for moral support." Theresa patted her tummy. "I'm glad I picked a forgiving style."

Theresa had selected an off-the-shoulder empire-waisted gown that flowed over her developing baby bump. The bridesmaid dresses were similar with low backs and v-necks. We'd resemble a bouquet when we posed together, with me in blue, Emi in green, and Liz Guiden in yellow. Flower girl Connie would wear pink. Ring-bearer Chad had an aqua cummerbund for his tiny tuxedo, as did the ushers, Connor Mayweather and David Guiden.

In my mind, I walked through the wedding, pausing when it occurred to me someone was missing. I couldn't believe we'd never discussed it.

"Theresa, who's escorting you down the aisle?"

"Didn't I tell you?" She stopped as the office door chimed.

I leaped and scurried to the front, skidding to an abrupt halt when I spotted Emi in the lobby. She wore jeans, and a faded FSU t-shirt and glanced around with a distracted expression like she didn't recognize the place.

I ran to her and wrapped her in a hug. "Hey, you."

"Sorry I haven't been in touch, but I've been under house arrest while the ribs healed." She winced and took a half step from me.

"Sorry, I forgot." I slipped an arm around her shoulders and squeezed more gently. "Theresa and I were just talking about you. We've got dress fittings this afternoon."

"Oh, yeah, the wedding." Emi squinted, drew her brows together, and looked past me. I suspected her dad made the wedding off-limits, too.

Emi shook her head, and the confused frown faded. "I need to see Tony."

My smile fell, and I knew this was it, the end. Emi had come to say goodbye.

"Sure, come on back." I choked on the last word and started down the hall so she couldn't see the tears.

Sean raised his head as we passed his office. I tapped on Tony's door frame but didn't bother trying to smile. "Visitor." My voice cracked.

Tony leaned back in his chair, his face set in grim resignation. "Hi, Emi, have a seat."

She slipped inside and closed the door behind her.

I wanted to rush in and beg her to stay, but didn't have the energy to do anything but turn away. Sean waited in the hallway, arms folded, scowling at Tony's closed door. I joined him and grabbed an elbow to steady myself.

I swiped at the tears on my cheeks. "This so sucks."

"Why is she here?" he asked.

"She didn't say, but I assume she's come to say goodbye to Tony." I brightened as I realized there was still hope. "He'll talk her out of it, won't he?"

Sean shook his head. "Even Tony has limits when it comes to manipulating people. If this is what she wants, we'll accept her decision."

I stomped a foot like a three-year-old. My voice even squeaked and trembled like a child's. "I bet she's even bowing out of Theresa's wedding, and after she has the baby, Theresa will leave, too. I hate this Sean, I want everything back the way it was."

Sean's features softened, and he rubbed my back with one hand. "I'm sorry things have gone so wrong, kid. We'll get a new team going."

"I don't want a new team, I want—"

Tony's door shot open. His head popped out, and he caught us with his dark, piercing eyes. "Get in here," he ordered. He turned his head and yelled down the other hall. "Theresa! My office."

I feared Emi had passed out or something, but she stood beside Tony's desk, hands folded demurely in front of her. Tony wore his half-smile as he resumed his seat. It was good to see that smile again, but I couldn't imagine what it meant. Theresa slipped in, stood next to me, and glowered at Tony.

Behind me, arms crossed over his chest, Sean leaned against the door frame, filling it. "Well?"

I was curious, though concerned I wouldn't enjoy what Emi had to say. If she was leaving, I was sure I'd lose it and be a basket case. Frustrated, I remembered Ray hadn't called all morning and wondered how Cinderella was getting along. I slipped my phone from my back pocket and opened my messages.

There was a text from Ray. "*Hi, hon, hope U R having a good Monday. Cinderella prefers your side of the bed, btw. See you 2nite.* My head jerked to Emi. My jaw dropped. While I read Ray's words to myself, Emi had spoken them out loud.

I squinted at her. "Did you just—"

Emi cocked her head in Theresa's direction, sighed, and smiled. Theresa stepped to Tony's desk and lifted an envelope from its corner. While Theresa studied the envelope silently, Emi said, "*Florida Association of Certified Public Accountants, 3800 Esplanade Way, Suite 210, Tallahassee, Florida.*"

Theresa extended the envelope toward Emi. "That's what it says." She screwed up her face. "But why am I reading it? I don't want to be reading people's mail." She tossed the envelope back on Tony's desk.

Emi clasped her hands behind her back, rocked on her heels, and grinned. Tony beamed like a proud dad as the realization hit the rest of us at once.

I screeched and ran to hug Emi, forgetting her sore ribs again. Theresa bounced to join us.

Sean's face paled, and his fists clenched at his sides. "This isn't possible."

"It was the trauma of the accident," Tony said. "Emi is now one of us. Emi is a practitioner."

*

Rather than move into the conference room, Sean pulled in chairs from his office so we could sit around Tony's desk. No one wanted to turn the celebration into a meeting.

"I woke up in the hospital with a killer headache," Emi said, "and my ribs hurt like hell, but otherwise, I felt fine. I remembered the accident and got my story straight in my head, ready for the cops."

"You were lucky," Tony said. "Remind me to give you a bunch of shit for following us."

"Later, I'm not on the clock yet. Anyway, when I gave my statement, I had it together but wondered what the cops thought of my story. While the detective wrote, I stretched my neck to read the guy's notes. He gave me a nasty look, so I cut my eyes away, but I heard his words. In my head! The cop didn't read out loud, but I heard him in my head."

Sean rested his elbows on his knees, dropped his head, and laughed.

Theresa chuckled, too. "I bet you freaked."

"I figured, cool, I have a new skill. I didn't understand I'd made the cop do it until days later when I was home with Pak, helping him register for the CPA prep classes. He got a text from work, and I could tell it bothered him, but he said to forget it. We kept working, but the message still distracted him, so I looked at him and thought, 'just read me the damn text,' and he did. He picked up his phone and read it, not out loud, but in my head."

Tony rested his elbows on his desk. "This is marvelous, Emi, but what about your dad? Andrew doesn't want you here, and I don't blame him after the accident."

I touched her hand. "I thought I'd lost my best friend forever."

She reared back and scowled. "You really believed I wasn't coming back?"

"Well, yeah, your dad told Sean you were done with Mayweather I said.

"That's Dad, not me. Like Tony, my dad sometimes forgets I'm old enough to make my own decisions," Emi said.

Tony scoffed and tapped a pen on his desk.

Emi waggled her head. "I kept my distance to keep the peace while I recovered, but I never agreed to give up my job and return to Knox. Dad tried to enlist Pak and Mom to talk me out of coming back, but they outnumbered him from the get-go. You know how much Pak loves this stuff. He blames me for being alone that night. And my mom adores Tony, heaven knows why."

Tony's smile broadened. "Caroline is a wonderfully perceptive woman."

"I'm sorry I didn't keep in touch, but I needed to respect Dad's feelings to make it easier to tell him there was no way I'd leave Mayweather. Also, I wanted to make sure this new skill was for real and wouldn't fade as I got better. It was hard to stay away." Tears pooled at the corners of Emi's dusty blue eyes. "I missed you guys so much."

Theresa rested a hand over her heart. "Thank God, I was afraid you were ditching my wedding."

"What's with you two?" Emi flopped her arms to her sides. "Ok, I get it, I was out of touch, but Pak's the best man, and there's no way Jen's passing up the opportunity to photograph Theresa's wedding. I took a few weeks off to rest and appease Dad, but I couldn't stay away forever."

Every muscle in me went limp with relief. "I'm so glad you're back."

"And I'm glad you're not ditching my wedding," Theresa said. "Don't forget the fitting this afternoon."

"Yeah, about that. I've been sitting on my butt for a while. There might be a lot of letting out to do."

Theresa patted her tummy. "You and me both."

"Please, no baby talk in my office," Tony said.

"We'll start slowly, but," Sean rubbed his hands together, "everyone come up with ways we can put Emi's new skills to work."

Chapter Thirty-seven

Mayweather Executive Solutions returned to full strength on Tuesday. Thrilled to be back at my reception desk, I cleared our calendar then filled it again when Harold Berman called with a job. We worked frantically to wrap up the case by Thursday of that short week. Sean ordered the office closed on Friday for last-minute wedding preparations, the rehearsal, and the reception to follow.

The weather promised to be cool but sunny for Theresa's outdoor wedding on Saturday morning in the Portal Paseo at the Mission San Luis. Friday was hectic through mid-afternoon. Emi and I picked up dresses, tuxedos, flowers, and favors for the guests. I helped Theresa with last-minute additions and cancelations. The three of us got our hair and nails done instead of eating lunch.

I ran home for a shower but still had the rehearsal to get through. After a full day of running errands, frenzied texting, and forgetting to eat, I was vulnerable and unprepared for the shocks delivered to my nervous system that evening.

The wedding party gathered late Friday afternoon to discuss last-minute changes with the caterers before the rehearsal. As we wrapped up our chat, I looked forward to my first real meal of the day when the first surprise of the evening walked in the door. At least it was a surprise to me when Maggie and Ricky Jacobs arrived. Theresa explained she'd asked Ricky Jacobs to walk her down the aisle. Somehow this missed getting mentioned to me. It was a happy surprise, though it shouldn't have been. Mayweather had deep ties with Knox.

Francine Guiden, Pak, Reggie, and Anderson worked at Knox. Theresa, Andrew Watson, Emi, and Tony used to work there. The more I considered, the more I realized that the two companies, Knox and Mayweather, were part of a large extended family. Emi was right. She couldn't go back to work at Knox and have no contact with Mayweather. The two companies were interwoven with shared people and history. Emi and I were doomed to remain friends. I'd been stupid to think otherwise. The realization amused me, and I eased into the rehearsal at peace for the first time in weeks.

We'd scheduled the rehearsal for late afternoon to take advantage of the waning December daylight. Everything went flawlessly, even with children involved. Reggie waited on the dais, wearing a black t-shirt labeled "groom" in gold script. His best man, Pak, stood at Reggie's side in a tuxedo t-shirt.

On the pianist's signal, Connie led the procession and mimed tossing rose petals on the imaginary white carpet running from the mission to the dais. My purple heart-shaped pillow stood in for the ring bearer's white satin cushion. Chad carried it proudly, wearing a huge grin. He resembled a miniature version of his dad, with his hair gelled into little spikes.

Behind the flower girl and ring-bearer, Emi was followed by me and then Liz Guiden. Theresa, in her white, gold-scripted "bride" t-shirt, walked the imaginary carpet on Ricky's arm. Ricky looked the part in his usual old-fashioned three-piece suit and silk tie.

Jeni dodged around, planning her shots as we walked through the ceremony and recessional, then it was inside for dinner. Mission San Luis would also be the reception site, so guests didn't have to drive across town then wait for the bride and groom to arrive.

The rehearsal dinner was more of a rehearsal reception with beer, wine, and finger foods. Theresa wanted a casual event to encourage mingling and chatting. I'd invited Ray to join us, and he appeared thirty minutes into it, having first stopped to change out of his uniform.

I stuck to wine, but I'd been too busy to eat much, so my head was already swimming when the next surprise hit.

It was dark by then and chilly, so the wedding party and their families gathered inside the hall. Fake candlelight flickered everywhere, and the intimate excitement of a party before the party filled the room. The atmosphere was spirited, and the buzz of conversation echoed off the high ceilings.

The chatting halted abruptly when a glass shattered on the tiled floor.

A server rushed to Theresa, who stood frozen, hand still curled though her glass lay in shards at her feet. She blinked twice, then strode forward to intercept a middle-aged couple entering the room arm-in-arm.

"Mom, Dad, what are you doing here?"

Woozy from the wine and the shock, I grasped the back of a chair as I spun to locate Emi. I spotted her next to Pak, and our eyes locked. She nodded, and we weaved our way discretely toward Theresa and her parents.

The party chatter resumed, though at a much lower volume. I suspected every gifted person and practitioner had one ear tuned in our direction like radar.

As Emi and I reached Theresa, her mother said, "We're much too busy for social media nonsense, but your friend Cory mentioned he'd seen the page for your wedding. You remember Cory, don't you? You haven't forgotten everyone at home?"

"Of course, I remember Cory, Mom, but why are you here?" Theresa asked.

Theresa's dad boomed in a deep, full-bodied voice capable of commanding a room. "Do we need a reason to attend our daughter's wedding and to meet the father of her baby?"

Theresa noticed us hovering and took a step backward. "I suppose not," she said with false cheerfulness. "Let me introduce you. These are my best friends, Emily Watson and Allison Francona. We work together. Guys, these are my parents, Emory and Louise Fitzgerald."

Emi offered her hand. "Pleased to meet you." She held onto Emory's hand a moment too long, and her glance suggested I should do my thing.

I began with Louise, wrapping both of my hands around one of hers. "You must be so excited with a new son-in-law and grandbaby coming your way."

Louise let me grasp her hand, but she didn't smile, not with her lips or with her eyes. "At least the wedding will come before the baby." She examined Theresa from head to toe. "And at least she isn't showing."

Emory huffed. "That's the way it's done these days, Lou. Not like in our day. Not like in our day at all."

I withdrew my hand but held my smile.

Emi said, "Theresa, why don't you relax with your folks before we introduce them to everyone." Emi inclined her head toward the crowd. I didn't need to read minds to understand she was telling me to alert the team.

"I'll send Reggie and Geraldine over first." I melted off into the party.

Fortunately, Reggie and his mom were together.

Reggie was stunned. "Her parents? She didn't mention inviting her parents. We've never discussed them much, actually."

"She didn't invite them," I said. "They just showed up."

"That's not good," Geraldine pronounced. "What's wrong with them?"

"They think Theresa's a witch." Mother and son laughed. "Seriously," I said, "they had a falling out when she left home. They're private people, down-homey."

"Hmm." Geraldine didn't care for that. She and Reggie were light-hearted and outgoing. "Come on, Reggie. Let's draw these folks out."

I wished them luck and searched up the guys. Without explaining, I pulled Tony away from Francine, dragging him across the room to where Sean was arguing with Anderson.

"What the hell is Theresa doing on Facebook?" Anderson snapped.

"She made a page for her wedding. One of Theresa's school chums brought it to her parents' attention. And here they are. Theresa left home on bad terms. She tried to explain her gift to them, but they're religious people and think she's a nut or in a cult. I read the mom, and she's suspicious as hell."

"Our strategy should be denial," Tony said.

Sean nodded thoughtfully. "Agreed, spread the word. Theresa has no special skills, she's never mentioned special skills, special skills don't exist. Theresa is our top researcher, nothing more."

"Got it," I said.

"And Anderson, kill that Facebook page," Sean ordered.

Anderson pulled out his phone. "On it."

I returned to Theresa and Reggie, who sat with their folks at one of the round banquet tables. Emi stood off to the side, examining the massive wooden beams on the ceiling. When I approached the group, Geraldine was explaining to a disbelieving Louise that Reggie's name was just Reggie, not Reginald. Emory interrogated Reggie about the decision not to have a church wedding. Reggie was holding his own, but relief flooded his face when I arrived.

"Ready to meet the team?" I asked with extra cheerleader perk in my voice. Theresa and Reggie rose, but Emory and Louise remained seated and scowling. They expected their daughter to handle the introductions.

Putting my two hands on Theresa's shoulders, I pulled her toward me in a chummy manner and whispered through my smile. "I'll set you up, start with Ray. You follow, but don't make it obvious."

Theresa responded with a nearly imperceptible nod.

There was no danger of Ray mentioning gifted people, and Emory and Louise would be impressed by a member of law enforcement, so we started there. I warned Ray Theresa's parents were tough nuts and left him with a quick kiss before scooting back to Sean.

"Gather up Melanie and the kids," he said. "We'll play the family angle."

"Got it," I said.

I found Connie, Connor, and Chad hiding under one of the banquet tables. I poked my head under the tablecloth. "Showtime kids."

Showtime was Sean's code to get cleaned and polished. I herded the kids to a water fountain and wiped their faces with napkins. The boys tucked in their shirts, and I combed everyone's hair.

"Connor, take Connie's hand and stand up straight. Chad, you're with me."

As I marched the troops to their parents, I passed Ray, who agreed with Emory that drug use among our nation's youth was a plague and a curse. I caught Theresa's eye to let her know the next act was on deck.

Sean shook Emory's hand like he was trying to sell him a car. Melanie introduced the children who stood in order of height, wearing practiced angelic smiles reserved for company.

"What a lovely family, Mr. Mayweather." Louise shook her head sadly. "You see so few intact families of this size these days."

Emory launched into a monologue regarding the divorce rate and its effect on the youth of our nation.

Sean let him rant, then leaned close to Emory and Louise. He spoke low, so his words wouldn't fall on delicate ears. "I couldn't agree more. That's why I'm so impressed Theresa and Reggie took the time to ensure their compatibility before jumping into marriage and a family."

Melanie added her two cents. "Sean and I were friends for years before we considered marriage." She patted Louise's hand. "You must be so proud."

"Yes," Louise responded without conviction.

I left Sean and Melanie to work on Theresa's parents while I hunted for Tony and Francine.

"Sean's playing the family angle. You two work on the dual-career thing. I'll get the twins."

My hunt for Liz and David began badly. I couldn't find them anywhere in the hall, then remembered they were fourteen and bored out of their skulls. By putting on my fourteen-year-old attitude, I located them drinking wine behind a hedge.

"Hey, you two," I said.

They jumped a foot apart, David to the right and Liz to the left.

"Don't tell Dad," Liz whispered loudly enough to be heard by passing aircraft.

"Not important now," I said. "Theresa's parents are here, and they're real hard-asses. Get over to your Mom and Dad and act like they're the best thing since Bluetooth. Do it now." I gathered their half-empty champagne glasses. "And pop a mint."

I ditched the glasses and joined the Guiden family as Theresa was making the introductions.

"Mom, Dad, this is Sean's business partner, Tony Guiden. Before coming to Mayweather, he was the chief financial officer of the big manufacturing firm where I used to work."

Impressed, Emory offered his hand.

"My wife, Francine, is a sales rep with Knox," Tony said.

Louise's eyes narrowed hard at Francine. "Have you always worked outside the home?"

"I used to feel differently, but then I realized responsibility for the financial security of the family is too important to leave to chance, don't you agree?" Francine nodded as she spoke. Unconsciously, Louise mimicked her, nodding in return. Tony wasn't the only member of the Guiden family with skills.

The twins stood between their mom and dad, uncertain smiles stretched across their faces.

"Our children have always had at least one parent available," Tony said. "You've never been neglected, have you, kids?"

"God no, Dad's always on our butts about something," David assured the Fitzgeralds.

"We can't cross the street without one of them asking ninety questions," Liz added.

This pleased Louise and Emory.

I paved the way for several more introductions, staying one step ahead of Theresa's parents. Maggie and Ricky Jacobs assured the Fitzgeralds that Theresa had been an ideal employee. This was not precisely the case, as Theresa had been spying on Knox for Deiner Equipment. When she was caught, the Jacobs had Tony interrogate Theresa in a manner that would send the conservative couple screaming for an exorcist.

Pak was the best, a natural actor. He had the Fitzgeralds eating out of his hands in minutes. With both arms wrapped around Emi, he told Emory, "Theresa and Reggie have encouraged us to take the plunge ourselves soon." He and Emi exchanged adoring glances seen only in sitcoms from the nineteen-fifties. "I've even moved my father into the house, so Emi has protection when I'm away."

How Emi didn't puke, I'll never know. Still, Theresa's folks were satisfied she and Pak were a devoted couple despite living in sin.

After an hour of bouncing around, I found my way back to Ray.

"I need fresh air," I said.

"You are a little flushed." He kissed my clammy forehead. "You've had quite a day."

"I'm wiped, and I've had too much to drink, and I've still got the wedding to get through tomorrow."

We held hands and strolled through the lawn that would be covered in one hundred white folding chairs in a few hours.

"You'll do fine," Ray said. "You're amazing and strong and beautiful, and I love you."

There they were, the words I never expected to hear, not spoken sincerely by a man like Ray, who wanted nothing in return. The shock was too much.

I collapsed into his arms and sobbed.

He laughed and hugged me.

"I'm sorry," I said between gulps of air. "I'm tired."

"As long as you're not crying because you don't love me back."

"I love you back just fine, but I need sleep." I stood on tip-toe and kissed his cheek.

We studied each other's eyes, then kissed properly until I pulled away and grinned an evil grin.

"Let's go to my car," I said.
"The Volkswagen? You're not suggesting that we—"
I sprinted to my car. Ray followed.

Chapter Thirty-eight

The spring day was sunny, warm, and breezy. Beneath an impossibly blue sky, my friends stood chatting on the deck surrounding Sean's pool as he flipped burgers on the grill. Melanie circulated with trays of sparkling pink champagne in plastic flutes.

I wore a rhinestone tiara with an attached net veil and a t-shirt with Bride written in gold script. Emi and Theresa wore pink bridesmaids' t-shirts. Ray was still in his uniform but wore a pink carnation in the top buttonhole and held Cinderella under his left arm.

My mom chatted with Caroline Watson. Mom looked young and pretty in a yellow sundress. Her hair was dyed more or less one color, and she wasn't cursing. Anderson led a conga line around the pool, which was filled with splashing children. Even Drew Watson enjoyed himself, slapping Tony on the shoulder and laughing.

As I watched my friends, my heart filled with so much joy, it threatened to burst. But the party got better when the one person who'd been missing arrived. Brilliant sunlight blinded me, obscuring his face as he stepped outside, but I knew it was him, and delight exploded from within me. I ran to him.

"Ben!"

"Allison, honey, we need to get back to the party. Everyone's leaving."

I blinked awake and raised my head from Ray's shoulder.

"Hey, are you okay? Did you have a bad dream?" he asked.

I couldn't respond.

With a forced smile, I pulled myself together enough to say goodnight to Ray and my friends, then drove home alone. That night, I revisited the dream over and over as if repeating it in my head could make it real.

Chapter Thirty-nine

Theresa's wedding didn't kick off until eleven the next morning, so I slept until eight, thinking three hours gave me plenty of time to get ready. What an idiot.

I fed, washed, and dressed the kids, then showered and dressed. Melanie did my hair, then we both cleaned up the kids again.

The twenty-minute drive to the Mission took thirty minutes. We arrived at ten-forty, ten minutes after the designated time to join Theresa, Emi, and Liz Guiden. Jeni Watson made herself obnoxious with her camera, and no matter how many times I reapplied gloss, my lips were dry.

Melanie herded Chad and Connie into the room. The two kids were suddenly not the least bit interested in being in a wedding. Theresa vibrated with nervous tension, and Emi fretted over a vision she'd had regarding Pak and ducks.

At ten-fifty-nine, Ricky entered the room, took Theresa's arm in his, and said, "Okay, people, let's get this show on the road."

We fell into line, and the procession began.

If there were slip-ups, nobody noticed. Theresa was radiant, the children adorable, the ceremony mercifully brief. The reception kicked off on schedule, and the tension surrounding the formalities evaporated.

I took my seat at the head table, slipped off my shoes, and downed a glass of champagne. Two more glasses disappeared during the toasts. Bridesmaid duties completed, I mingled with Ray at my side.

Detached, I watched the party from another dimension, a symptom of too much stress and champagne. I was struck by how most stuff seemed so ordinary, while other things appeared so weird.

Pak and Emi leaned on each other while posing for pictures, the perfect couple. Nothing odd there. Theresa talked calmly with her parents, then hugged her mom. That was weird.

Ray and I chatted with Martin Clendennon, who was more pleasant than I'd remembered. Then again, he wasn't investigating a murder anymore. Ray explained that Martin was pumping fists and patting backs because he was running for an open county council seat. I wished him luck. I knew zip about local politics, but Clendennon seemed like an amiable guy. At least Tony appeared interested in what he had to say.

We returned to our seats for lunch. Eating made me more alert, but not for long. By the time cake-cutting began, I wanted naptime with Ray. I giggled into his ear, and his flushed-face response told me we were on the same page. When we returned, the party was in full swing, and I felt more dazed and out of it than ever.

Emory and Louise Fitzgerald slow danced to YMCA. Pak overdid the champagne and sang *"You Are So Beautiful"* to no one in particular. Francine whispered that Tony had agreed to be Martin Clendennon's campaign treasurer. Connie dozed under the gift table while her brothers had a sword fight with the ornamental baguettes.

Afterward, we all agreed the wedding had been grand, absolutely grand.

The kids fell asleep in the van on the way home from the reception. At eight, I showered, changed into an oversized tee, and crawled into bed. I'd had two long, eventful days. I ached for rest, both physically and emotionally, but took time to review the wedding photos Jeni Watson emailed me.

My favorite, the one I planned to make into a screensaver, featured my friends and me. Theresa and Reggie were in the center. Geraldine and Maggie and Ricky Jacobs stood behind them, looking on like the proud parents they weren't.

To the right of the bride and groom, Emi and Pak clung to each other. Behind them, Caroline and Andrew Watson beamed beside Andrej and Zabel Zacharia.

Ray and I stood to the left of the bride and groom. Melanie and Sean Mayweather posed behind us, hands on our shoulders. I'd never dreamed such a picture of me would ever exist, but there I was, happy, in love, surrounded by friends and family. I studied the shot for a long time, then reached to switch off my lamp. As I did, the door opened, and Sean stepped into my room.

My hand twitched, and I gasped. Sean understood what I'd experience while growing up, so he never entered my room unannounced. This breach of his personal code did not bode well.

"Hey," I said.

"Hey, yourself." Sean sat on the foot of my bed. Curiouser and curiouser. I drew my knees up and rested my chin on them.

"Is there a problem?"

"Yes," he said, and my heart sank.

"Is the problem with me?" I asked.

"Yes."

My heart sank further, slipping down into my gut as I reviewed the stupid things I'd done over the last few days. Oh yeah. Me and Ray in the VW at the rehearsal dinner. Someone had probably seen us. If Sean was breaking his rule regarding my personal space, it must have been a kid or, God forbid, the Fitzgeralds.

We'd just gotten our relationship back on track, and I was too tired to deal with getting thrown out again. I lowered my forehead to my knees to avoid Sean's eyes. "Now, what have I done?"

"Not much. Just become amazing." He crossed his legs and wrapped a hand around his raised knee. "You're more of an asset to my business than I ever imagined. You make everyone smile, and you've wormed your pesky little self into the hearts of my wife and kids. You've totally changed our lives, and I'm struggling to find a way to repay you."

The warmth filling my heart caused it to float back to its proper place in my chest. I raised my head from my knees. "You've done a few things for me, too."

"There's one more thing I can do. It came to me last night. I don't know why it didn't occur to me sooner. Busy, I guess."

He stood and rubbed his hands down the front of his slacks.

I smiled up at him. "Sean, you've done everything for me. When we met, I was only seventeen and ready to give up on life, but you and Melanie turned me around. You made my last few months of school a dream. You've given me a job that's beyond a dream, beyond imagining. I have friends, family, and a home, everything I lacked when I was a kid. What could you possibly do for me you haven't already done?"

"Find your brother," he said, and left.

END

Thank you for reading *Not Deep Enough*. If you've enjoyed this novel, please leave a review. If not, please let me know how I can improve your experience by emailing me at kelly@kellyzimmerauthor.com

For more adventures with Emi Watson and her friends, read

Book One

The Magic in Me

And

Book Two

Dying to Return

To read free Emi Watson short stories, visit:

www.kellyzimmerauthor.com

Don't miss out!

Visit the website below and you can sign up to receive emails whenever Kelly Zimmer publishes a new book. There's no charge and no obligation.

https://books2read.com/r/B-A-NIDN-DOMLB

BOOKS 2 READ

Connecting independent readers to independent writers.